the Renegade

and the Lodestar

LAURA K MAURER

For more information,
address: laura@bookishgirls.com

First paperback edition June 2024

Book design by Vanessa Mendozzi

ISBN 979-8-9904868-0-5 (paperback)
ISBN 979-8-9904868-1-2 (ebook)

www.therenegadeandthelodestar.com
www.laurakmaurer.com

For Mom and Dad, who filled our house with books,
and gave me my first book of Greek Mythology.

For Doug, who said I could do anything.

And for Luke, #44, my ray of sunshine.

GREEK MYTHS WERE NOT
ABOUT RIGHT VERSUS WRONG.
THEY WERE ABOUT JUST
VERSUS UNJUST.

PROLOGUE

Hades stood on the precipice of a terrible yawning distance, a vast cavern that dwarfed his divine frame. Perched on a rock teetering at the edge of the abyss, one misstep and both he and the rock would cascade into the blackness.

But Hades rarely mis-stepped.

Hades's eyes glowed as he surveyed the Underworld. The whites of his immortal eyes were the only light in the immense cavern. The hushed whisper of an empty wind slid from a tangle of passageways that led off into every conceivable direction. A sense of loss permeated the air.

"It's more terrible than I imagined."

Zeus emerged from a tunnel, clasping his thunderbolt. The weapon illuminated the great open space of the Underworld, but Hades saw nothing more in the newfound light.

The rugged walls shone, dripping with what felt like tears from uncountable ages. Pillars stretched from the floor to the ceiling, unevenly spaced, crooked as an old man's spine. Jagged cones of rock rose out of the ground, as if reaching for salvation, but finding only bitter hopelessness. A dull black river snaked along the bottom of the ravine, unevenly slicing the massive space in two: the Styx.

"The stench is awful."

Hades felt a stabbing pain in his chest. The pain wrenched his heart, making it hard to breathe. How could Persephone be in such a place?

"What now?" Zeus kicked away a rodent the size of his muscled forearm. The creature tumbled to its demise far below.

Hades's eyes narrowed.

"Now we find her. And take her back."

CHAPTER 1

Persephone's simple ivory dress contrasted with the vibrant green of her eyes. She wore a belt of braided grass around her waist and thin braids in her hair. The braids framing her face were interwoven with little white flowers. The rest of her dark brown hair hung wildly, blowing in the breeze.

She stood on the edge of Mount Olympus, beaming at the land that spread out before her. Trees and grasses sprouted from the once-charred earth, filling Persephone with a palpable sense of hope. She took a deep breath, smelling new growth and the tanginess of the nearby sea. A peaceful land for the first time, Persephone rejoiced in the sunlight that warmed her skin, its sweet warmth feeding her the way it fed the plants she created.

The fear that had been an integral part of all the young gods' lives had been sliced off, the way a sculptor cuts away extraneous stone, leaving only beauty behind. Fear and darkness were vanquished as Hades and his brothers led the gods to victory over Kronos, his Titans, and their terrifying giant army. Chaos had been overthrown and hope poured in in its place.

Persephone's face clouded as she remembered the war and the toll it took on the earth and the gods—and on her favorite god, most of all.

She lifted her gaze. The vast open sky, she knew, was a sight she would never tire of seeing. She would never stop feeling grateful for it. The expansiveness, the openness, the feeling it instilled in her that there was no end to the beauty of the world—it invigorated her, filling her with promise and possibility. She smiled.

Persephone wriggled her toes, digging them into the earth, feeling the soil beneath her feet. She felt grounded to the earth, a part of it, even as she coaxed life from it.

She tucked her dress behind her and knelt. She waved her hands over the ground, feeling each grain of dirt as a pulse of energy against her skin, a possibility. She closed her eyes and visualized lush green leaves vibrant with life. When she felt the plants rise out of the soil, she opened her eyes. Sprouts grew from the formerly barren spot, clamoring up between her fingers.

The plants grew until they were as high as her shoulders. She laughed and stood before they encircled her and covered her completely. That had happened before, and she'd had to dig her way out.

She stepped back and tripped over a pair of armored feet. She lost her footing, and would have fallen had Hades not caught her.

Hades. Persephone's cheeks flooded with warmth. Her skin prickled as if it were coming to life. Hades held her arm with one hand, his other arm was wrapped around her waist. He had a firm but gentle hold on her. Persephone looked up at him. He took her breath away.

The god smiled down at her indulgently. Then a quizzical look came over his face, as if he recognized something he'd not noticed before. He cleared his throat and righted her, placing her back on her feet with a gentleness that made tears come to her eyes.

"Sorry I startled you," Hades said.

His fingers lingered around her waist just long enough for her to feel them even after he'd moved them.

"I should have been paying attention," Persephone said, embarrassed, pushing a stray hair out of her eye. "My mother says my attention is too often someplace other than where it should be."

Hades gave her a small smile but said nothing more, so she studied his face, watching him as he turned to look at the land below them. He was taking it all in, the way she'd done before he arrived. She knew that he, perhaps more than all of them, appreciated the peaceful, hopeful world they'd fought valiantly to build.

"Isn't it magnificent?" She nodded at the scene before them, forgetting to be nervous around the stunning god.

"It can be," justice-loving Hades answered, equivocating.

"It already is."

Hades shook his head. "There is so much to be done before the world matches what I have in my mind."

Persephone started at the unfamiliar rawness in Hades's voice. Wide-eyed, she watched cares descend over his face, cares he hid from the other gods as he dazzled them with his vision and brazenly led them into action. She had never seen Hades like this, vulnerable and doubting. While a small part of her felt fear at his uncertainty, the larger part of her felt even more drawn to him. So moved by his need for partnership, comfort, and understanding that she forgot her own doubts and fears, Persephone stepped in front of him.

She slowly took off his armored gloves, remnants from the war that he still put on every day. She dropped them to the ground. Then she took his hands in hers.

She held his hands—their bare skin touching. She wanted to reassure him, to tell him that she was with him, that she believed in him. She acted without thinking, for if she had thought, she would have stopped herself, telling herself that Hades, of all the gods, needed neither help nor reassurance.

But he did need those things. And for them to come from her was like magic.

Persephone had never touched Hades's bare skin before, and her innocent act of support and intimacy ignited a passion between the two young immortals. The spark had been there, waiting to be fed. The attraction between them, the respect, the mutual admiration now blazed with all the intensity of their youth and unfettered power.

Hades felt heat rise in his face, and thought he grew ten feet taller. Comfort and excitement filled him at the same time. He felt as if he—who had lead for as long as he could remember—had found someone to lean on.

Hades looked into Persephone's eyes and knew that he loved her—that his love had been there lying in wait to be awakened by her touch. Love for her flowed through his body, as if that was what now sustained him. This wisp of a goddess with her pink lips and gentle nature held the most powerful god in the palm of her hand. He touched her dark hair and found his hand trembled at her beauty. He was hers, he realized.

Forever.

The two young gods stared at one another as if seeing each other for the first time. They held one another's gaze until the sky darkened. Not wanting his view of her dimmed, or their moment to end, Hades wrenched his focus from Persephone. In one swift, clean motion, he hurled his thunderbolt into the sky. The thunderbolt whistled and soared until it reached the mass of clouds that had obscured the sun. It pierced the clouds, tearing a hole in them, and releasing a single brilliant ray of light onto Persephone.

Persephone smiled up at Hades with such joy and gratitude it nearly knocked him to the ground. It was startling to see her delicate features express such broad emotion. Long eyelashes framed her sparkling green eyes. She exuded vibrance and exuberance but in a restrained way, until she took you in as a trusted friend. Her voice was so sweet it nearly dripped with honey, but its sincerity could make you weep. You couldn't help but want her to like you, to approve of you, so you could feel good and strong and worthy.

And that was how Hades felt now: good, strong, and worthy. He knew he would chase that feeling all his immortal days.

Persephone closed her eyes and tilted her head back, feeling herself grow stronger with each breath, with each moment in the sun. Hades took her hands again and felt an immense satisfaction at being able to provide her with the sun she craved. He realized that he wanted to give her whatever she needed. Always.

"We have a chance," Persephone said to him, her face glowing even brighter in the focused light of the sun. The sunlight itself grew brighter and more intense where it touched her. She looked for a moment like a vision, her body shimmering in the light. Hades squeezed her hands to make sure she was real, that she was there, in the flesh. With him.

She opened her eyes to see Hades's lean, handsome face full of emotion and want. "The darkness that filled the world has been banished," she said boldly. "Now we can make a world of light and beauty."

"Yes," Hades said, his voice breaking. He nearly wept at the understanding in her eyes, this girl he hadn't realized had grown into a woman.

"That is what's been in my mind. That's what I fought for. Night is over," he whispered.

Persephone cupped Hades's face in her hands and beamed.

"Let us welcome the dawn."

CHAPTER 2

Persephone gasped, gulping for air. She inhaled deep, rib-expanding breaths. Each breath filled her body a little more, reviving her. The air tasted musty and ancient. It stunk of stagnation and rot—but she was grateful for it.

Persephone's body felt stiff. She stretched her arms overhead, then quickly pulled them back in close. The ground beneath her was cold and hard, topped with a thin layer of mucus. She wiped the gooey ooze on her dress, peeling the sticky substance off her fingers.

She was afraid to open her eyes. She had the overwhelming sense that she was far from home. She felt no life around her. A distant memory haunted her thoughts, a memory of pain and loss. But the dream that woke her had been of Hades.

"I am waking from a dream," she said quietly. "I will open my eyes and find myself having fallen asleep by the marsh."

The marsh had running water, permeated by the sulfurous smell of the rotting giants who'd perished there in the war between gods and Titans.

"I'm afraid not, little lamb," came a gruff voice. "But you know that. You know where you are, and you remember how you got here."

Persephone shivered and shut her eyes tighter, willing herself to be somewhere, anywhere, else.

But it was no use. She remembered. Of course she remembered. Tears streamed down her face, waterfalls of pain.

"You need no coin, my lady," the boatman said gently. He reached out a gnarled hand and lifted her to her feet with surprising ease. "Come with me."

Persephone opened her eyes. The sight of the pitch-black cavern filled her with horror. She'd never seen it before, but she knew where she was.

A terrible memory flashed in her mind. She looked down at the slashed and burned hole in her dress. She gingerly peeled aside the remnants of gossamer fabric. Her trembling fingers hovered over her chest, not daring to touch what she found there, where her smooth glowing skin used to be.

Persephone froze, unable to do anything other than breathe. Her thoughts were scattered, torn between memories of her past and now-impossible dreams for her future.

It was over. It was all over.

The raggedly cloaked boatman gently took her hand. He put his other arm around her waist and led her to where his modest vessel bobbed in the dull water. He stepped into the boat, then turned to reach for her.

Persephone roused herself from her shock, forcing herself to move before he could touch her again. She pulled her arms close and crossed them tightly, as if they could offer her protection from what was inevitably to come. Her toes lingered at the edge of the water, clinging to the rocky shore. The black water lapped perilously close to her feet. She edged away from it.

"I'm not yet across the river," she said to herself. Then more loudly: "I'm not yet across the river." Persephone took a step back from the water. She pinched her arms and felt the pinch. She dared to hope. "I'm still here. I haven't crossed the Styx. I can return!"

"None can return," Charon said sadly. "Ask him."

Persephone's gaze followed Charon's gnarled finger to a huge three-headed dog with monstrous red eyes. Kerberos crouched in front of a wide opening in the cavern. His yellow fangs were as tall as Persephone. His dragon's tail swished behind him in warning, its dagger-like spikes scraping the cavern floor as it swept side to side, making a high-pitched screech that turned Persephone's stomach. The hound growled, a sound so menacing that Persephone's knees went weak. Then a foul Underworld gale swept in and pushed her. She tumbled forward into the boat.

"Kerberos guards the entrance to the Underworld." Charon shook his head, leaning forward to help her. "No one living gets in, no shades get out."

Kerberos' foul breath had blown her into the boat. She glared at him, her chest heaving in anger, her hands trembling with fear.

"But I'm a goddess!" she protested from her hands and knees in the little boat, her body swaying uneasily with the water's movements.

"I know, lamb. But you Olympians have no control over what lies here. You know this. This isn't your realm. This is the realm of none but the dead."

The boatman spoke tenderly in his graveled voice, as if addressing a child.

"What lives down here is more ancient than the gods, older than you can imagine. If you're here, you're supposed to be here—no matter who you are. And I must take you across."

Persephone sunk lower into the boat.

"How can that be?" she whispered fearfully, knowing the ferryman was right, but wishing he wasn't. Wishing she didn't believe him.

Dazed, she pressed her cheek against the side of the vessel and stared into the black water. Charon effortlessly dug his long oar through the Styx, and the boat moved forward with silent melancholy.

Persephone watched the water as they made their slow progress through it. She couldn't see to the bottom. Perhaps it went on endlessly. It was so unlike water in the world above. It had no sound, no echoes of life within, sustained by it. It didn't reflect. Persephone couldn't see her image in it. But then, Persephone thought, maybe she no longer had a reflection.

Persephone stared blankly into the water, feeling as empty it was. She had no sense of how long they'd been on the Styx—or how long she'd stared into its blankness—when small ripples appeared on its surface.

She bolted upright. Persephone clung to the side of the boat and leaned over the water. Something was rising from the depths. Oddly, she felt no fear about what was coming, but rather, was drawn ever closer to it—until her face nearly touched the water.

"Wait!" she called to the boatman. "Stop! Stop the boat! We're passing it!"

Charon expertly maneuvered the boat, stopping it midstream, then turning it so she could see what the Styx had to show her.

It was a face. It looked like a reflection, but was it? Could it be? Dangling over the side of the boat, Persephone found herself looking not into her own face, but the face she loved best.

Wordlessly, Persephone reached out to Hades's face. Her fingers grazed the water and felt his chiseled cheek. She traced the line of his jaw up to the sharp peak on his forehead. She ran her fingers through his hair and reveled in the smile he gave her. His teeth gleamed, his smile creasing the skin around his dark eyes.

Persephone smiled. She put her hand on her heart and held it there, her other hand not leaving Hade's face. The water from the Styx was thick and viscous—it dripped from her palm and soaked her dress, but she didn't feel it. Her skin was warm beneath her hand, as she remembered the warmth of Hades's skin on hers.

The boat bobbed in the water. Charon patiently watched and waited for the goddess to be ready to move on, something he could not recall having done in the countless times he ferried souls over the same dark water.

Hades's face was still there, smiling at Persephone from the water. It was the face of a man so capable, so worthy and strong, that he was the king of the gods themselves.

But this? Persephone hung her head. This obstacle was too much—even for him. This—she tried not to think the word but it slipped into her mind—this *separation* was insurmountable.

Persephone reached out to hold Hades's face, a desperate need filling her: the need to bring him closer, as if he could take her away from this place. Away from what seemed to be her Fate. But as she tried to clasp him to pull him towards her, his face vanished. She gasped.

No trace of his image remained. It disappeared completely, as if had never existed. The Styx was calm and still; it was as though she had only imagined Hades's face. As though she had only ever imagined it...

Charon looked on silently from where he stood in the boat. His usually hardened face was full of pity.

"Hades," Persephone whispered to the now-glasslike surface of the Styx. The loss of his image tore the last frail fragment hope out of her. She didn't know she could feel such emptiness. "I—I—"

Her shoulders sagged and she collapsed over the side of the boat. She stared hard at the place where Hades's image had been. The current had begun pulling the boat away, but she kept her eyes firmly fixed on the place where she had seen Hades.

She knew he hadn't really been there, but she had felt him. It had seemed so real it was like the Underworld had ripped him away from her a second time. She felt this second loss shattered her in two.

"I'm sorry," she whispered. "I'm so sorry..."

"It's me who's sorry, my lady," she heard Charon say. The boatman gripped her shoulders, gently settling her back into the boat. "Even down here, I know of your kindness."

Charon eased a desolate Persephone back onto the boat's well-worn seat. He took the oar again in his ancient hands and turned the boat around, taking Persephone farther from where she had seen Hades's face. Persephone watched the spot until it was out of sight.

She closed her eyes. She felt weak. Boneless. Defeated.

She let the boat carry her forward. Charon's oar splashed in quiet rhythm. The sound reminded her that she wasn't alone. At that thought, Persephone knew she wanted to be strong. She didn't know what was going to happen next—none of the gods knew what awaited those who went to the Underworld. They knew only that no god wanted to venture there. All they knew of were the terrible stories told by the Titans and by Kronos, enemies they had overcome.

Persephone knew she needed to be prepared and ready to meet whatever came next.

Trembling, she fought to regain her composure. She opened her eyes. She dried her arms on her stained and tattered dress, then put her hands beside her on the seat. As she touched the smooth, ancient wood, thousands of faces flashed before her eyes, faces of those who had been in Charon's boat before her.

Humans. So many of them...

"Is there any light where we're going?" She focused on the ferryman's conical hat to distract herself from the myriad of other thoughts vying for her attention. "Any glimmer of sun that pierces the blackness?"

"No, my lady." Charon shook his head as he rowed them slowly towards the other side of the Styx, towards the shore she saw in the distance.

"Well, now, that's not quite right," he said, changing his mind and nearly smiling. "Now you are the light."

At that, Persephone shut her eyes and didn't even try to stop the tears from gushing out.

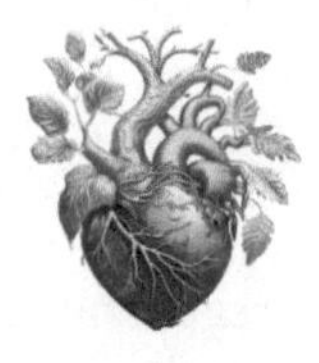

CHAPTER 3

Persephone rested her head on Hades's chest, moving slightly with his rising and falling breath. He was so solid, a part of the ground beneath her as much as Mt. Olympus was. She traced her fingers along his bare skin. Hades grinned, eyes closed, and squeezed her to him.

Persephone laughed—she'd thought he was asleep. She shifted and placed her chin on his chest and gazed at his face.

Hades's dark eyes were wide-set, giving the impression that nothing could happen without him seeing it. His dark brown hair reached just below the nape of his neck. He had a habit of raking his hands through it when he was thinking. His hairline came to a point on his forehead, which made him look at once predatory and noble.

"Do you know how much you terrify me?" Hades said, his eyes still closed.

"What?" Persephone asked, startled. The trees that had been swaying in the breeze stilled. Lying in tall grass in the midst of a grove, the sun warmed Persephone's skin through an opening she'd requested of the leaves.

Hades opened his eyes. She thought she might melt under their intense beauty.

"I said you terrify me," he repeated.

"I find that hard to believe," Persephone teased.

"Believe it. You're the most dangerous of all the gods," he said.

"Oh, really?" Persephone tugged playfully on a strand of Hades's hair. "I make plants grow. How can I be the most dangerous?"

In response, a darkness came over Hades's face that made Persephone feel at once sad and frightened.

"What are you saying?" she asked, her playful mood gone.

"If anything happened to you, Persephone, it would destroy me. Or I would destroy everything else."

Persephone sat up, a chill running down her spine. She had never thought about them being separated—the possibility had never entered her mind before that moment. She only knew that she loved Hades. That her love for him sometimes felt it would overwhelm her and swallow her whole.

"I go where you go. Where I go, you follow. We'll always be together—you and I," she assured him. "Now that I have you—" Persephone forced a smile, attempting to erase the worry from Hades's face. "I'm not about to let you go."

She pushed aside the unease that had bubbled up in her along with his words and leaned over to kiss him. He pulled her down and wrapped her in his arms. The trees entwined their branches, shading and sheltering the young gods from the rest of the world.

. . .

Persephone woke with a start. The boat was still. Charon was gone. She was alone and it was quiet. The stillness was profound. Terrifying.

Despair returned to her in the darkness, and she whispered Hades's name. It gave her strength.

She could still feel his lips on hers, his arms holding her like she was the only thing in the world. In his world. In the only world that mattered.

But she wasn't in that world any longer.

Persephone had been sleeping on her hair and it was now a knotted tangle. Strands stuck to her face like a spider's web.

She found herself straightening it with her fingers, sitting up and tidying herself, smoothing out her burned and torn dress.

Charon had pulled the boat onto shore while she slept. She forced herself to look around at this new place. She was overcome with panic at what she saw. The boat ride had been longer than she anticipated. When had she fallen asleep? She wasn't merely across the river from where she began; she was somewhere else entirely. She had no idea what to expect next. She could see rugged forms in the blackness, the rough walls of the cavern, but still no light. No clear pathway. Nothing moving or living. What awaited her once she stepped out of the boat?

Persephone's thoughts turned to her mother. She missed her calm, warm presence. What would her mother do once she found her gone? How savagely would Demeter grieve her loss? Persephone had never been without her mother—their lives, their work were entwined like vines.

She shook her head, gathering her strength once more.

If I get out of this boat, if I set foot on that side of the river, there is no turning back.

"I'm not moving from this spot," she declared. She threw her shoulders back bravely, but her whole body trembled.

"You will, my lady," the ferryman said, his lined face forlorn as he emerged from the darkness. His sudden appearance and the silence with which he moved made Persephone start.

"I don't know how or why you will leave the boat," Charon said. "But I know you will."

He planted his oar in the ground beside the worn vessel and leaned against it, looking at her with resignation.

Persephone crossed her arms.

"Nothing will make me move from this spot," she vowed.

Then she heard it.

The scream. It came from the darkness. A cry for help.

Persephone leaned forward, uncrossing her arms. It was a heart-wrenching sound. She searched for signs of movement in the dark, but found nothing.

"Help please! Someone help me!" came another plea. A tiny red light appeared in the blackness. "Help me!"

The light flickered.

"Who is that?" Persephone asked, shuddering.

She rose and turned to the ferryman.

"Why do you just stand there?" she demanded. "Go to her! Help her!"

Charon shook his head.

"That's not for me to do," he said. "It's not my task."

Another scream pierced the darkness. The red light grew, glowing orange.

"What do you mean not your task? If someone needs aid, you help them!"

"No," he said. "I don't."

The goddess shook her head at him, disappointed. "Well, I do."

She took a deep breath and raised her foot. She paused, foot lifted, and thought of Hades. And her mother, and the warmth of the sun. She thought about the way the light shone on the grass, making it glow. She thought of the sea and how it cradled the shore, and gleamed in the sun like starlight.

Persephone said a silent farewell to the world she loved and everyone in it. And stepped out of the boat.

Charon sighed.

"I told you. No one can resist. Your goodness was used against you. I am sorry my lady. So very sorry."

He removed his hat, crushing and wringing it as a tear slid down his wrinkled face. "It is a cold, cruel world," he bemoaned. "And the Underworld is no different."

Persephone watched from shore as the ferryman pushed his boat back into the Styx, climbing into it with a speed and nimbleness that belied his ancient appearance. He put his mangled hat back on his head and dipped his oar into the water with a silent splash.

"I've been called again," he said as he rowed away from her, not turning back to look. "My task is never done. I wish you peace, lady, though there is none to be had here."

As she watched Charon float away, Persephone caught her breath. The weight of what she'd done crushed the air from her lungs. She covered her face with her hands and crumpled to the ground. Her bare legs were cold in the wet black sand. She had never felt cold before.

"Help!" came another desperate scream, the loudest one yet.

Persephone looked up. She sniffed and wiped the tears from her face. Then she stood and ran to the red-orange light, which expanded with her approach until it was large enough to be a doorway. She ran straight through it, and into the heart of the Underworld.

CHAPTER 4

"I'll bring her back," Hades had said. "I'm going to find her and bring her back."

Zeus had listened. He had let Hades rail and shout and destroy. Zeus had grieved and stood by his brother as he grieved. It was unthinkable that Persephone was gone. The longer she was gone, the more the earth itself mourned.

Zeus knew it wasn't the earth mourning, but rather the grieving of the gods who ruled it: Persephone's mother was as devastated as Hades. As Hades battled with the ground itself to make his way to the Underworld to find Persephone, Zeus watched the crops and trees around them wither, dry up, and die.

The air grew cold. The sun vanished behind the clouds. The wind carried the mourning cries of Demeter.

"You cannot reach her." Zeus shook his head sadly, trying now to soothe his brother and bring him back from the brink of what felt like madness. Hades was always the one to see and speak reason. "You know you cannot. Persephone cannot return from where she's gone."

Zeus flicked away a grasshopper that landed on his shoulder. The air was dry and dusty. Grasshoppers swarmed in the dead grass.

"Hades, we agreed," Zeus reminded his brother again. They stood side by side at the edge of a great chasm, the chasm left when Persephone had been dragged into the Underworld. "We all agreed, we twelve. Our border is the Underworld. We won't go beyond that border. We won't grasp for realms beyond what we've already chosen."

"I changed my mind."

"That's something I would do," Zeus said. "Not you."

"It doesn't matter." Hades knelt and dug his fingers into the dirt at the edge of the chasm. "Laws, rules, mine, yours. It's all nothing."

Hades clenched his fist so tightly that the dirt he was holding disappeared. It vanished, as Hades's great love had. Like his hopes and dreams had vanished the instant Persephone was taken away from him.

"Without Persephone, there is nothing."

"No!" Zeus said angrily. "Look around you! There is the world you led us to found and rule. The world that is now dying because Persephone is gone. You are the king of that world. The king of the gods. Persephone wouldn't want you to let everything we worked for die."

Hades nodded slowly. "You're right." He opened his fist to see that what it once grasped was gone. "We are gods," he said quietly, more to himself than to Zeus. "I am king of the gods."

A fearsome look crept over Hades's face. The whites of his eyes grew brighter in contrast to the darkening sky. Thunder rumbled and filled the air as Hades stood, towering over the jagged trench ripped in the earth when Persephone died. Zeus watched Hades's anger grow until it burst out of him like a storm.

"I am king of the gods. I am the most powerful creature in our universe!" Hades roared, his eyes shining. "Nothing can stop me from getting what I want!"

"I know what you want, and you know it can't be done!" Zeus yelled back at him. He stood firm, unwavering, amid Hades's growing storm. "Hades, you—of all of us—you know we don't control the Underworld. We cannot cross that border! You know our power has limits."

"Then that will change," Hades vowed. He twirled the glowing thunderbolt in his hand, his face eerily lit by the bolt, while everything surrounding him was drenched in darkness.

"Even our father dared not challenge that truth," Zeus countered. "What lies in the Underworld are dangers and forces so ancient we can't understand them, let alone tangle with them!"

"We can untangle them."

"Hades." Zeus shook his head, exasperated. "Even you, brother. Even you cannot win this fight. I would follow you anywhere, but the Underworld—the Underworld is worse than the bedlam our father reigned over. It's mad and dark and hopeless."

"And you want me to leave her there?"

Hades turned his anguished face from Zeus and glared at the silent earth that held Persephone prisoner. He stomped on the ground, and a tornado rose from beneath his foot. As it grew, its roar became deafening.

The tornado tore over the ground, churning up grass and trees, inhaling them into its soaring, unforgiving funnel cloud. Hurling boulders from the ground as if they were grains of sand, the funnel cloud sucked the huge rocks up and then spat them out. The sound was ear-splitting.

Hades raised his arms, conducting the tornado like a symphony, guiding it to dig deeper. It was a furious beast made of wind and rage, racing back and forth over the trench in a desperate search for his beloved Persephone.

"Hades, stop!" Zeus pressed his massive hands into Hades's forearms, crushing them into his sides. "Brother." Zeus spoke through gritted teeth, struggling to hold down his brother's arms before the now-gaping trench and the still-roaring tornado. "She is lost! You will tear apart the earth and kill every living thing on it, but it will not bring her back!"

Hades threw his head back and howled, a terrible wail of grief and fury. He yanked his arms out of Zeus's hands.

"She is lost!" Zeus yelled.

"She's not lost," Hades growled, his dark eyes flashing. "I feel her...I still feel her!"

Hades pounded his chest with an intensity that would have made a mortal man fall over dead. He staggered and dropped to his knees.

Zeus took Hades by the shoulders and lifted him to his feet. Debris flew all around them, a god's rage unleashed. The two most powerful gods stood nose to nose, in the eye of the storm.

"Brother." Zeus spoke in the soothing tone he used to calm untamed beasts. His hands gripped Hades's shoulders, his knuckles white with the effort of holding his brother in place to try to make him understand. "She's in the Underworld now." Zeus spoke slowly and carefully. "Persephone is in the Underworld. And that is where she must remain."

"I cannot leave her to that for the rest of existence," Hades said softly. "I cannot..."

"I know," Zeus answered. "I know..."

Hades looked into Zeus's eyes, then bowed his head. The tornado vanished. The rocks and branches in its grasp dropped to the ground. A stillness permeated the air, matching the destruction wreaked by the funnel cloud. The jagged trench was now a canyon that nearly split the ground in half.

Hades looked up at his brother.

Zeus raised an eyebrow. It wasn't over. He knew by the look in Hades's eyes, and the man Hades was, that Hades hadn't given up. He wouldn't give up. Hades would find Persephone. Or destroy himself trying.

Zeus had to think fast. He stroked his chiseled chin and paced, circling Hades slowly, attempting to outwit the most brilliant god.

"Let's say you tried it. If you defied our law—and me—how would you find the Underworld?" Zeus asked. "No one with breath in his body has seen the entrance to it. No one knows where to find it and, between the two of us, you and I have seen every corner of this world."

Hades was quiet and calm. But Zeus knew his little brother was thinking, calculating.

"Digging wasn't getting us anywhere," Zeus said, appealing

again to his brother's strong sense of reason. "I think you could crack the earth in two, wake every kind of horror, but still not find the gate to the Underworld.

"But let's say we did find the entrance," Zeus went on, driving in the dagger. "She will not be able to come back to the surface. She died, Hades. She belongs to the Underworld now."

Zeus knew that doubt had crept into his brother's mind. He felt a twinge of guilt for not encouraging his brother's hope. Even when it looked like Kronos and the Titans were going to defeat them in the darkest days of the war, Zeus hadn't seen his brother doubt, let alone give up. But now Hades had to give up. Zeus wasn't ready to let his brother cross the Styx—and to find Persephone, that's what Hades would have to do.

Zeus mercilessly knocked the twinge of guilt to the ground and waited for Hades's response.

"What good is it?" Hades asked, searching his brother's startled face for answers.

"What good is what?"

"Everything we fought for." Hades shook his head. "The war we started. The war we fought against our own father. We fought the Titans—Kronos' race of creatures three times our size. We fought the giants—stinking, stupid, filthy beasts who would have eaten us limb by limb if they'd captured us. For what? So we would be gods over all? Why? It was vanity. Arrogance. It's all worthless without her...if I cannot bring her back..."

And then Hades broke down and wept like a child. Zeus held him, wishing he could take away his brother's pain, cursing that he could not make this right.

"It was for good," Zeus answered, his voice cracking. "You had a vision of a world that could be pulled out of the darkness and into the light. You imagined a world ruled by order and justice. You made it happen. And Persephone loved you for it."

"Without sunlight," Hades said, more to himself than to Zeus, not seeming to hear his brother, "what will happen to her? She needs the light. She needs the sun."

"I know," Zeus whispered. "I know. I loved her too."

"I cannot be without her."

"She is gone," Zeus said. "She is gone."

After a few quiet moments, Hades angrily threw off his brother's arm.

"NO." Hades gritted his gleaming white teeth. His thunderbolt, the weapon Hephaistos forged for him for the war against Kronos, the weapon he'd used to kill Kronos, glowed an angry red in Hades's hand.

"She is not gone," Hades snarled. "I know what you want me to do, but do you think I will just let her go? Would you? Could you?"

Zeus didn't respond.

"She is not gone," Hades said. "We know where she is."

Hades squatted down and dug his fingers into the earth once more.

"I'm going after her," he vowed. "I'm bringing her back. And I will destroy anything that stands in my way."

Hades's dark eyes burned with fire. Zeus exhaled, knowing he was the defeated one.

"Then I'm going with you."

CHAPTER 5

Persephone edged closer to the screams. The cries had quieted, but she had nothing else to do but try to find their source. No other task, no other purpose. She had to find the creature she believed needed help, needed her. That task, that goal, kept her from breaking down completely.

And so she walked. The further she walked into the Underworld, the more Persephone realized she was walking into the strange orange light she'd seen from Charon's boat.

Soon, she was enveloped in that red-orange light, and it was all she could see. It was a strange sensation, for it wasn't the warm nourishing light of the sun, but something else. It made her feel oddly cool. And afraid. She shivered, wrapping her arms around her waist as she took another deliberate step.

"Hello?" she called. "Is anyone there?"

Silence. Stillness.

"Where did you go?" Persephone whispered.

"Naïve girl," an angry whisper came back to her.

"What?" Persephone spun around, air swirling near her face. Was that the flap of wings?

"Where are you?" Persephone called. "Who are you?"

"Stupid girl. Goddess—? Hah! You are nothing now."

The cruel whisper was in her other ear now. Or was it a different voice? Something swooped and swirled around her. Shadows flew inside the red-orange light; they were a blur.

Persephone turned again, reaching out.

"Stop. Please," she pleaded. "Talk to me. Who are you? What happens now? What do I do now?"

"You are like the rest of us now," the voice spat. It was a female voice, full of bitterness. "You are nothing."

Persephone's head ached. It was the light, she realized. It was brighter now, and made her whole body ache. Her head pounded as the creature circled her in a wild orbit, swirling around her, staying just out of reach.

Persephone closed her eyes, but the light seeped in behind her eyelids. She felt herself growing weaker and colder. She had no idea that cold could bring such pain. The cold spread through every part of her body. It stung and burned her skin like fire.

Persephone collapsed, landing hard on her knees. She fell forward, clapping her palms to the ground. She felt only hard, impenetrable rock. Her eyes still shut tightly, she traced the ground with surprising calm, until she felt what she was hoping for.

The tiniest grains, soft and fertile: soil.

The pain in her head was like someone stabbing her behind her eyes. She curled into a ball, retreating into herself, as if she could escape the pain. The soil still clasped in her hands, Persephone squeezed. She poured her energy into the seemingly-insignificant soil. She thought of her mother. She thought of the sun and rain. She concentrated with all the fervor she could muster on the infant grains of earth.

Persephone's breath grew faint, but she kept her focus on the soil, holding onto it as if holding onto her own existence. Just as she was about to sink into unconsciousness, tiny stalks sprouted from between her clenched fingers.

She uncurled her fingers. Life reached out from her hands. Vines slunk up along the walls of the wide tunnel, reaching, growing, entwining and protecting Persephone.

Persephone felt the noose of the poisonous light grow faint. The pain in her head eased. Relieved, she felt a twinge of exhilaration.

She opened her eyes.

The walls of the Underworld tunnel were overgrown with dark green vines that drowned out the painful red light. The vines were smooth, with spiked leaves and golden-yellow flowers. They covered the tunnel and went as far as she could see.

Persephone eased herself onto her feet. Her body was stiff, but she felt a glimmer of hope. She hadn't expected to have any power in the Underworld, but this proved she wasn't powerless. She caressed a shiny leaf and exhaled deeply. The leaf's thick red veins pulsed with life.

Persephone heard movement nearby. She turned and saw a silhouette in the distance. She knew it was the creature who had taunted her.

"You're still here," Persephone said, grateful. She was not alone.

She walked towards the creature, and realized it was two creatures. Their heads were pressed close together. It looked like they were arguing.

"Who are you?" Persephone said. "Come where I can see you."

"You're not a goddess here," one creature hissed. "You cannot order us to do your will."

"I thought perhaps there were more than one of you."

"What do you want?"

"I want to help you."

"Help me what?"

"You screamed for help."

"That was a ruse. I don't need your help."

"I hear the pain in your voice." Persephone drew closer. "You do."

"That was a nice trick," the voice said, ignoring Persephone's observation. "With the plants."

"It wasn't a trick. It was creation. Feel them—you can feel the life beating through them. What's your name?"

"How did you do that?" came a second, higher-pitched, voice. "How did you make life down here, where everything is death and decay?"

"Be quiet," admonished the first voice.

"What if she can help us?"

"There is no help for us. You know that. There's no help for anyone here."

While the two figures resumed arguing, Persephone edged closer to get a better look at them. She started in horror at what she saw.

The creatures were more than twice her size. They had women's faces, but the eyes, bodies, and beaks of eagles. Large, ragged wings were folded at their sides, and they had sharp yellow talons for feet.

Persephone reached for the wall and clutched a handful of leaves. She took a deep breath to compose herself, then approached the winged women.

"Your wing is torn," Persephone said in a shaking voice. "Does it hurt?"

"Yes, it hurts!" the first winged creature snapped, lifting her head to glare at Persephone. Her eyes were sharply intelligent, bright yellow with large black pupils. They were full of pain and anger, yet so sad that Persephone's heart ached.

"Everything hurts and it hurts all the time," the creature hissed. "Every breath I take pains my body and kills me a little more. I was forced to call to you, but I would have called you anyway."

"Let me help you," Persephone said, undeterred. She reached out a trembling hand. The figure snapped her beak angrily, and the goddess drew back.

"What kind of creatures are you?" Persephone asked.

"Creatures? What kind of 'creatures'?" The first creature mocked and cackled. "We are your nightmares."

"We're harpies," the other said sadly. "But we were not always this way."

The first harpy took wing, her injured wing half-folded even in flight, so that she flew unevenly—alternately soaring and dropping. Her companion followed her into flight. Persephone chased them down the tunnel, until it opened into another vast dark cave.

"Take care, goddess," said the kind harpy as she swooped back around, hovering before an astonished Persephone. "And try to hide. Maybe he won't find you."

"Wait—what? Hide? Hide from who?"

"You're frightening her for nothing," the other harpy called from the distance. "We can change nothing here…you should know that by now. We must go."

"Wait—don't leave. Please. What are you talking about? Hide? But why?"

The goddess looked more delicate than ever beside the hulking figure of the harpy, whose wings stretched into the darkness as she hovered before the goddess. The harpy's beak was cracked but sharp as a dagger. Her eyes were the size of Persephone's face, and she looked as if she could open her mouth and swallow Persephone whole.

"I don't understand." Persephone shook her head, trembling from head to toe. The glimmer of hope she'd felt moments earlier was dashed against the Underworld rocks like a wave extinguishing a flame. "Hide from what? This is the Underworld. Isn't this the end?"

The harpy tilted her head.

"No," she said, blinking her enormous eyes. "I'm afraid not. It's the beginning…of something I don't dare try to explain."

The kind harpy's eyes were full of sympathy. "It will be difficult for you to hide here," she said, assessing Persephone. "You still smell like life. A freshness shines from you like a beacon. It's a scent so strong I feel like I can touch it. And your skin, you radiate. Even here. With a faint light, like hope…

"The Underworld is a maze of tunnels, interspersed with caverns. Find a tunnel like the one you just came through and take it. Follow it until you get lost in it. Stay quiet, stay in the dark. And you might keep a kind of freedom." The harpy gave her one last pitying look, then swooped around to join her injured comrade.

Together the harpies rose, flying in circles, higher and higher up into the vast cavern until they were out of sight.

"Wait!" Persephone ran after them, waving her arms. "Come back! Please don't leave!"

But on they flew.

"Stop!" Persephone cried. "Please come back!"

But they didn't turn back. Persephone was alone again.

CHAPTER 6

The young gods surveyed the monstrous gash in the earth. The two immortals looked like ants beside the huge rift in the ground, rather than the most powerful gods in the world. On Zeus's wide, chiseled face was trepidation, and on Hades's, bitter resolve. A swath of charred ground marked the earth near the fissure, and went as far as the eye could see.

Zeus stomped over the blackened soot, sandals crunching, calves bulging. He grew angrier with every step he took. The ground trembled as he walked. His thunderbolt was lost beneath the ground. He'd thrown it into the fissure, attempting to send it to the Underworld, but the earth closed around the bolt, keeping it.

"I vowed to do this with you," Zeus said. "But, as I expected, this isn't working. We know this was the place where Persephone disappeared, but it leads us nowhere. The ground fights against us! We will not find the Underworld this way."

"Look at this," Hades said from where he knelt deep in the fissure. Digging gently, he pointed to a small white root. "I thought every living thing had been destroyed by my storm and then by the thunderbolt—but look. This is new. And growing. Watch."

At Hades's touch, the root grew, spreading deeper into the soil like a claw stretching out. "Did you see that?"

"I did."

Zeus knelt beside Hades. He put his hand on the root. The

root grew thicker and dug deeper into the soil. Then another root sprouted up beside it.

"What are they? And what do they mean?" Hades asked.

Zeus shook his head, not knowing.

The high-pitched screech of a falcon made both gods turn to the sky. The lone bird soared through the cloudless blue sky, its scream filling the air, the sound more mournful than predatory.

The falcon circled the gods, its wings spread. A trail of sparrows flapped crookedly behind it, their movements choppy and sporadic compared to the majestic calm of the bird of prey.

"They will lead you to her," came a mournful voice.

Hades and Zeus watched Demeter transform from the falcon into a woman, as she landed at the edge of the crevasse.

Hades leapt up at the sight of Persephone's mother. Her face was partially obscured by her blue cloak, but Hades could see that Demeter's eyes were haunted by loss. Her usually tanned and blooming cheeks were hollow and colorless. She reached out and gripped Hades's arms tightly as he approached, as if he were the last link to her daughter.

"I've scoured the whole of the earth, Hades," Demeter said hoarsely, searching his eyes for a glimmer of hope. "She is no longer above—she is in the world below."

"I know," he said, bowing his head, finding it almost unbearable to take Demeter's pain along with his own.

"That is a new beginning," Demeter said, glancing at the tiny roots, the lone life in a landscape wrecked by Persephone's disappearance and Hades's furious attempts to go after her. "That plant is not from a seed of my making, nor is it Persephone's—I can feel and see her on everything she creates. She always leaves a little piece of herself behind, and I can follow it like a trail of light…"

Demeter paused, lost in remembrance, a peaceful look coming over her face.

Zeus and Hades exchanged glances. Zeus prompted, "And these roots, Demeter? What about them? How will they lead us to her?"

"We need to make them grow," Demeter said. With one look from the goddess of the harvest, the roots began to shake. They squirmed through the ground like worms. "This plant tells me it was created when Persephone was struck down. It's the path to the Underworld. It's the path to her." Demeter's face contorted in pain and Hades held her firmly.

"The earth loves Persephone," Demeter explained dreamily, pulling away from Hades. "It wants her to be returned to us."

"She will be," Hades vowed.

Demeter nodded. She turned to the tangle of roots. She threw off her hood, closed her eyes, and inhaled deeply. She raised her arms, wordlessly commanding the roots to grow.

In answer, they did grow. They grew until they became a tree, a laurel that creaked and stretched as it grew and expanded in every direction. Its bark thickened, its branches spread upward and reached out until they towered over the gods. Simultaneously, the roots dug down with urgency and force.

"Now," Demeter ordered Hades from the shade of the laurel, "follow the roots to the Underworld. Find her, Hades. Find my daughter and bring her home."

"I will," Hades said, his fists clenched.

Zeus came to his side.

Demeter pulled her cloak back over her head. The goddess stood motionless, staring at the tree's roots, and seemed to have forgotten the other gods' presence. The air grew colder still. In the distance, fields of grain withered, and a cold wind chased away any remnants of the sun's warmth. Fruit rotted and fell from its branches. Demeter closed her ears to the pleas and prayers of the people who worshipped her. She wouldn't hear their bellies ache with emptiness. She shut out the sounds of hungry children, of parents bemoaning how their goddess had forsaken them. She shut out everything, except her desire for the return of her daughter.

"We need to move fast," Zeus said to his brother. "Or everything we've done will have been for nothing. We need to find Persephone if we want any kind of world to return her to.

Or, in her grief, Demeter will kill everything we've created."

Hades reached out and tore a forked branch from the laurel tree. He tossed his thunderbolt to Zeus, who easily reached out to catch it.

Hades pointed his staff at the laurel's roots.

"Down we go."

CHAPTER 7

"Where are you going?" a voice demanded, stopping Zeus and Hades in their tracks.

Hurtling out of the sky like a stone, grey-eyed Athena landed with a clang of bronze. The impact against the compacted dirt sent soil and stones flying.

Athena narrowed her eyes at Zeus and Hades's breastplates and helmets. "And dressed for battle?"

Not one to miss out on a fight, she was working herself up to release a tirade at her father and uncle for leaving her behind. Then she spotted the motionless, transfixed Demeter. She paused, then looked back at Zeus and Hades's grim faces.

"It's true then?" Athena said, horrified. "Persephone? I thought—well—I thought it couldn't be—how can this have happened?" She turned to Hades. "I'm so sorry."

Hades nodded, unable to speak. He had no answers.

A stunned Athena turned to Zeus. The glare off his gold breastplate was so bright she had to squint to see the images of the Gigantomachy that Zeus had Hephaistos engrave there. The Gigantomachy was what she named the war that the gods had waged against the Titans and giants to gain control of the world.

Athena's reflection looked back at her through the images of war. She saw her own wide-set eyes, her image wavy in the metal. She looked a bit like the owl who was never far from her side.

Athena shifted her focus back to the scenes on Zeus's armor. She remembered every scene depicted there—she'd fought in most of them, earning her place as the goddess of war and wisdom with her bravery and cunning. But the last scene, the one engraved in the center of Zeus's chest, was Hades's battle alone. It was the battle that decided the outcome of the war: the fight between Kronos and Hades.

Athena inhaled and turned back to Hades. His armor was unadorned and oxidized, so darkened it was black. She looked at Hades's face, hardened with grim purpose, and knew where Hades and Zeus were going. And she knew what they were planning to do there. Or try to do. It was almost unthinkable—going to the Underworld to bring someone back. But if any god would dare attempt it, it would be the two gods who stood before her.

Or her.

"Can I go with you?" she asked quietly.

"No," Zeus said.

Uncharacteristically, Athena didn't debate his answer.

"You lead while we're gone," Hades said as he leapt into the crevasse and landed on a thick, newly-sprouted laurel branch.

"Me?" Athena stepped forward, following Hades to the edge of the chasm. "Not Poseidon?"

"Ha!" Zeus scoffed. "He may be my brother, but I wouldn't trust him with my dog. And I don't even have a dog."

"It must be you," Hades agreed, his face serious, set like a statue. "You must lead the gods, Athena. They cannot be left rudderless."

"Or who knows where they'll end up," Zeus added. Then he said gently, his tone more a question than a command. "Please stay. We need you here."

Athena paused for a moment, then nodded very slightly, acquiescing but making sure Zeus knew she was not entirely pleased to be left behind. She raised an eyebrow. "I need to know. Are you planning to do what I think you're planning to do?"

"Probably," Zeus answered with a twinkle in his eye.

"You're going to the Underworld."

"Yes," Hades nodded. He was sharpening the tips of his staff to dagger-sharp points.

Zeus approached his daughter. He took off Athena's helmet. Beneath her imposing headpiece, Athena had her father's wavy hair. It was the rich burgundy color of unwatered wine. The shade contrasted sharply with her fair skin and grey eyes, the color of which varied according to her mood. Her eyes were a soft dove grey when she was content, a stormy grey in anger.

Her nose, usually covered by the nosepiece of her helmet, was sizeable and emphasized the look of fierce focus and concentration she usually wore. The purple plume atop her helmet was motionless—Athena realized there was no wind to blow it about.

The world had paused, its breath held, awaiting the gods' response to Persephone's death.

Zeus kissed the top of Athena's head. Then he replaced her helmet and said with a smile, clasping her arms, "I trust *you* with everything."

Athena hadn't been afraid since the day Hades had battled Kronos in single combat. She could only nod in reply.

She watched Hades and Zeus race down towards the Underworld, descending in leaps from branch to branch, then sliding down the laurel's trunk until they reached the tangle of smooth grey roots. It looked as though they were navigating a nest of giant serpents, since the roots, with Demeter's help, had swelled to the circumference of broad tree trunks.

With Hades in the lead, Athena watched as the earth opened up for them. Her two favorite and most beloved gods didn't hesitate. Balancing lightly and easily on a root, they disappeared into the earth as if they had been swallowed by it.

"Be careful," she whispered to the two most powerful gods in the world, clasping her spear to her chest. "And please come back."

CHAPTER 8

The goddess of love sauntered out of the sea, her damp hair trailing below her waist. A thin layer of salt coated her bare collarbone. Her dress was laced with slits from her ankles to her waist, so that with each sway of her hips, it looked tantalizingly close to falling to pieces.

Aphrodite strode past Persephone and leaned against a tree. She crossed her arms and glanced at Persephone's tangle of plants with a disinterested air. She sighed, bored, but perked up at the sound of men's voices.

Aphrodite turned to see Hades, Poseidon, and Ares approach. Poseidon and Ares shouted at one another, their arms flailing, Ares's face reddening. Water spurted from Poseidon's fingertips. Ares's fingers spouted a dark substance—Aphrodite squinted and then grimaced when she realized it was blood.

Hades stood in front of the two other gods, attempting to calm them down. He held out a hand to each god in turn and spoke in firm, measured tones.

Aphrodite raised an eyebrow as Hades mediated the argument between the two hot-tempered gods.

She sighed, a languid, longing sigh, and leaned back against the tree.

"He's the best of them," Aphrodite said, her heavy-lidded eyes on Hades. "He'll love like no other."

She turned to where Persephone knelt in the grass, elbow-deep in dirt.

"You're lucky," Aphrodite told Persephone. She tilted her head. "I can see what he sees in you. He's lucky, too." Aphrodite smiled. "Don't let him forget it."

Persephone blushed.

Aphrodite laughed. The birds who had followed her from the sea began to sing. Cooing doves and squawking gulls took flight, swooping, circling, and diving. Eventually, they landed in a great flock around Aphrodite's bare feet.

Each bird brought the goddess an offering. Some brought twigs, others feathers. The last gull placed a gleaming pearl in front of Aphrodite's toes.

Aphrodite squealed in delight and picked up the pearl. Persephone heard the grass she'd just created sigh with pleasure.

"You're strong," Aphrodite said to Persephone, holding up the pearl to inspect it. "Stronger than you know. You and Hades are worthy of each other."

Aphrodite looked to Ares as he cleaned his teeth with a knife and spat angrily at Hades's decision.

"It's rare to find the kind of love you share with Hades," Aphrodite said with a sigh. "Believe me. I know…"

CHAPTER 9

Persephone thought about what the harpy had said about her scent and skin, and was buoyed by the revelation that she was leaving a trail behind her. She knew the image she'd seen of Hades in the Styx was only that—an image. But, what if he did come to the Underworld to find her? If any god dared to attempt it, it would be him. And she was leaving a trail he could follow.

She stood a little bit taller. She felt a little bit stronger. She refused to let herself think about how impossible it was, how it was against the rules that she and the other Olympians had put in place. She wanted, for a moment at least, to cling to the notion that Hades could come after her.

But the harpy had told her about her scent and her light as a warning. Because Persephone trusted the harpy, the warning also made her uneasy. She smiled grimly—she hadn't thought she could feel any more uneasy than she'd felt the moment she awoke in the Underworld.

"What kind of dangers lurk in these dark corners? Other than going mad with loneliness…"

Persephone called to a strand of her vines. They braided themselves into her hair.

"That's better," Persephone said, and the little flowers shimmied in agreement.

Persephone sighed softly. It was a relief to not be entirely alone.

She sniffed her skin but could detect nothing other than the stale, rotten smell that permeated the Underworld. Even her new flowers didn't smell sweet. They absorbed the forlorn smell of their surroundings.

"We need fresh air," Persephone said to her vines. "Is that possible here?"

The vines and flowers had no answer.

"You know what we need to do," Persephone said to her creations. "Follow the water. The river must lead to an opening." She felt excitement rise in her chest. "And an opening could mean a way out."

Trembling with hope, Persephone turned back the way she came. She hurried, taking long strides, back towards the river Styx. Her tunnel of vines followed her, growing thickly along the cave walls as she walked.

Persephone stopped when she reached a fork in the tunnel.

"I don't remember this. I've gone too far. I didn't walk that far to find the harpies."

She spun around, and suddenly there were four tunnel openings.

"No!" she cried.

Two more openings appeared.

"No!" Persephone fell to her knees. "I need to get out! Which one is the way out!"

She collapsed into a heap, Charon's words echoing in her head. *There is no way out, my lady.*

The vines and flowers tried to comfort her, growing around her, surrounding her with thick foliage, but she was inconsolable. She was still crying when she felt something move past her. She looked up, wiping tears away with the back of her hand. Her mouth fell open at what she saw.

A person had walked by her. But then, it wasn't a person. It was a shade, a transparent figure, and it floated away from her.

Persephone chased it.

"Wait!" she called. "Who are you? Where are you going?"

The shade didn't reply. It couldn't reply. It was devoid of life. Persephone knew that at a glance. She felt that as it swept past her. Desperate, she followed it anyway. Hastening to keep up with its pace, Persephone began to run.

"Wait!" she called again, in spite of its uselessness. When she arrived at the end of the tunnel, Persephone froze.

Thousands of shades floated in a vast cavernous room. They swept in and out of a tangle of hundreds of tunnel openings.

Persephone stared. Shades floated past her as if she wasn't there. She had no idea how long she stood there, transfixed, but something fell from above and landed on her foot: a feather.

Persephone reached down to pick up the feather and was faced with something else she hadn't anticipated: she was hungry.

CHAPTER 10

"The war is over," justice-loving Hades declared to the gathering of gods on Mount Olympus.

He stood on a plateau in the shadow of the great mountain's peak. The gods gathered in front of Hades and Zeus, curving before them like a crescent moon.

"The dark age of Kronos and the Titans is over," Zeus declared to shouts and cheers from the other gods.

Newborn stars shot up into the bright sky as the gods celebrated. The trees encircling the gods atop the mountain swayed in approval.

"It was a terrible fight," Hades said. "We fought and destroyed and suffered. But we did it for..." Hades paused and looked to Persephone, who stood—small in stature but glowing with pride—at her place among the twelve formidable and jubilant gods. "Light." He smiled and she gave a brilliant smile of her own.

"We fought for light," Hades repeated. "Now we can bring order to the world. Now we create anew. The tide has turned. Now we are the builders and masters of the ships. Let us lead them to the morning."

Murmurs and nods of approval flowed through the divine group.

"We know what it can be," Hades continued, the thunderbolt in his grasp humming, feeding off his restrained energy. "This world can be a place of beauty and art, hope and ideas. Each of you have gifts—each of you can bring meaning to this place we call home."

"We are Olympians," Zeus said from his place beside his brother. "Gods of Mount Olympus, the highest mountain standing."

The twelve gods looked to the sky in unison. With an exhale, Zeus lit up the sky until it was a vibrant orange, sweeping and swirling with pink and fuchsia. From their place atop Olympus, the gods watched the sun lower at Zeus's bidding.

"And who will lead this glorious new world?" Poseidon sneered, pausing the sun with a flash of his hand. He stepped forward. "Little brother." Poseidon's eyes were on Hades. "Do you think it should be you?"

The three brothers stood apart from the rest of the Olympians.

"You, Hades, and I are the strongest," Zeus told Poseidon. "We will take the greatest responsibilities."

"And what are the greatest responsibilities?" Ares spat.

"Someone has to rule the sky," Aphrodite offered, her bare leg winding around Ares's muscular thigh. Ares grinned wolfishly and turned away from the discussion, distracted.

"That same god should be our leader: ruler of the sky is ruler of the Olympians," Athena added, disgusted as usual with Ares and Aphrodite.

"Agreed," said Hades.

"Agreed," the rest of the gods answered in chorus.

Demeter stepped forward. She took laurel and olive branches from a basket hanging on her arm. The branches wove themselves into a crown.

Demeter handed Persephone the basket, then approached the three brothers with the crown. The gathering of gods was silent as she stood before Zeus, Poseidon, and Hades: the three most powerful gods.

Demeter turned first to Poseidon. She looked into the stormy blue eyes beneath his unruly black eyebrows. Her long, narrow face was small beside his large head and wild, dark hair.

"Powerful shoulders, fiery temper, at peace in the water, you are vengeful, quick-tempered, and terrible when roused. You are competitive but not the leader of men. You need your own separate kingdom, over which you can rule without submitting to the guiding forces of others. You should rule the vast ocean."

"But—" Poseidon began to object, but Zeus silenced his slightly shorter brother with a menacing look. Poseidon glared, simmering.

Next, Demeter moved to Zeus. He grinned, but ever-serious Demeter was immune to his irrepressible charm. She narrowed her eyes, and broad-chested Zeus fidgeted under her gaze. Hades quietly laughed.

Not yet speaking, Demeter moved in front of Hades. Hades grew silent.

Demeter lowered her head and Hades, understanding, did the same. She placed the crown on Hades's head. Its leaves turned to gleaming gold. The gods gasped, then hushed as the sun dipped beneath the horizon. A great green flash lit up the sky.

Next came a tremendous creaking and smashing. The stunned gods watched a great throne rise in their midst, breaking free of the stone of Mt. Olympus.

"Hades." Demeter spoke in measured tones. "You are far-thinking. You have vision and determination. You possess patience and commitment, much like the farmer needs, if he is to cultivate what he's planted and feed the fruits of his labor to sustain his family.

"Justice-loving, far-thinking Hades, you will be god of the sky. And god over all."

Persephone held her breath. Hades closed his eyes, absorbing Demeter's words, feeling the weight of the responsibility she'd placed on his head. Zeus clapped his mighty hand on Hades's shoulder approvingly, and Hades grinned. The new king of the gods opened his eyes to see his fellow gods staring at him, most of them approvingly. One or two of the twelve looked dubious or jealous, but not Zeus. Never Zeus.

"Zeus," Demeter began, but Hades was distracted. Again, he found Persephone's face beaming at him from among the divine, the most beautiful to him out of the most beautiful that ever existed.

"Zeus," Demeter repeated. "You burn with a fire like the sun.

Fire creates and destroys. You create and destroy. You are selfish and vain, but loyal. And in the end, you choose right—or you make things right. You are dependable despite your frequent foolishness. Your vibrancy and passion are unmatched except by the brightest star in our sky. You should command the sun."

"Who said you could decide, Demeter?" Poseidon growled, his trident spewing water like a fountain as he stepped forward threateningly.

"No." Zeus's massive hand kept Poseidon back, a glance from him freezing the trident's water into a sculpture of ice. "She's right. We all know she's right."

"He's the youngest!" Poseidon shouted, dissatisfied. "Hades is younger than you and me! Zeus, this is an insult. Rightfully, one of us should rule over all."

"*Rightfully?*" Zeus asked. "Rightfully—," Zeus mocked. He strutted back and forth, his arms outstretched. "Rightfully, Kronos would still be alive and we would be living in hiding and fear and filth. Who among us wants that? Who among us wants to return to the days before the war, before Hades plotted and planned and led us to freedom?"

Zeus's question was met with silence, as he knew it would be.

"I thought as much."

Zeus stood shoulder to shoulder with Hades.

"Hades will lead us now as he led us in the war to overthrow our father. I will follow him anywhere," he vowed.

Then he raised his lightning bolt, the matching one to Hades's.

"Hades," Zeus roared. "God of the Olympians!"

Hades did the same, and their bolts lit up the sky—their combined power making even the most confident of the other gods feel cowed.

CHAPTER 11

Hades and Zeus raced along the tunnel carved by the laurel tree's roots for three days and three nights. When the tunnel finally ended, it left the gods at the brink of a dark chasm.

Zeus peered over the edge, slashing his thunderbolt at the craven many-legged insects that had trailed them into the deep, the new gods a curiosity for the ancient creatures of the habitual dark.

Hades and Zeus stood side by side. Hades tightened his grasp on his forked staff. With a glance, he transformed the branch into bronze.

"Down we go," he said to Zeus for the second time. Then Hades raised the bronze staff and dove head-first into the abyss.

Zeus zapped one more hideous bug, this one with glowing eyes, before he dove after his brother. The gods fell for as many days as they had run, before landing on solid ground.

Hades landed lightly on his feet. Zeus, at his heels, landed with a thundering, decisive thud.

A low growl immediately filled the dark space in answer to their arrival.

"What is that?" Zeus grimaced, his back to the sound. The growl came again, this time bringing with it the stench of rotting meat.

Hades, his lanky body buzzing with unspent energy, looked over Zeus's shoulder and answered, "A sign that we've arrived."

Zeus turned to see a monstrous canine beast snarling and

snapping three massive jaws. The gods stood with their backs to the shaft through which they'd plummeted to get into the Underworld, and Hades wasn't willing to take one step backward. He had arrived, and nothing would stand in his way.

Pools of saliva formed in front of Kerberos as he whipped his spiked dragon tail back and forth. His filthy back paws stood in the Styx. He was challenging them to come closer, to dare to try to cross to the other side, to where Persephone must be.

Zeus flexed his muscles.

"Welcome to the Underworld, brother."

. . .

The gods stood their ground as Kerberos gnashed his fangs at them, forbidding them to go any further. Yellow saliva dripped from his three jaws and formed puddles that fed into the winding Styx. Kerberos' six red eyes narrowed and he pawed at the ground, his front claws so sharp they dug into the rock floor. They sliced gashes into the stone that were deep enough for a man to lie down in. The ground was wildly uneven, littered with his scrapes and scratches, full of pits and valleys.

Kerberos swished his tail. Two of his massive heads howled, while his center head focused on Hades.

The Underworld vibrated with Kerberos' howls, as if alive. Zeus snarled in reply, raising his thunderbolt and ready to strike, but Hades put his hand on Zeus's arm. Zeus held firm but didn't lower his weapon.

Hades planted his forked staff in the ground. He stepped forward into the hot, damp air that was heavy with Kerberos' stinking breath.

Like all the gods, far-thinking Hades moved with grace. He approached the gnawing, snapping jaws of Kerberos with the slow and reigned-in movements of a prowling cat. No grand flourishes, Hades moved with economy, straight-backed and controlled, reserving his power for thinking and bursts of activity.

Zeus, on the other hand, was all grand flourish. No subtlety. Impatiently, he twirled his bolt in his hand, his fierce gaze not moving from Kerberos's jaws.

"You need to let us pass." Hades spoke calmly to the center head of Kerberos. The other heads on the hound barked and snarled, and the volume of the sound pressed Hades back a little.

"You're reasoning with him? I think he wants to eat you," Zeus warned, his lightning bolt at the ready.

Hades didn't take his eyes from Kerberos. He stepped closer to the beast. The king of the gods would fit easily inside any one of Kerberos' huge mouths.

"There is someone I need to find," Hades said quietly.

Kerberos tilted his head, listening.

"She's on the other side of the Styx," Hades went on. "You need to let us pass so I can find her."

Zeus bowed his head, pained by the pleading in Hades's voice.

"Her name is Persephone. She is like the sun," Hades explained, reaching a hand in a slow measured fashion towards the great hound's center head.

Kerberos' center head snarled at his noisy heads on either side. They quieted, all six eyes focused on Hades.

"She is my sun," Hades said. His legs were knee-deep in a pool of the dog's saliva. "Have you seen her? She would be like a bright glowing light here." His eyes never moving from Kerberos, Hades asked again, "Has she passed this way?"

The mighty guard of the Underworld lowered his dragon tail, slunk down, and bowed his heads. Hades stroked the animal's nose.

"You will let us pass," Hades instructed, standing tall and letting his hand fall to his side. "And lead us to her."

Kerberos barked in ascent.

"The hound of Hades," Zeus marveled.

He pulled Hades's staff out of the ground and followed his brother and Kerberos into the Styx.

CHAPTER 12

Hades reached out to the granite throne that had emerged from Mt. Olympus for him. At his touch, the throne flashed, and its surface transformed into gleaming white marble.

Hades sat on the throne in the shadow of Olympus's craggy peak. Eleven other chairs then rose out of the groaning rock. The brightly colored chairs fanned out in a circle from Hades's throne, majestic in gold, red and blue. The circle of gods was open to the sky, so that the gods could see the stars. And the stars could see the gods.

Hades's throne was perched slightly above the rest, with narrow green glass steps leading from the black and white checkered marble floor up to his seat.

The remaining eleven Olympians took their seats. Persephone sat at Hades's right hand.

"We all knew it would be you, Hades," Athena said, beaming with pride from beside Zeus, who took his place directly across from Hades. "That it should be you. King of the gods."

She held up a cup of ambrosia and all the other gods did the same, toasting the new king of the gods and their new world.

CHAPTER 13

Hades waded into the Styx. The river water was dense, the consistency of blood. Each step took effort.

Kerberos paused and lapped up the dark Styx water thirstily.

"Argh!" Zeus shouted, covering his face. "I'd rather not drink whatever is in this foul-smelling liquid."

Hades silently waited for Kerberos to finish drinking, until he saw something that made him catch his breath: Persephone's face was in the water. Without a thought, he dove towards her, disappearing into the depths.

"Hades!" Zeus yelled. Then he cursed.

Kerberos barked and Zeus shouted for the dog to swing his tail over to him. The beast obliged, and Zeus leapt onto the scaly dragon tail, a weapon in each hand, and watched for Hades to resurface.

Perched atop Kerberos' tail, Zeus pointed his lightning bolt at the water. He swirled it around, stirring up the water, but found nothing beneath the surface. No life. No death. No Persephone. Just more black, murky liquid. He was relieved when Hades's head popped up around a bend in the river soon after.

"Where did she go?" Hades called. "I've lost sight of her!"

"I never saw her!" Zeus answered. He shook his head. "I saw nothing."

Kerberos spun and bounded to where Hades was treading water. Zeus nearly tumbled off the three-headed beast. He grabbed a tangle of grossly matted fur and held on.

"You saw Persephone?" Zeus held out a hand to help Hades from the water.

Hades climbed onto Kerberos, straddling the hound's middle neck. Zeus settled uneasily back onto the hound's tail.

Hades was soaked. Droplets of viscous Styx water clung to his face and hands. Zeus fought the urge to wipe the water off his brother.

"She is close, Zeus," Hades said. "She was in the water. I reached out and nearly had her. But she vanished…"

At this, Kerberos barked again and lowered his heads.

Zeus eyed the hound suspiciously. "Was it really her, Hades? Or is this place leading you in the wrong direction? Don't forget where we are…"

"It was her," Hades said, his dark eyes intense. "She was close."

Zeus nodded but then said grimly, "I've seen nothing in the water."

A quizzical look came over Hades's face.

"Do you think it was a trick of the water?" he asked. "Or that I only saw what I wanted to see?"

"I think we are in the Underworld, brother. And we don't know yet what we are dealing with."

Hades patted Kerberos. Then he took his staff from Zeus.

"Then let us find out."

Hades pointed his staff at the Styx. The eerily silent water divided at his unspoken command. The water was pressed aside, stacking upon the riverbanks in great black walls until the floor of the Styx was as empty as a cracked wine jar.

What the gods saw when the water receded was a muddy trench. Nothing more. There was nothing living or dead beneath the surface—nothing.

Zeus looked at Hades and felt a stab of pain at his brother's disappointment.

"She was here," Hades said. "We will find her again."

Kerberos sloshed through the mud, carrying the two gods in between the noisy, rushing walls of black water. The water swirled but was held in place, allowing them to pass.

The three of them forged on in silence, the two gods not knowing where they were going or where they should be going, just moving forward. Hades pinned his hopes on Kerberos knowing where to lead them.

"Do you think this beast knows where he's going?" Zeus asked with a nod to the hound. "Do think he understands what you wanted? And if he does, that he'll just take us to Persephone?" He polished his breastplate with a handful of Kerberos' fur, swaying along with the hound's uneven strides. "I don't know if it's wise for us to follow him blindly, deeper into the depths of this uncharted, stinking—"

Hades held up a hand and Zeus quieted. Kerberos stopped, his massive front paw halted in air mid-stride.

Hades leapt off the hound, sinking up to his shins in the stench-filled muck. He closed his eyes.

Persephone's voice. It echoed inside Hades's head, tumbling among his own thoughts. He let her honey-toned voice wash over him. It washed away the pain of her loss. It filled him and soothed him. She was back. Persephone was with him, and all was right again.

She was beside him, whispering into his ear. Hades felt the soft swish of her breath against his skin and turned towards it. He opened his eyes to see her.

But Persephone wasn't there. Confused, he turned. As he did, he sank into the mud.

Hades put a hand to his cheek. His skin was warm where her breath touched him. But where did she go?

"Persephone?" Hades was confused. "Persephone!" he called, his voice laced with urgency and desperation. "Come back! I've come—where are you?"

And then, all the pain of her loss came flooding back to Hades, tenfold. Persephone had been ripped away from him again. After having found her, the loss was even deeper.

Zeus cursed the Underworld and jumped off the hound, splattering mud onto his armor and onto Kerberos' nearest face. He stared at his brother, his eyes ablaze with concern.

With his square jaw and broad shoulders, Zeus was the most physically imposing of his gods. He often used his size to impose his will without having to say a word. He had a cleft in his chin that drove women wild. He rubbed it now, thinking.

Hades called Persephone again, and Zeus cringed. There was no sign of Persephone that he could see.

Zeus squatted down and pressed his weight into the mud that had begun pulling and sucking him downwards. With a grunt, he leapt up into the air, then landed softly in front of Hades. He spread his legs wide to keep himself from sinking into the riverbed again.

Hades repeated Persephone's name, calling her again and again. Each time, the echo of Hades's voice came back to them, but nothing more. Persephone didn't answer. Zeus wondered if she couldn't answer.

As if reading Zeus's mind, Hades called her again, this time both frantic and angry.

"Persephone!" Hades called, spinning like a compass that had lost its true north. The more Hades spoke, the more he moved. And the more he moved, the deeper he was pulled into the mud. But he either didn't notice or didn't care.

Finally, Zeus reached out and yanked Hades from the possessive muck, where the king of the gods had sunk to his waist. He set Hades on more solid ground at the edge of the riverbed, near the wall of water.

Zeus exhaled. Then he felt a prickling on the back of his neck, like something crawling up his skin. He looked over his shoulder. He held his buzzing thunderbolt, prepared to strike. A shriek echoed through the darkness as a dense fog slid towards them. He could hardly see it against the black walls of the Underworld and the Styx. Was there no color here?

Zeus cursed.

The fog gained speed. It hurtled towards them, its shrieking getting louder with its approach.

Zeus hurled his thunderbolt. The fog howled in pain as the weapon struck it. In an instant, the fog dissipated.

"Maybe we should proceed with more stealth," Zeus suggested wryly, with raised eyebrows. He picked up his bolt from where it fell after piercing the fog. It was caked with a sticky black substance. "Try to go at least slightly unnoticed by the terrors here?" He wiped the weapon on Kerberos' filthy fur.

"Did you hear her?" Hades asked softly. "Did you hear Persephone?"

"I heard nothing but this beast's loud breathing." He looked at Hades. "And you."

"I heard her, Zeus. I did. And I felt her—as though she was right beside me." Hades shook his head, confused. "You heard nothing?"

"I heard nothing."

Hades tightened his grip on his forked staff.

"But I believe you heard her voice," Zeus lied. "I believe it was real." He put a reassuring hand on his brother's shoulder. "The two of you are still connected. That's a good sign. Maybe she knows you're here. Looking for her. Let us hope that's the case."

"Yes," Hades said, his dark eyes darting from place to place. "Let us hope."

Hope—it was a word that seemed very fragile now to the king of the gods.

CHAPTER 14

"I think I'm hungry."

Persephone spoke, finding comfort in the sound of her own voice.

"Does that mean I'm still alive?"

She was utterly lost. She'd thought it was impossible for her to feel more alone, more isolated, but she was wrong. She kept talking, thinking that might calm the strange new feeling in her chest.

She felt her heart fluttering, like it was preparing to fly away. Then it thumped once, weakly, beneath the charred hole in her dress. All the while, Persephone spoke to herself, afraid of the abyss of fear she'd fall into if she stayed silent.

"Gods don't get hungry—not like this," she chattered. "Does this mean I'm human? How could that be? That's not possible." She closed her eyes and exhaled. "What is happening?"

"I can shed some light on that for you."

Persephone spun around at the sound of the voice. What she saw shocked her.

She saw a man. A human man. Or, someone who used to be a human man. He was now a shade. He looked almost alive but for the translucence of his skin, and the fact that half of his face and rib cage were bare of flesh, nothing more than white bone.

Instantly, Persephone was more fearful of him than she'd yet been of anything in the Underworld.

"Who are you?" she asked, trembling. A sick feeling in the pit of her stomach told her that this was the man the harpy had warned her about, the man she was told to avoid at all costs.

Persephone saw an evil in the man before her that she hadn't seen since the war with Kronos. His narrowly set eyes were devoid of warmth. His voice was high for a man, and had an edge to it. He had small ears and a sharp chin. He was thin and slightly shorter than Persephone, but he looked strong. He had a hardness about him, a cruelty that shone out of his small eyes. He laughed a high, unsettling girlish giggle.

"I'm the one who called you here," he boasted. "My name is Sisyphus. King Sisyphus. I'm king of the Underworld. And you are my prize."

Persephone gasped. When she exhaled, the air from her lungs flew out. It wove in and out of the labyrinth of tunnel, until it reached Hades's cheek. It swept against Hades's skin, and he paused.

He put his hand to his face. Then he leapt back onto Kerberos, Zeus right beside him— urging the beast on toward he knew not what.

CHAPTER 15

Hades and Zeus huddled together, repelled by the stench of the smoking, decaying giant's body on the other side of the ridge in front of them. The rancid smell stung the gods' skin and made their eyes water.

"Hephaistos needs to make us better helmets," Zeus said, tossing his half-melted helmet with its cracked nosepiece aside. "Giants are repulsive. I need armor that covers my entire face."

"Or, we could stop setting giants ablaze," Hades suggested.

"How better to rid ourselves of them?" Zeus asked.

"Their bones will make mountains in our new world."

"Our new world," Zeus grinned. "I like the sound of that."

Hades wiped the ash from his forehead and looked over at the teeming carcass. "This one will burn for a long time. He was immense. The fire goes so deep, I think it will never go out."

"A volcano then."

"Yes," Hades nodded. "I think this will be another volcano."

Hades stepped out from beneath the rock ledge where he and Zeus had taken shelter. He put his hands on his hips and surveyed the land that, until their last battle, had stretched uniformly into the distance. It had once been a vast, solid land, but now it was in pieces. Hundreds of small islands were now strewn and dotted across a dark blue sea, like so many stars in the sky. The gods hid at the top ridge of a crescent-shaped island.

"Athena asked me if we are destroying too much." Zeus eased himself into a more comfortable position under the ledge. "If there can be a recovery once the war is won."

"Creation needs destruction," Hades answered from where he stood. "We must tear down the old before we can build something new."

"That's what I told her you'd say."

Hades smiled. "She agreed, didn't she?"

"Of course."

"Sometimes," Hades said quietly. "At times like these, when everything is still and silent, I see his face."

"Whose?"

"Our father's."

"That's unfortunate," Zeus growled.

"I see Kronos' face the moment he realized we were rising against him."

"Ah—" Zeus threw his spear at an incoming chunk of rock, and it shattered into pieces. The spear kept going until it was nearly out of sight. Then it curved and started to return to where the gods rested.

"He was surprised," Hades said. "And yet, he must have known it would happen. He must have expected it, that we wouldn't tolerate his cruelty forever, not after we'd we had grown strong enough."

"He never imagined we'd grow strong enough. He tried to keep us from growing at all," Zeus snarled. "He wished we had never existed—and still does."

Zeus reached his muscled arm out and caught the spear as it returned to him.

"He killed his father to become ruler. And now we're trying to overthrow and destroy him. It's a cycle," Hades concluded. "And it's a waste. We'll break free of it."

"We'll end it." Zeus leaned out and smashed another boulder that was headed towards him. He slammed it with his bare fist, then ducked. Splinters and jagged stones burst out of the boulder and flew in every direction. It was one of Kronos' favorite weapons—exploding boulders filled with piercing rocks and wood. Zeus shielded himself with his armored forearms.

"How are the plans going with Hephaistos?" Zeus asked, yanking Hades back to a safer place under the rock ridge. Kronos' storm of rocks wasn't going to end for a while. "We need your new weapon," he added, collapsing onto the ground beside Hades. "With the Titans joining Kronos, it's almost too much for us to overcome." Zeus hung his head, too tired to fight off his discouragement, not needing to hide it from his brother the way he hid it from the other gods.

"Soon," Hades answered, his belief not faltering. "We're close, brother. We have the right material to keep the weapon strong, to make it indestructible. And we know how to harness the energy it requires. Now, we just have to catch the energy, the light and fire itself."

"And we can do that up here?" Zeus asked.

Hades looked up into the smoky black void of sky.

"We're getting close. We just need to go a little higher…"

CHAPTER 16

"What did you say?" Persephone whispered, disbelieving.

"I said I called you here," Sisyphus answered. He reached out his intact arm, which Persephone noted was layered with gold bracelets. How did he have those in the Underworld? No one was allowed to bring possessions from life down into the depths.

"I will make you comfortable here," Sisyphus said with the assurance of a man accustomed to getting what he wanted. "I'm sorry I was late. Unfortunately, things don't always go according to plan, even for me." Sisyphus looked around at his Underworld surroundings with an ironic grin. Then he laughed a high-pitched laugh that made Persephone cringe.

"Now," he continued conspiratorially, tucking Persephone's arm beneath his own good arm. "The first thing we must do is get you some food. It's not as bad down here as you think." He leaned in to whisper into her ear. His breath reeked of death and decay, and Persephone stifled a cough. How long had he been in the Underworld?

"How…" Persephone pulled her arm out from his and stepped away from him. She turned her face away from his and inhaled deeply. "How could you have called me here? And why?"

"It's nothing that needs to concern you," he said, dismissing her questions with a flick of his boney wrist. He reached out to touch one of the flowers in her hair. "Remarkable."

At his touch, Persephone's knees weakened in disgust. She stumbled. Sisyphus pulled her to her feet.

"You need sustenance," he said. "Now."

Persephone wanted to object, but her vision blurred. She leaned against Sisyphus. She felt as if everything around her was vanishing into darkness. She felt like she would slip away or float away like a shade. Sisyphus pressed something into her palm. Persephone opened her hand and saw six pomegranate seeds.

Sisyphus guided her hand towards her mouth. She dropped the seeds in.

She felt them, small and cold on her tongue. The seeds were so small. It didn't feel like she was giving in, but rather like she was allowing herself to live. Sustenance here wasn't a betrayal of her wishes to return above; it was survival. Her head swam, and she felt dizzy. And so she ate.

Crunchy and slightly bitter, she finished the seeds and felt herself regaining strength. She pulled away from Sisyphus and stood tall, looking at him with new strength. Anger flashed in her eyes.

Thump. She felt her heart beat again, stronger this time.

. . .

Across the Underworld, Hades froze. He felt her heart beat inside his own chest.

"Persephone," he whispered. "I'm coming."

CHAPTER 17

thena sat across from Hades's empty throne on Olympus. She reached over to Zeus's bright red chair and traced its lion's paw arm with her fingertips. A fleck of red peeled off at her touch. Athena inhaled sharply. It was the tiniest crumb of stone, but Athena feared what it meant—was the gods' power crumbling? Would they fail so soon after they'd begun? Would the world they bled for wither and die?

Athena arched an eyebrow—not on her watch. She cricked her helmeted head, alert.

It was silent in the circle of gods' thrones, except for the lone scraping of dry leaves tumbling across the floor. Athena tightened her hold on her spear and narrowed her watchful grey eyes. Her nostrils flared as the bitter scent of burning flesh filled her nose. Her feet grew hot. She sat calmly as the heat intensified and rose from the floor, as though a snake had unhinged its jaw and was devouring her from the ankles upward, its hot breath creeping up her flesh.

Athena watched Ares approach the circle of the gods' empty thrones. He stomped into view, his back to her. He crushed the scattered leaves beneath his feet, his footsteps falling heavily onto the marble floor.

Bloody-minded Ares wore no helmet. His wide forehead jutted out over dark, squinted eyes. His scant, scraggly beard looked as though it was about to grow thicker, but never did. It gave him a slovenly look, less dignified than the other gods. His face was stuck in a permanent scowl, as though something had irritated him and he had a blow wound up, ever ready to repay the insult, whether real or imagined.

Ares paused at the foot of the steps leading to Hades's throne. He looked covetously up at Hades's seat of power, like a child who wanted a new toy.

Sneering, Ares lifted an armored elbow, thrust it downward, and smashed the glass steps.

The opaque glass shattered. Ares threw his head back and laughed. He spread his arms out, reveling in this small victory. Then he closed his hands into fists and blew. The glass shards shot down from Olympus, and rained towards an unsuspecting town below.

Athena narrowed her eyes, and the glass pieces stopped in mid-air. They swirled around in great swooping circles. Before they could reach the roofs of the homes in the town, the shards soared back up to Olympus. The whirlwind of glass circled Ares before remaking itself into steps.

Ares cursed as the steps reformed. With one last glance at Hades's throne, he turned to stalk away.

"It was you," Athena said.

Ares paused. He looked over his shoulder.

"You sent Persephone down below," Athena accused him, rising from her seat.

"Why would I do that?"

"That's what I want to know."

Ares shrugged. "What's done is done."

"Unless it can be undone."

"She's gone." Ares curled his mouth in a satisfied sneer. "Even the *magnificent* Hades cannot undo *that*. And that's the beauty of it."

In a blink, Athena was standing directly in front of Ares.

"So it was jealousy?" Athena asked, shaking her head. "That made you take Persephone's life? We are all of us Olympians,

Ares. We are family. We worked together to make this world and now you would destroy one of us and fracture our victory out of simple envy?"

"Simple," Ares repeated, confused. "Simple?" For a moment, his face softened as though he thought he might find some understanding in Athena, but he quickly shook away that hope. Hardness returned to his countenance. "It's not my reasons that concern you," Ares hissed. "It's that you didn't think I was clever enough to come up with a plan that could outsmart you and your precious Hades."

"I didn't think you could get any lower in my estimation." The look on Athena's face was one of undisguised distaste.

"Lower?" Ares shook with laughter. "Lower?"

He stalked away from her, prowling around the circle of thrones, his arms outstretched like he was claiming them all for himself. "That's funny." He looked at Athena and made a face. "Wait, you haven't figured it out." He paused. "Now, that does surprise me. That weasel of a man is smarter than I thought."

Athena's calm demeanor was swept away in the face of Ares's unfounded arrogance. It gave way to her rage at what he had done to Persephone.

"What *you* haven't figured out," Athena began, "is that you can never outwit me. Or Hades. And that you will pay for what you've done. You think because you're Hera's darling, because you make men bleed and fight and act without humanity that you are better than me? Wars are not won with might alone, Ares. And that is why you will always fail. And I—and Hades—will always win."

"You don't scare me." Ares spoke with malice but leaned back into his heels.

"Liar."

Ares paused. A guilty looked flashed on his face for the briefest moment. Then he smiled. "I am a liar. But this time I have you beaten." His smiled turned into a smirk. "You all believed the Underworld was beyond us." Malevolence glinted in his eyes.

"That we couldn't tame it. But my connection to the Underworld is vast. My reach there is strong, and it gives me power. Think about it, oh brilliant one. My role is bringer of death! Most of those shades are there because I sent them there!" He laughed, and Athena felt humans and animals shudder and quail at the sound. "I am fed by greed, envy, jealousy AND death! Those, not pale ambrosia, are what give me life!"

Athena watched Ares grow stronger as he spoke about the Underworld. His armor started to vibrate. It hummed a horrible, sharp sound, like a death cry. Had she been less strong, it would have made her cover her ears.

"It's good to be me, Athena. It's good to be the god of war. War is the great leveler, as you like to say. War is simple. It's pure. It devours good men and women, as well as bad. War doesn't care about good or evil, right or wrong. And neither do I. I don't care about Hades or Persephone. I care about glory and power."

"Which is why I will defeat you every time." Athena's voice was rich and deep. "Because you should care. I, too, am god of war—or have you forgotten already? But I am also god of wisdom. And war without wisdom is like tossing stones in a bucket, and saying you're building a palace. You end up with nothing but a useless mess." Athena shook her head, disgusted. "Your wars are unjust. What you did to Persephone was unjust and you will pay for it."

"Justice," Ares spat, his spittle leaving little pools of slime on Olympus' shining floor. "What is that? What is justice compared to power? Hades is stupid in his devotion to justice."

Ares leaned forward, eye to eye with Athena. She didn't move back, even though every aspect of Ares was rank to her. Finally, Ares shrank slightly under the power of her glare, the first of the two gods to pull away.

"I can make men and women do my bidding," he said to her unmoving face. "Whatever I want, I can make them give me. No one defies me. That is being a god. And it is good. It is very good."

"That's not what being a god is."

"Says who? Hades?" Ares looked around, dramatically.

"Because he's not here, is he? Why should I do what he wants? He's not here to make me."

"But I am," Athena said and, as she spoke, she seemed to grow even taller, enlarged by her graceful dignity.

"We are equals, you and I," Ares dismissed, his mouth curling into a distorted grin. "You don't rule me. And, you know, I don't see Zeus here either. You need to think about who holds your loyalty, Athena. You know no one ever returns from the Underworld. It looks to me like Olympus needs a new king. I've won already. You just don't know it yet."

Athena smiled, and it was terrifying. "Like I said. I have all the wisdom."

With a leer and a grunt, Ares vanished. Only a puddle of blood, spit, and vomit remained where he had been standing on the once-gleaming floor.

Athena turned to the owl perched on her shoulder. "Call the gods together," she instructed. "We have a problem."

CHAPTER 18

Hades sputtered and coughed. After feeling Persephone's beating heart in his own chest, Hades had leapt blindly into the nearest tunnel, nearly flying through it until reaching the vast open space Persephone had found when she was chasing the harpies. Zeus bolted after him. As he arrived at Hades's side, shade after shade descended upon the gods, who were not where they were supposed to be. Trespassers onto the world of the dead and despairing, Hades and Zeus were soon surrounded by thousands of shades.

Zeus slashed at the shades with his thunderbolt, its heat blasting the dead until they slammed against cavern walls. But more swarmed in to take their place. Hades had dropped his forked staff when he flew off Kerberos, so he used his tremendous strength to try to push the shades away. But he found that they were insubstantial; he could not touch them with his body. Rather, the numberless dead flowed through him.

Zeus's arms flew so quickly that his moves were a blur. The brightness of the thunderbolt drew more shades, rather than frightening them away. The earth-shaking sound of the bolt had no effect on them. Hades gasped for breath, drowning beneath a sea of shades. Zeus targeted the shades with the heat of his bolt, sending them flying off his brother, but they were immediately replaced by more and more and more.

The shades were drawn to Hades as if pleading for his help, but in doing so, they were destroying him. Zeus frenetically blasted shade after shade until finally Kerberos bounded over, gnarling and snapping his massive jaws at the innumerable blank-faced shades.

Terrified of the three-headed dog, the shades floated away, crossing over and through one another, heading in every direction. They disappeared into the tunnels and up into the vast darkness of the immense cavern's roof. Some looked longingly back at Hades. Zeus shivered at the strangeness of the need he sensed from the dead, creatures he'd assumed were devoid of feeling and thought.

Kerberos chased the last few shades away, until none remained in sight.

Hades sat up and breathed deeply. He raked his fingers through his hair. Kerberos pranced over to him proudly, then lowered his heads in submission, awaiting his master's praise.

"What took you so long?" Zeus admonished the beast, trying to shake off the feeling that the shades wanted to keep Hades for their own. It gave him an even greater urgency to get them out of the Underworld before it was too late, with or without Persephone.

"He was too big to get through that tunnel," Hades said, absently scratching behind one of Kerberos' ears, while one of the beast's other heads rested near his lap. "I should never have left without you. We don't know what lies ahead. Every step leads to a new world. I acted without thinking."

"Unusual for you, and generally forgivable—but not here. Not in the Underworld." Zeus paced anxiously, eventually settling down beside Hades. "We have to stay together," he said quietly. "Or we won't make it out of here."

"Yes," Hades replied, nodding. "You're right." He turned to his brother. "Thank you for coming with me, Zeus."

Zeus shook his head. "Where else would I be? Here. Drink." He held out a cup.

"Now? No," Hades scoffed.

"Now, Hades."

Hades acquiesced and drank the ambrosia. Then Zeus gulped the rest down, wiping his mouth on his forearm.

"Those creatures," Hades said. "The shades. Did you feel like they wanted something from us?"

"No, but then, I was busy trying to keep you alive."

Hades shook his head and grinned sheepishly. "Right."

"Now where?" Zeus asked, changing the subject.

"I don't know." Hades looked at the ground, his mind filling with visions of the wan-faced shades, creatures with the spark of life extinguished from them. Their shoulders slouched, with no muscle and no hope to hold them up and give them substance. He shook his head and cleared his thoughts.

"I think we have to go lower."

CHAPTER 19

Kerberos' heads lay in a pool of his own saliva. A satisfied rumble emanated from his throats.

"What's that noise?" Zeus raised an eyebrow. He pointed at Kerberos with Hades's staff before tossing it to him. "Is that creature purring?"

Hades ignored his question. He let the weapon fall to the ground with a clang.

"Do you know what I felt in those shades?" Hades asked.

"A clinging despair? Inescapable malaise? If that's what you felt, then yes," Zeus replied grimly. He didn't mention the need he'd also felt from them, specifically the desire to keep Hades among them.

"It was heart-wrenching. I don't know what I expected to find here, but I thought there would be some semblance of...."

"Peace?"

"Perhaps. And order..." Hades shook his head. "It was a chaotic mass of need. It felt like they had nowhere to go. Is it possible—"

"What?" Zeus asked.

"Is it possible that we aren't in the Underworld yet? Is this just a waiting place? Those shades were lost. They were asking me to take them home..."

Zeus felt a chill fly up his spine. He needed to distract Hades from thinking about what the shades wanted.

"Look what I found," Zeus said, an eager look on his face.

He held out his hand and showed Hades a fistful of shiny dark vines. Zeus had taken them from the tunnel where Persephone created them. They had passed through the tunnel just before they'd been attacked by the shades.

Hades saw the vines and ran back to the place which offered hope amid the rot and fear and darkness. He held his breath and marveled. The tunnel was thick with vines on all sides, so thick it virtually thumped with life in a place that was devoid of life. Hades knew only one reason for those plants to be in the Underworld.

"I didn't see this when I came through before," he whispered, barely able to speak. The relief he felt at seeing this sign of life nearly overwhelmed him. He knelt. The foliage had spread to the floor too. Every Underworld surface in the tunnel was layered with Persephone's creation. It was so thick with leaves and flowers that the cave walls were hidden entirely. Hades reached out and lovingly picked a golden flower.

"She was here," Hades said. Tears filled his eyes. Zeus immediately turned away, wiping his own eyes.

"And she is well," Zeus said, clearing his throat. "She makes every place better, even this barren wasteland. She was able to do this, to grow these." He pointed to the lush plants. "Here! With no sunlight."

"There is hope," Hades whispered.

"Yes, brother," Zeus reassured him, allowing himself to feel reassured too. "There is."

"Kerberos," Hades commanded. "Take us lower. Take us down. Find Persephone."

He held the flower up to Kerberos' nose. The hound of Hades sniffed, and then howled.

Hades leapt upon the creature's back, still clasping the flower. Zeus steeled himself, then joined his brother astride the smelly beast.

CHAPTER 20

isyphus led Persephone by the arm. She felt disoriented since eating the seeds. As the path Sisyphus pulled her along grew darker and more narrow, she blinked to try to clear her vision. She struggled to focus, trying to take in details so she'd be able to return the same way once she was free of him. Her stomach clenched—she was afraid of going deeper, fearful that the deeper she went into the Underworld, the less likely it was that she could ever leave. Or perhaps it was the seeds…

She hadn't imagined they could go any deeper into the earth, and yet they kept descending. They finally arrived at a staircase. Ancient rock had been roughly carved into tall, uneven steps. She stumbled on a loose rock and fell. Her arm slid from Sisyphus's grasp. She sat where she fell on the narrow stair, refusing to cry—even though it felt like the room, the entire Underworld, the ground itself, was closing in around her.

She shivered.

"I can't breathe." Persephone trembled. She looked at her hands, which quivered uncontrollably. "It's too far from the sun. Too far from the sky. I can't go any further below. I can't bear it…"

"You can. And you will," Sisyphus demanded, unwilling to let his prize go, vastly annoyed that she wasn't at least a little grateful to him for helping her. For wanting her.

Persephone clasped her hands to her chest and closed her eyes.

"By all the gods, you are beautiful," Sisyphus marveled. "Do you hear that?" His voice grew determinedly softer. He pointed a bone-finger towards the unknown of the deeper, further darkness. "I have gifts for you," he said, having no understanding of the woman he was trying to tempt. "I can hear some of them now. Come. Come see where I have brought you."

He continued down the stairs.

"Come," he called from below, as if Persephone were a dog to be commanded. "You're nearly there. Come see your new home, Persephone."

This would never be home.

She shouldn't have eaten the seeds. She had seen the shades. They had no memories of life above. No gut-wrenching sadness of missing those they loved most. It was supposed to be over in the Underworld. You were supposed to disappear into a shade of who you once were. Maybe eating the seeds was a mistake, trying to go on may have been a mistake...

Persephone felt the walls of the narrow stairway closing in around her. Why didn't she disappear? Why wouldn't she disappear?

Then she heard it.

"Persephone," she heard. "I'm coming."

Persephone's eyes flashed open.

"Hades?"

She heard only a low roar in reply.

"Hades," she repeated, his name a prayer on her lips. It was real. He was real. He was still coming for her.

Sisyphus was far beneath her now. She could just make out the whites of his cruel little eyes as he looked up at her, waiting, expectant. She turned from him and looked up the crooked stairs she'd just descended. She was tempted to run up them, back to where she felt Hades was. Where he was looking for her.

But then she heard something else: a distant screech. A familiar screech. It was coming from beyond Sisyphus, and it gave her pause.

Persephone pulled herself up. Using the cold, damp wall as support, Persephone rose and moved forward. Slowly, carefully, gracefully, she descended the last remaining steps, moving towards the screeches and the ever-increasing volume of another sound she recognized.

"There is running water," she whispered, feeling a rekindling of hope. "Keep coming, Hades," she called softly. "Ever further below…"

On the last step, Persephone's foot landed in water.

She gasped. The water was warm and clear. She fell to her knees, soaking her skirt and legs. She cupped her hands, filling them with water, and poured it over her face. She rubbed her cheeks and chest. She cleaned her arms and ran damp fingers through her hair.

She sighed, feeling a sense of renewal. She glowed with satisfaction.

"Kronos," Sisyphus swore reverently, as he came back to meet her. "Look at you. I am your slave, your king." He bowed before her, taking her hands in his.

Persephone clenched her hands into fists. Sisyphus squeezed her hands painfully tight; from his right hand, she heard the sharp scrape of bone against bone.

Persephone tried to pull her hands from his grasp, but his hold on her was shockingly strong. Unnaturally so. Something immortal was at work in this man, this shade.

"Let me go," she said. Fear rose up in her again. What was he? She wanted to run away from him, but her desire to follow the fresh water made her stand her ground. She would follow this creature to find where the water began. And then, Hades would find her, or she would find a way out.

"You'll change your mind," Sisyphus said, kissing her closed fists ravenously. "About me. And my kingdom."

Persephone's horrified look made him shrug his shoulders.

"Or, you won't," he acknowledged. "It doesn't matter, I suppose, but I would prefer if you didn't despise me. I know Hades is a difficult man to forget. But you don't have much choice."

Sisyphus dropped her hands unceremoniously. Then he turned and walked ahead of her again. Not bothering to turning back, he waved her on.

"Come," he beckoned with his bone-white hand. "Come see your new home."

Persephone forged ahead, her feet sloshing through the welcome pool of shallow water. With fresh water, there must be more life in the Underworld than she'd imagined.

Who rules it? she wondered. The water. It wasn't Poseidon, for it was fresh water, not salt. She could see or hear no nymphs. So who controlled the water here? Whom did it obey?

Persephone paused. The roar they walked towards had become so loud it drowned out the sound of familiar, returning screeches. Her head cleared as she recognized what the roar was, what it meant. She began to run, the powerful sound buoying her, giving her unexpected strength.

She turned a corner and saw it. A waterfall. It blocked the path ahead like a wall. She looked up—the waterfall soared so high she couldn't see where it began. It was a majestic sight, the graceful beauty and power of the water glowing, carving its way through the dark depths of the Underworld.

She could see no way out from the deep pool where the waterfall ended. The water seemed to lead nowhere—only up. She gazed up with longing, knowing all her dreams and loves were above her.

She tried to speak to the water, to ask it to help her, to lift her up and carry her to where it began. It was fresh water, so it must have origins beyond the Underworld. But the water had no response. Persephone couldn't be sure if it was ignoring her, or if it was unable to reply.

Sisyphus spoke instead, but the roar of the falls was louder than his voice. Persephone closed her eyes and stood motionless, listening to the consistent, insistent rush of the water.

His patience spent, Sisyphus reached through the water and pulled Persephone through it. Soaking wet, her dress clung to her body. Sisyphus gaped at her, thrilled by her beauty.

Persephone ignored his stares. She found herself in yet another huge cavern. It was different from the others she'd encountered. This one was brightly lit, glowing with warm, otherworldly light.

With the waterfall at her back, she stood on a narrow cusp of land that appeared to be an entrance to a whole new world.

Lava spilled down the walls of the cavern in bright orange trails. It looked like the sun was weeping, leaving heat and light as a comfort in its pity for Persephone. A lone trail led forward from the waterfall. On either side of the narrow spit of land was a sea of hot, glowing lava.

The cavern was warm, like a midsummer afternoon. Its warmth was thick. Persephone could almost imagine she was above the surface in the sun's embracing light. She could almost feel the sun touching her, pressing upon her skin. She was warmer and more comfortable than she'd been since arriving in the Underworld, which made her feel even more wretched. This Underworld place was trying to emulate the earth she loved, as though she wouldn't find it pale and pitiful in comparison.

Persephone wanted to laugh, but felt too close to crying. She would never forget that she was not above. The roof over her head could never be like the magnificent star-dotted sky. It would always be a prison of stone and soil and separation.

She heard the familiar screeching again. This time it was close. Very close. It had become a welcome sound to her, the call of the harpies—the closest things she had to friends in this vast unknown realm.

"They're welcoming you," Sisyphus said, puffed up with pride. "My gift. We're nearly there. Come."

Did he know that she had already met them? It seemed he did not. Persephone bit her tongue at again being called like a dog. Staying well out of his reach, she followed Sisyphus. He led her along the slippery trail over the softly bubbling lava sea.

Persephone kept her eyes on her feet. One wrong step and she would fall into boiling lava. A pebble slipped from beneath her foot and tumbled into the lava flow below. It floated, then glowed and burned, melting. Another thing taken by the Underworld.

"There it is."

Sisyphus pointed a bony finger, an unsettling giggle escaping his lips. Persephone looked up. She caught her breath at what she saw. This was not the Underworld she expected.

Sisyphus saw that she was impressed. He was pleased.

"Your new home."

The scope and beauty of what lay before her astonished her. An island stood amid a vast lava sea. Perched on the island was a sweeping palace. Topped with seven azure spires, the palace was unspeakably elegant. Its soaring windows were set into cream-colored stone. Each window was made of colored glass. Diamond-shaped panels of green, red, blue, and yellow glass made mosaics of the windows, which shone brilliantly like rainbows. Delicate gold trimmed each blue spire like lace.

High walls surrounded the island, enclosing the palace like a fortress, a fortress set against the lava and against escape—a reminder that this palace was to be Persephone's magnificent prison.

A narrow stone bridge led to a golden door behind an imposing bronze gate.

Swooping around the palace were what looked like huge birds. Persephone recognized the harpies. There were at least a dozen of them. They screeched and howled—whether in warning or in greeting, Persephone couldn't tell. One of them dipped and angled in awkward flight, and Persephone knew it was the angry, injured harpy, even though she was too far away to see her face.

"Harpies," Sisyphus explained, clearly unaware that Persephone had already met them. "They are your slaves. My gift to you. Your wedding present."

"Wedding?" Persephone saw armored creatures with bows and arrows aimed at the harpies, presumably to shoot them if they dared to fly away. If they dared escape.

The harpies screeched again. Persephone heard their screeches as cries for help. She felt her own body screech too, a silent cry for help of her own.

"I assume you mean our wedding?" Persephone said with a shudder, barely able to utter the words. "Yours and mine?"

"Of course," Sisyphus said blankly. "That's why you're here."

"That's why I'm here," Persephone repeated. She felt like the room was spinning. She thought she might fall into the lava and it would be a welcome end. But no—she clenched her fists.

"You will be my queen. You were given to me. Promised."

"By whom?" Persephone's surprise and outrage morphed into anger.

"By me."

Persephone spun around at the sound of a familiar voice.

Ares stood like an island in the midst of the lava lake. Appearing from out of nowhere. In the Underworld. Alive. And against the law of the gods and everything she believed to be possible, there he was. He looked immensely proud of himself.

The glowing lava coursed around Ares, not burning him into ash or melting him into liquid, but rather, giving him strength. Then, before Persephone's furious, startled eyes, Ares's armor turned blood red. Ares's narrowed eyes were full of hate. And victory.

Rage coursed through Persephone's body. Her body shook with fury for everything he'd taken away from her. The light. Her mother. Hades.

"Ares?" Persephone demanded, bewildered, grieving, angry. "Is this true? Can this be true?"

"Of course it is. Surprised?" Ares's teeth shone in a malicious grin. He shook his head. "This will be a difficult for you at first, I know. But look where I've sent you!" He waved his armored hand ambiguously at the palace like a prince waving halfheartedly at an adoring crowd.

Ares strode towards Persephone in his red armor. The lava spluttered and splashed out of his way. With each step he took, more spikes sprouted from his armor.

Persephone backed away as he approached, his new appearance shocking and horrifying her. It wasn't just the sight of his armor that horrified her. Or his proud admission that he ruined her life by taking it from her, and promising her to a dead villain. His armor shrieked as he walked—rather than creak, it reverberated with terror-filled screams. All the carnage he had been a part of, all the agonizing wails he had incited, had become absorbed by his clothing. He wore them like a prize.

Sisyphus tried to wrap his arm around Persephone to comfort her, but she thrust him away. She edged away from both men, coming perilously close to the edge of the land. Something she had never felt before coursed through her as she looked at Ares: hatred.

"Listen," Ares said, attempting to appease her. "Something had to change up above. The world we were making with Hades and Zeus in charge wasn't what they promised us. And you—you weren't helping. You weren't just growing plants. You were making humans as weak and meek as you are," Ares said. "Someone had to put a stop to it. Of course, removing your influence from above is only an added benefit of sending you here. Encouraging men to be kind to one another, to help one another." Ares shook his head in disgust then spoke slowly, as if to a child. "If men see one another as equals, if they believe men are basically good, why would they fight each another? If they forgive and share, there's no room for greed and envy. And where does that leave me—as god of war? Not very busy, that's where. A little bored if you must know..."

"So, you want to encourage humans to destroy the beauty and order that we created? You want to ruin everything we fought for? You took my life...because..." Persephone sputtered. "Because you're bored?"

"Yes," Ares answered matter-of-factly. "I do. But, to be fair, which I know you appreciate, it was all for what is beauty to me. Discord, battle, war."

Ares pointed an armored hand to his chest, then shook his head patronizingly. "I'm surprised you hadn't figured this out already. You always seemed fairly clever. But, in your defense, you don't think that way. You're not inclined to see the dark side of gods or men. The main reason for getting rid of you was, of course, to remove Hades from Olympus. So I can take over as king of the gods."

Persephone was stunned. That he would do that to her was terrible enough, but that he also dared defy Hades and Zeus, and the rest of the Olympians, infuriated her.

"You could never defeat Hades."

Ares burst into laughter and the Underworld felt a shade darker, colder, and more frightening. "I know! That's why I led him here, by killing you! Hades is here in the Underworld. Looking for you! But he'll never find you. Sisyphus will make sure of that."

Sisyphus smirked and narrowed his eyes, then made a small nod in agreement. She turned to Sisyphus, and realized she had underestimated him.

Ares's laughter eventually died down, but it left her feeling as though the air was being squeezed from her lungs.

"Hades," Ares went on, "will be destroyed by this place, by his endless searching for you. He'll lose his senses. You should see him. It's happening already! He'll never return to the surface. And I will be king of the gods, king of all the world."

"Impossible."

"It is possible!" Ares snapped. "Hades's love for you will destroy him. And the world he created."

Persephone couldn't believe what was happening. Everything was growing dark, drowned out by blackness. She thought, for a moment, that it was all a horrific, vivid dream. But she knew that was a lie. Persephone had to face the fact that she was not having a nightmare: she was living one.

Ares whispered in her ear, his rancid breath hot upon her skin.

"I told Aphrodite she is my perfect match, for love is even more destructive than war. Hades's love for you will be his end."

Persephone spun away from Ares, unable to stand the sight of him. Her head pounded. The bottom of her once-beautiful dress slipped into the lava. Sisyphus pulled it up and stamped out the fire that had ignited on the fabric.

"Zeus and Athena will stop you," Persephone vowed.

"No," Ares said. "I've taken care of Zeus, too. He's here with Hades, of course. Inseparable as always. He will be lost here forever with his beloved Hades. Athena," he snarled, "I'll deal with."

Ares grinned with satisfaction, towering over the goddess, who refused to look back at him. Then he dove into the lava and was gone.

King Sisyphus snapped his fingers. Two harpies swooped in to lift Persephone up and fly her to her new palace. Her prison. Supremely satisfied, Sisyphus followed on foot, surveying his underground kingdom as he went.

CHAPTER 21

It was dark, as it always was before the Olympians won the war. Day or night, it made no difference. There was no day or night. The sky was always grey.

"Is this it?" Zeus asked, his eyes wide.

The two gods had resumed climbing once Kronos' rock shard and splinter attack was over, and they had finally summited the highest peak in the land. The going was treacherous. They had to keep an eye out for signs of Kronos and his allies through the heavy mist of the clouds while, at the same time, not falling off the mountain. Gravel slid beneath their feet and made them skid uncontrollably. Eventually, Hades and Zeus had to scale the vertical face of the rock to reach the top.

"This is the place." Hades stood tall. Zeus rested after swinging himself up to the precipice of the peak. "The clouds gather here at this time every day. We just need to wait for them."

Zeus pointed. "Storm clouds approach."

At the peak of Mt. Olympus, the two young gods would have looked insignificant if they'd been visible through the burgeoning clouds. A storm began to rage above and around the mountain. Sounds like a stampede of wild boars filled the air, and the reverberations nearly knocked the gods off their feet.

"What do you need from the storm?" Zeus yelled, holding his arm protectively over his head. His armor was pelted with rain, and with clanking hail the size of his fists.

"I'll show you," Hades answered, standing firm, his focus keeping him steadier amid the wind and rain than his larger brother.

"Here," Hades shouted over the howling wind. "Take this!" He handed Zeus the lid from a large clay jar he'd carried up the mountain. "Be ready to throw it onto the jar when I tell you."

Zeus lay down his spear, took the lid and nodded.

Lightning flashed, a web of light and power electrifying the sky.

"Are you thinking—" Zeus began, once he saw how intently Hades watched the lightning. "Are you going to catch the lightning?"

Hades grinned, not taking his focus off the tempest in the sky.

"That's the weapon," Zeus said, putting it all together, marveling again at his brother's brilliance. "It's lightning."

Hades crouched, his arm cupped around the clay jar, ready to pounce. The jagged hailstones fell all around Hades, but none touched him.

"We're going to harness the lightning," Hades said. "And use it."

A monstrous clap of thunder erupted, and a lightning flash lit up the sky. Hades leapt up and vanished into the brightness. Zeus squinted as the light stung his eyes. It felt like someone stabbed him in the head. He willed himself not to crush the clay lid his brother had given him. He opened his eyes and searched the sky for signs of Hades.

"Throw the lid!" Hades shouted as he hurtled down from the heavens like a shooting star. He held the jar out in front of his chest. The jar blazed with brilliant, quivering light.

Zeus hurled the lid like a discus. It spun through the air and found its target, perfectly topping the jar. Hades placed his hand on top of the lid to hold it in place, and landed on Olympus with a crash.

He dropped to his knees and tumbled forward. He was sprawled on his stomach, holding onto the frantically shaking jar.

Zeus looked at his younger brother in awe. "That," he said as he ran to help steady to jar, "was impressive."

Hades, his face blackened with char from the lightning, laughed.

Relief mingled with excitement as the prospect of victory against their father and his monsters was once again in their sights. Hades and Zeus sighed and embraced, for they knew what they held in their hands.

The jar was full of hope.

CHAPTER 22

Hades and Zeus brought the jar—the jar that held their best hope for victory—to one of the hundreds of islands in the wild and roaring sea. They brought it to a cave on that island and set it down before Hephaistos.

With the waves at their backs, Zeus glanced back periodically to ensure the unruly and uncontrollable water didn't edge too close to them. They awaited the blacksmith's inspection of the lightning.

The smell in the cave was acrid, a pungent combination of sulfur and smoke. Hephaistos had taken over an active volcanic island. He used the lava that flowed out of the sporadically erupting volcano to feed the fires of his forge. His forge was as long as the cave itself, which stretched the length of the island.

At that forge, Hephaistos had discovered he could make a substance stronger than rock—he could make metal. Zeus knew, with one eye on the water, that Kronos would love to put out the fires of their forge if he knew it existed or what its purpose was.

The gods Poseidon and Dionysius rolled wheelbarrows full of rocks they'd mined from the mountain into Hephaistos' workshop, where Hera and Athena smashed the rocks, pulling out the minerals for the blacksmith god to turn into metal.

Bronze. It was a momentous discovery for the young gods. Kronos and his horde of giants and Titans had only weapons of rock and wood and fire to compound their strength. The lightning, in addition to the bronze, could win the gods the war. It could win them the world.

All the activity in the workshop paused as the gods stood watching, hoping Hades had found the key to their victory. Hephaistos held the twitching jar steady on his workbench. He leaned against the bench, and reached a muscled arm into the jar.

Sweat poured down Hephaistos' charcoal-black skin. His eyes glowed white. His head was round and hairless, as smooth as the skin on the rest of his body. His dark arm lit up as if from within as his hand grasped the lightning.

Hephaistos clenched his teeth. Hades reached over to pull the blacksmith's arm from the jar, but Hephaistos shook his head. Hades backed away slightly.

The light spread up Hephaistos' arm towards his face. The blacksmith god closed his eyes and then yanked his arm out. He slammed the lid back onto the jar.

He exhaled and wiped his forehead with the back of his huge hand. He grinned at Hades. His white teeth glowed with nearly the same brightness as the lightning.

"It's what we needed," he told Hades in a deep, joyful voice. "I can make the weapon with this."

Zeus clapped Hades on the back. Hades nodded at fire-taming Hephaistos, his face grim with purpose and anticipation.

"Zeus!"

Hera ran up to Zeus, smoothing the rock dust out of her glossy hair. She flung a chunk of rock behind her and beamed at the eldest of the young gods. "That was brilliantly done," she said effusively.

Zeus grinned down at her, a twinkle in his eye.

"It may win us the war," he said, looking proudly at Hades, who was deep in conversation with Hephaistos. The blacksmith kept one hand on the still-vibrating jar.

"You're remarkable," Hera praised. As always, she held her head high, formal and dignified even in the dusty confines of Hephaistos' steaming hot cave.

Zeus nodded, drinking in her admiration.

"I won't disagree."

Zeus leaned against the rough cave wall and Hera sidled up under his outstretched arm. She gazed up at him with inviting eyes. He moved his other arm towards her elegant, bare shoulder, but paused before touching her, as something else caught his eye.

"Persephone!" Zeus sprang out from under shrewd Hera's net. "Let me help you," he offered.

Hera scowled to find her advances thwarted by the sudden arrival of the naïve slip of a goddess.

The youngest of the gods, Persephone was completely disheveled. Her dress was torn, falling off one shoulder. Her face was filthy, and her hair was a tangle of tiny braids and knots. She was struggling to push an overloaded wheelbarrow piled high with jagged rocks.

"You look like a wild animal, Persephone," Hera admonished, trailing Zeus and making no move to help the younger goddess. "What have you been doing? You were supposed to help us pull the minerals Hephaistos needs from the rocks. What are these?" Irritated, she picked up a rock, inspected it, then tossed it back onto the pile. "These aren't even the rocks that have the minerals we need to make metal."

"I know," Persephone began apologetically, blowing a strand of hair from her eyes. "I saw a light when I was in the tunnel. It was coming from the rocks in the distance."

Persephone looked with wide-eyed innocence and excitement to Zeus, who tilted his head, awaiting the rest of her story. Hera raised an eyebrow, disbelieving.

"I followed the trail of light," Persephone began. "And when I reached its source, I found this."

Persephone held out her hand. In her palm was a rugged stone in a surprising shade of dark green.

"What is it?" Zeus asked, putting his face very close to it.

"It's her getting out of her work again," huffed Hera.

"It's a precious stone," Persephone said softly, lovingly eyeing the rock. "There is beauty in the world already. You see? Amid all the madness and darkness, beauty hides beneath the earth, just as power does. The power Hephaistos found, the strength and might of metal, is matched by *beauty*. We gods won't need to create all the beauty we seek. It's already here. We just need to uncover it."

"How does this help us, Persephone?" Hera asked disdainfully. "You were shirking your task. You'll have to finish where I've left off because I need a rest."

"I think it's marvelous, Persephone." Zeus held the emerald up, turning it around and around, inspecting it.

Hera was just about to change her opinion to mirror Zeus's when Hades approached.

"What's that?" Hades asked his brother.

"Nothing," Hera dismissed. She took the stone from Zeus and tossed it to Hades. "Persephone is wasting time again."

"It's a precious stone," Persephone whispered, melting a little in the proximity of gorgeous, justice-loving Hades. He caught the stone. "Truly," she said, composing herself as he crooked his head, awaiting further explanation. "Hold it up to the light. You'll see it glow."

Persephone felt like Hades's intense, dark eyes bore into her heart, wrapping themselves around everything that made her who she was, inspecting her, trying to understand her. She relaxed into his intelligent gaze. She leaned towards him, hoping she could explain in words what she saw in her mind, knowing that it matched what he desired for their world.

"It's beauty," she said, looking up into his fathomless eyes and nearly getting lost there. She pointed to the emerald in his hand. "That's what it is. Already here. In our world. It's in the depths, waiting for us to uncover it and bring it to light."

Hades's expression softened. He studied the stone in his hand. Then he looked back to Persephone. He gazed at her thoughtfully, as if trying to identify a thought or a feeling.

"Hades!" Hephaistos called.

Hades's gaze lingered on a blushing Persephone for moment longer, before he tucked the emerald into his armor. He turned to help the blacksmith in his struggle to contain the lightning as he separated a piece of it from what was in the jar. Zeus was also quick to help, leaving Hera shaking her head at Persephone.

Hera regarded the younger goddess as one would an annoying little sister. She picked up one of the shiny, yet rough, precious stones from Persephone's wheelbarrow. She turned it around, then blew on it, twirling it as she blew.

"Ah!" Hera squealed as her breath polished the stone until it gleamed. She held it up to the light of the fires, and it glowed a brilliant red. Well, my girl," she said, holding the garnet up to her finger. "Maybe you did find something here."

Persephone sighed, watching Hades with longing.

"Yes. I think I did."

CHAPTER 23

Persephone traced the facets of a garnet on the bracelet Sisyphus had pressed onto her wrist. Her gaze lingered on the deep red jewel. The sight of it took her back to the day in Hephaistos's cave when she first discovered precious stones. It was the day Hades first had a glimpse of the woman Persephone was, a woman that shared his thoughts and dreams. A woman worthy of him. A woman he could love.

Persephone glared at the stacks of gold jewelry on a delicate little table Sisyphus had given her in the hope of winning her over. In the hope he could eradicate her disgust and sorrow with the gleam of metal and jewels.

Persephone stood alone in the room where she'd been brought after Ares proudly confessed his betrayal. In spite of herself, she'd slept after he locked her in. She had no idea how long she'd been there, shut inside. She had no way to measure the passing of time. It was disorienting to have no sunrise and sunset. She'd grown accustomed to the order that she and the other Olympians had brought to their world.

In the Underworld, there was no order. It was like time had reversed itself, as if the sun had gone backwards, unraveling the spool of time, and leaving a mess of the gods' pains and care. Here there was only the Underworld. Only Sisyphus and his terrifying longing. And a palpable sense of despair.

Persephone felt the smoothness of the polished garnet again. Then she twisted the cuff off her wrist, scraping and reddening her skin in her haste to remove the trinket. She strode over to the window, pushed it open, and flung the bracelet out. She watched as the precious piece of art plunged into the lava, landing softly as if on a feather pillow, and then sinking into the molten fire.

Persephone paused at the window and surveyed the Underworld. She watched Sisyphus's guards scuttle back and forth along the narrow causeway over the lava. She took note of the towering height of the gate Sisyphus believed would keep her contained—its tall, spear-like prongs, and its connection to the palace's thick, soaring walls.

She watched a line of lava snake down the black cave wall and into the lake beneath her. She couldn't tell where the lava came from—it oozed out of the walls of the home of the dead.

And then there was the waterfall. Persephone stared at it. She watched where it ran into the lava lake and created a cloud of steam as the cool, fresh water slammed into the ancient, scorching lava.

Persephone took a deep breath. Ares had said Hades was in the Underworld, that he was searching for her. Persephone had felt his presence. She'd heard him. She knew he was looking for her. All of this she knew and believed. What she hadn't suspected was that he could be in danger.

Could brilliant and strong Hades, vanquisher of Kronos and king of the gods, be defeated by the endless, cruel labyrinth of the Underworld? What if Ares, for once, wasn't lying or boasting to try to impress? If Hades really was trapped in the Underworld, could Ares take power on the surface and plummet their beautiful, peaceful world back into darkness and despair?

Persephone couldn't wait for Hades to find her. She had to find him.

Persephone turned on her heel and strode across the room. She stood before two massive doors. They were ornately carved, designed to awe, their size intended to make Sisyphus's guest feel small. And helpless.

Persephone reached for the doors. The handles were made of red carnelian, carved in the shape of roaring lions with tiny black pearls for eyes. She exhaled, pulled on the lions, heard a click like a lock releasing, and flung the doors wide open.

It was surprisingly quiet in the hallway outside her room. The floor was made of swirling green marble. The walls were coated in etched gold. A mosaic band ran along the top of the walls, made with rare blue stones and pearls, to look like foam-crested waves. Persephone was mystified to find such richness and beauty in the Underworld. The hallway was so richly decorated it was beyond anything even the gods possessed. She scraped the wall with her fingernail to see what lay beneath the overlay of gold. She found nothing—it was solid gold.

As she stood there, astonished, a scent crept upon her. She turned from one way to the other. The smell permeated the hall. She turned her nose up at the odor, which was like a poor perfume, a clumsy mixture of disparate flowers. Underlying the sickly-sweet perfume was a more subtle scent, one that the floral smell was designed to cover: the sour smell of decay.

Persephone stepped closer to inspect one of the lava-filled torches that lined the hall's golden walls.

"Who made this place?"

"Slaves," came a quick, resigned answer. "Who else?"

Persephone spun around to see a small man with a stylus and clay tablet standing outside her door. He hunched over his tablet, scribbling while he spoke.

"Sisyphus has an unending supply of slaves in the Underworld," said the busy little man. "Each shade comes here with a talent, a gift they had in life. Artists, builders, cooks. He learns their skills and then he uses them. They're shades. They require no food, no pay, no relief. And so they—we—will spend eternity under his thumb, forced to do as he commands."

"Who are you?" Persephone asked, startled.

"I'm Philos. I was a philosopher. Now I'm Sisyphus's slave." The philosopher put his stylus behind his ear and looked blankly at Persephone. "I am how he finds out the talents of the new shades that come here. I assign them their tasks."

Philos stood only as high as Persephone's shoulders. When he was hunched over his tablet, he was even smaller. He walked off, scribbling, his eyes on his work.

Persephone followed him. Philos's hair was white, what few strands were left of it. And it was unkempt, as though he'd never thought to brush it, or that the thought of doing so was deemed a waste of time. His skin had the translucence of the other shades she had seen, but he didn't have their wan, vapid look. His eyes had a spark of life in them.

"What happens to the shades who come here who don't have talents that Sisyphus finds useful?" Persephone asked.

"Ah, well." Philos paused and scratched his head with his stylus. He looked up at Persephone. "They're left to wander. They wander the Underworld, aimless, searching for meaning, for anything. But they never find it. There is nothing to find. There is only rot and fear and emptiness." Philos resumed walking. "I think it's better to be a slave."

Persephone was devastated to hear this. The gods dreamed and worked and pledged to make life good for humans. But they hadn't given any thought to what would happen to the humans after they died.

Persephone ran to catch up with Philos, who was surprisingly quick. She reached out and touched his shoulder, wanting him to stop. She had so many questions.

Philos froze at her touch. He dropped his tablet and it shattered. He turned to the goddess, his eyes full of tears.

Persephone pulled her hand away and clasped it with her other hand.

"Are you all right?" His body had the strangest feel, somewhere between solid and mist.

Philos looked into Persephone's eyes with awe and wonder.

"I saw my family," he whispered. "When you touched me, I remembered my wife. Our daughters. Our granddaughter..."

He put a shaking hand to his temple.

"It was as if they'd been pulled through a fog I didn't know was there. That I didn't know was keeping them from me. You returned them to me—you returned my life to me."

The old philosopher stood a bit taller.

"I remember my life," he said quietly, his eyes glistening. "And the people in it." He smiled wistfully. "I know they still love me. They remember me. They honor my memory. I can feel our connection now, my family's and mine. It has not been broken with my death. They have not forgotten me."

Philos bent over to pick up his stylus. He tucked the small piece behind his ear, and sighed with a sort of contentment. "Ask for my aid. I'll do whatever you ask of me," he told the goddess, his aged face earnest. "Whatever you need, my lady. You gave me a gift I can never fully repay. Now the countless number of days I'll spend here won't feel as empty. I'm not alone now—because my family remembers me..."

Persephone smiled. "I'm glad I brought you comfort," she said kindly. As she looked at Philos, a thought gnawed at her. Perhaps she could help other shades as well—

But Hades came first. She had to find him and a way out for them both. They had to return to the surface to stop Ares. Then they could return and help the shades. The seeds she ate had not slipped her mind. Yes, she had eaten the pomegranate seeds and, yes, that should mean that she was tethered to the Underworld forever; but hadn't they—the almighty gods—broken and remade the world before? Couldn't they do so again?

"Tell me, Philos," she began. "How does time pass here?"

"Slowly," was his reply. Then he thought for a moment, tapping his cheek with a crooked finger. "The boatman comes with what feels like regularity. I think he comes once a day with new shades."

"You think that every time you see him, it is a new day?"

"I cannot be sure, but that is how it feels."

"Please begin to take count of his appearances. I want to be aware of the passing of the days."

"I will do that for you, my lady." Philos bowed. If he'd still had bones, Persephone imagined she would hear them creak as he bent.

"Thank you," Persephone smiled. "Another thing." She swallowed. "How does Ares come and go from the Underworld?"

Before he could answer, Philos's eyes widened. The old philosopher whispered to Persephone, his way of warning her of King Sisyphus's return.

"I will find out."

Philos scurried away, again hunched over, even though the remains of his tablet were crushed under Sisyphus's feet as he approached Persephone.

"I will see you at the boat, Philos," Sisyphus ordered over her shoulder. "As usual."

Philos nodded as he hurried away, not turning back.

Sisyphus turned his attention to Persephone.

"You came out of your room!" he said, his tone condescending, as if speaking to a child.

He opened his arms wide, expecting her to run into his embrace. Two hulking black armored creatures were at his back. Persephone wondered what those monsters were, that trailed the self-proclaimed Underworld King.

She shrunk away from Sisyphus. He pulled her in and embraced her, in spite of her clear disdain. His skeletal arm and protruding ribs were rough to the touch, but the rest of him felt fleshy yet gossamer, as if her finger could pierce through the illusion of his skin. She shivered being so close to him, keeping her own arms firmly by her sides. Her gaze was on his gargantuan guards.

Stay calm, she told herself, thinking she might be able to lull him into complacency. She needed to learn as much as she could about him and his so-called kingdom. She wriggled out of his grasp and he beamed at her, finding her disgust somehow charming.

"What do you think of your palace now that you've begun exploring it?"

Sisyphus shooed the hulking creatures away. As they went, Persephone saw that they each had three feet and five arms. Like great, humanized spiders. She didn't want to see what was under their helmets, which had menacing, black pincers where their faces would be.

"Where did you get all of this gold?" she asked, ignoring his question. "The pearls, the gems? Where did it all come from?"

King Sisyphus narrowed his eyes and tilted his head at the unexpected question. His lips curled and he smiled, deciding to humor his future queen.

"It's right in front of you. It's all around you."

"You found it in the Underworld?"

"Exactly," Sisyphus answered. "The earth is full of gold, precious stones, metals, and more."

"I know that."

"You do? Excellent," he said with a patronizing pat of her hand. Persephone fought the urge to roll her eyes. "Well, the Underworld is richer than anything that you've seen above ground. And it's all mine."

"According to whom?" Persephone was defiant, thinking of the pathetic numberless shades.

"According to me," Sisyphus preened. "Ares and I are partners. And now you are a partner to me, of a different kind. Less a partner, I suppose, and more like a reward."

Persephone's eyes widened with shock, floored by this creature's arrogance. She felt her fingertips heat up with anger at being spoken to with such insufferable superiority. She'd never felt so much power well up in her body before. She wasn't sure what would happen if she unleashed it—the pincers on the face of the spider guard nearest her began to wriggle as if sensing her power rise—so she reigned it in.

Sisyphus was smart. He was clearly the mind behind Ares's plan. She would have to be careful if she wanted to learn everything he planned so she could tell Hades and Zeus when she found them.

"Ares needs bronze," Sisyphus went on, happy to boast of his own genius. He reached over to take something off the wall behind her.

He held up a dagger for her to see. Its blade glimmered in the light of the lava torches.

"Ares needed weapons. Weapons, weapons, and more weapons if he is to take over the rule of the gods. And I needed a kingdom to replace the one that was ripped from me when I was sent here."

Sisyphus grimaced at the stinging memory. He advanced down the hall and turned down another richly appointed hallway. Persephone trailed behind him, out of arm's reach, listening intently.

"And so, we are partners, Ares and I." Sisyphus turned to face Persephone. "I mine metals for him. And he made me King of the Underworld. And gave you to me to be my Queen."

Persephone's rage rekindled. She felt her hands simmer with anger and power. Ares had betrayed them all. What he had done to her hit her again—with the same force of the spear she now remembered had come from his hand and pierced her chest. She stumbled back against the wall. She fought the urge to touch her chest, the place from which Ares had stolen her life and her love and her light. She clenched her fists, her hands buzzing with energy and fury.

She wrung her hands, squeezing the power that had welled up in them, feeling it travel up her arms and into her chest. Sadness and fear overtook her anger as she thought of her mother. Demeter would be wandering the earth above, bemoaning Persephone's death. She knew her mother's grief would be long and terrible, and that the entire earth would feel it.

Persephone looked around. This place—she gathered herself before the self-centered Sisyphus could realize how affected she was by the confirmation of this news—would be full of thousands of new shades if Persephone couldn't find a way to stop Sisyphus and Ares.

Demeter's grief would mean the end of things growing on earth. There would be no fruit, no grain, no harvest. Humans would starve. Ares hoped Hades's grief would trap him in the Underworld, so there would be no one to coax Demeter back to reason. And Zeus would be trapped with him. Humans would be caught up in a war waged between the gods, sending even more shades to the hopeless depths.

Persephone stared at the self-proclaimed king of the Underworld as he twirled his dagger. Its tip pierced the exposed bone of his finger, but he made no motion that he felt it, that he was capable of feeling pain.

Persephone glanced at the mirrored wall behind him. Unlike any mirror Persephone had seen before, the golden mirrors that covered the walls in this hallway were as smooth as calm water. They didn't mar the image they reflected—there was no distortion in the glass.

Persephone looked at her reflection and caught her breath when she saw a figure by her side. Her heart thumped in relief and joy.

In the mirror, Hades was beside her.

He stood tall and strong and dashing. His dark eyes looked into hers, full of love. Persephone reached forward to touch Hades's face, but when her finger grazed the mirror, Hades transformed. She could only watch as he shrank and shriveled until he became Sisyphus.

Persephone backed away. Sisyphus stood beside her, admiring the way he looked beside the evanescent goddess in the reflection.

"I knew," Sisyphus said from beside her with smug satisfaction. "I knew, once I was satisfied with all the gold and the treasure, I would need a queen." He turned to Persephone, his eyes alight with something like madness. "And so, I built this palace for you."

Hades's striking face flashed in her mind. Her heart nearly thumped again, but Sisyphus vowed, "You *will* be my wife."

Persephone's heart went quiet.

CHAPTER 24

Zeus sighed once Hades was finally asleep.

"Ambrosia—" he said with a half-grin. "It works every time."

It was indicative of how much the encounter with the shades had cost Hades that he had allowed Zeus to give him the ambrosia, knowing he'd sleep soon after drinking it.

Hades held Persephone's vines in a white-knuckled grasp. Yellow petals poked out from in between his fingers.

"Persephone," Zeus whispered, staring at the petals. "Where are you?"

Suddenly, without warning, the flowers began to wilt. The edges of the petals turned brown, then black. Zeus opened Hades's hand and the whole vine disintegrated into ash.

"Please don't let that mean what I think it means…"

Kerberos gave a little whimper and Zeus hushed him. He didn't want Hades to wake up and see what happened to the plant he'd clung to, as if it was Persephone herself.

Zeus sighed. Then he raised an eyebrow. He sensed that something, or someone, was watching them.

He swung around. In the distance, he saw two great bat-like creatures peering into the tunnel. Zeus scowled and took a step towards them, but Kerberos had picked up their scent. The hound yanked its neck out of the tunnel and bounded after them as they swooped away.

Zeus sat with a thunk beside Hades's sleeping form and put his head in his hands. He had no idea what to do next.

CHAPTER 25

Persephone forced herself to throw off her dread and horror, her pain and sadness. She had nothing to lose by defying this mad-man. Everything of value had already been taken from her. She thought of her mother and Hades and the life-giving sun. She allowed her anger to overtake her. Her rage grew. She grew in size with her fury, and everything before her eyes turned red.

"You forget that I am a goddess!"

Persephone spoke in a voice so unlike her usual honeyed tones that Sisyphus backed away. The suddenly unrecognizable force in front of him took him by complete surprise. The halls shook and the mirrors cracked. Cracks splayed across the mirrors like an army of spiders' webs.

"I have powers you cannot begin to understand," she declared. "Do not presume to own me, to plan for me. I've heard your plan. The plan you made regardless of my thoughts and desires. And now I can tell you to forget your selfish dream. I'll never be your Queen. I'd never marry you."

Sisyphus stood, frozen. Persephone's anger and strength was unexpected. A smile crept up on his lips. He couldn't take his eyes off her. He had never desired her more. After a few tense moments, he gathered himself. His narrow-set eyes lit up with a plan.

He walked gingerly towards Persephone, holding his arms up as if surrendering.

She, of course, knew otherwise. Persephone watched him think, his wicked brain working out a new plan. When a calmness came over his face, she knew he had his plan. His hands fell to his sides.

From where he stood, Sisyphus said simply, "Marry me or I will torture Hades."

Persephone fought to keep her expression unreadable.

"I *can* keep him in the labyrinth of the Underworld until time runs out," Sisyphus gloated, casually inspecting his sharp yellow fingernails. "I can send armies of shades to torture him. I can drown him in the Styx, revive him and drown him again. Everything I promised Ares I could do and more... I will do to your *beloved* Hades." He coldly looked Persephone in the eyes. "Or, marry me and I will let him leave the Underworld. Without you, of course."

This was what she wanted. Unbeknownst to Sisyphus, he had given her exactly what she wanted: Hades's safety. The promise of Hades's safe return to Olympus, where he and Zeus and Athena could defeat Ares in the blink of an eye.

Mirroring his calm with calm of her own, she asked, "What happened to you, Sisyphus? How did you die?"

"Oh, this?" He tore open his tunic to reveal a chest stripped of skin down to the bone. Persephone covered her mouth, shocked at the extent of the graphic wound.

"This is where your lover killed me."

Persephone's mouth dropped open.

"Yes," Sisyphus chortled. "Now things begin to be clear to you. This is what it looks to be hit with Hades's thunderbolt."

A dark expression came over Sisyphus's face.

"It's a powerful weapon."

He stepped towards Persephone. He traced his bony finger along her cheek. "Though, perhaps not powerful enough." He smirked and let his hand drop. "But this is not all about revenge." His tone became frighteningly conciliatory. "It's a love story, too. You see, I saw you once. Above."

Persephone closed her eyes, remembering life when she was

still on earth, when she'd never set foot in the Underworld.

"You were with your women," Sisyphus went on. "You were picking wildflowers. You were...glorious. Your face was a revelation. You moved with such grace. Such goodness. I had to possess you. I had to take you for myself. But how? You're a goddess, as you just reminded me. I am but a man."

Persephone opened her eyes and glared at the man who presumed to control her.

"You are just a man," she said, vitriol in her voice. "So we agree."

"I am a man," he concurred. "But not just any man. I'm the man who pulled himself out of the stupor of being a lifeless shade with my own will and ambition. I am the man who made Ares realize he could be of use to him. In more ways than one.

"I could provide him with all the bronze he needed for his weapons *and* I could rid him of a hated rival. At the same time, I could get my revenge on Hades for ruining my life by sending me to this place, when I was at the pinnacle of power on earth!"

Sisyphus was yelling now, all pretense of calm control gone. He pounded his chest, rattling his bones.

"Hades took everything from me! I was a king! I was feared! I was obeyed! I was rich! I had any woman I wanted. Now I'm not even a man—I'm what is left of a man after Hades kills him." He paused. "And I will have my revenge."

"You must have been truly evil," Persephone said.

Sisyphus roared and smashed his fists into the cracked mirrors on both sides of the corridor. Shards of glass flew out of the wall like daggers.

He took a deep breath. A vindictive look in his beady eyes, he snarled, "I think it's time for me to tell you something. But you aren't going to like it."

Persephone held still, waiting, dread crawling up her spine like a chill in the night.

"You can never leave this place," Sisyphus said. "The Underworld. Ever."

"You lie."

"Yes, I do." Sisyphus laughed, echoing Ares. The sound made her stomach turn. "But I am not lying now."

"Ares comes and goes when he pleases."

"But he didn't die. You did."

"I am a god!"

"And now you are a god of the Underworld."

Persephone's eyes filled with tears. They fell, soaking her face. "I don't believe it has to be that way."

"No matter what you think. No matter how you scheme and try, no matter how you cling to the notion that your immortality makes you special, you can never leave, because you have eaten here," Sisyphus said with callous satisfaction. "That sealed your fate."

"I've taken no food here!"

"I thought you might have forgotten them."

"Forgotten what?"

"The seeds."

Persephone's face fell. The seeds. She had pushed that memory to the back of her mind. She made the choice and she knew what it meant. She wanted to survive, no matter the cost. It was her choice and now she had to live with it.

The gods had decided their boundary was the Underworld, and that no god was to willingly cross that line. But if you did, if you ate food from the Underworld, there would be no return.

She knew that, she knew it, and yet…she'd done it. The seeds were so small, so insignificant, part of her thought she could dismiss them like she would flick a fly off her shoulder. Part of her thought they might not matter—the Olympians had remade so many rules with their ascension.

But the seeds did matter. As she inevitably knew they would. She had wanted to survive—whatever that meant—and so she had done it. If she hadn't she would have become a shade like the tens of thousands who roamed listless and lost all around her. Now she had to figure out what survival in the Underworld meant.

"Six pomegranate seeds," Sisyphus said with a smirk. "That's all it took. Now you're truly here forever."

CHAPTER 26

Hades started in his sleep.

"What? Why are you saying this?" he shouted, then sat up. His eyes flashed open. His breathing was quick. His hair was damp with sweat. He shook his head, his far-seeing eyes full of confusion and disbelief.

Zeus rushed to his brother's side. "What is it?"

Kerberos lowered his huge head over Hades and whimpered.

"It can't be." Hades shook his head.

"What can't be?"

"Persephone."

"You heard Persephone again?"

With slight wave of his hand, Zeus swept the ashes, the remnants of Persephone's vines, from Hades's skin.

"I saw her," Hades said, his mind still foggy with sleep.

"You saw her?"

"We were looking at our reflection in a golden mirror. I was right beside her." His lips curled into a slight, brief smile before the smile was extinguished. "She was afraid."

Zeus bit his lip.

"She told me to leave," Hades said, wrinkling his brow in confusion. "To go home and leave her here. She pleaded with me…"

Zeus stood. He paced around the low-ceilinged cavern he'd found for Hades to rest in. It seemed an insignificant enough spot, ideal to avoid unwanted encounters with shades or other unsavory Underworld creatures.

It was a small space, so Kerberos' body lay outside the door. The great hound stretched his neck to fit a single head inside. Zeus's sandaled feet were sunk to his ankles in unidentifiable black muck. He hesitated before saying, "Maybe she's right."

Hades dismissed the idea and stood up. "It was a dream." He picked up the bronze staff he'd laid down when he rested after drinking the ambrosia.

Of course, he saw the ashes.

Of course, he felt the absence of Persephone's vines.

But he didn't mention them, nor did he question what happened while he slept.

"It was just a dream," Hades repeated. "Nothing more."

"A dream or a vision? Maybe she's trying to tell you something."

"Why would she tell me to leave her?" Hades admonished, disbelieving. "To stop coming for her? Why would she do that?"

Reliving the harrowing experience with the shades who seemed hungry for Hades, Zeus offered softly, "To save you."

"Save me from what?"

"From yourself."

CHAPTER 27

"Come." Sisyphus attempted to temper his command with an entreating look that came across more like annoyance than an invitation. He was a volcano that might erupt at any moment. One moment it was calm and quiet, the next moment smoke puffed out and the explosion followed. His volatility, the ever-present danger of his reactions, was gravely unsettling.

Sisyphus took Persephone's hand. She allowed Sisyphus to pull her along like a child. She should have been relieved that she was able to save Hades, and that he and Zeus would return to the world above to save it and punish Ares. And yet, confronted for the first time with the realization that she really was stuck in the Underworld forever, she was dazed and heartbroken at the loss of all hope of leaving. Even the tiniest morsel of hope she had been nurturing had been snuffed out by six tiny seeds.

"Here, my darling," Sisyphus interrupted her thoughts. "Remember your wedding gift. Look. See them. It will make you feel better."

They must have descended below the palace. It had grown so hot that they had to be nearly touching the lava—or beneath it. Persephone wiped her forehead wearily and glanced up. She saw a huge boulder that fit into the wall like a puzzle piece. Sisyphus pointed, and his guards, who reappeared out of nowhere, scrambled to heave the stone away from the wall.

Sisyphus nodded at the opening. Persephone peered into the darkness and saw the huddled forms of the harpies.

"Why are they chained?" she demanded, the terrible state of the harpies yanking her from her self-pity.

"They're your slaves," Sisyphus explained slowly.

"Remove their chains," Persephone commanded. "At once!"

"Why?"

"I said, remove their chains! All of them! The harpies are mine and I will do with them what I like."

Sisyphus shrugged. "If they attempt escape and get themselves shot, you'll have only yourself to blame."

"Take off their chains," she repeated. "They can fly free now. They are bound to me and will not try to escape.

"And I agree," she added, smoothing a wayward strand of hair from her face and composing herself. "I agree to your bargain. Let Hades and Zeus leave this place. Let them return safely to the surface. And I will be your Queen." Persephone paused, stumbling over her next words. "I will marry you."

An eager smile crept across Sisyphus's face.

"Hmmm, I assured Ares that I would keep Hades here in the Underworld," he mused.

"What do you want?" Persephone blazed. "More gold? Or me?"

"Remove the harpies' chains!" Sisyphus ordered. He turned to Persephone, his beady eyes glowing with victory.

"I will let Hades and Zeus leave. I will even show them the way out. You, my darling, are all I need," Sisyphus simpered, holding her graceful hands high. He kissed her hands and then swept out of the room, letting Persephone assume he was off to fulfill his promise to his future wife.

"Do nothing," Sisyphus told a guard once he was out of Persephone's hearing. "The Underworld will destroy Hades and Zeus, and Persephone will never be the wiser. Ares will be content.

"And she will be content in the palace island I built for her— she'll never leave it, and Hades will never find it. Persephone will forget about Hades, in time. He will certainly forget about her."

The guards grunted their understanding. Sisyphus sauntered off, his beastly guard in tow.

. . .

Six more massive, armored spider creatures appeared from nowhere to unlock each harpy from where their taloned feet were chained to the wall.

Persephone rushed into the hot, dark cell. Her presence was immediately felt in the cell, a freshness wafting into the room, a lightness lifting the spirits of the dejected creatures who had dwelt there for so long. Persephone headed straight for the angry harpy, who looked sicker than before. She knelt beside her.

"He's gone." Persephone spoke to all the harpies as she inspected the angry harpy's wing. "Sisyphus won't hurt you again. I won't allow it."

"You fool yourself if you believe you have power," the angry harpy scoffed. She was too weak, however, to protest Persephone's ministrations.

"I have some power," Persephone said. "And you'd be smart to see that. Now, try to lift your wing."

Begrudgingly, the harpy did so, as the other fourteen harpies gathered around and watched.

"Tell me." Persephone turned to the kind harpy, finding her in the cell by her stripe down her yellow beak. "Is there any light here? Besides the lava? Any sun?"

"No, my lady. And we have flown to nearly all corners of this place."

"Nearly all? Not all?"

"No," answered a harpy with dark wings spotted with white feathers. "The Underworld is so vast and changeable we can't be sure we've seen it all. And before you arrived, we were not all allowed to leave freely."

"Then that is your first task. Map this place. Do it in an

organized fashion, so you can be sure of what you've seen, and what you still need to see. You six," Persephone pointed. "Go. Map the Underworld and find me daylight if there is any."

The six harpies nodded in salute and then swooped out to follow Persephone's orders.

"Now you, my girl," Persephone said to the kind harpy. "Take the others and fly. Fly up that waterfall and find the source of that water. And bring back as many vases of water as you can. I need to grow a plant that will heal her wing, and it's going to require water."

Again, the harpies responded with military precision, following Persephone's orders.

Persephone tore off a piece of her dress, a brilliant white gown that she'd been wearing when she awoke in Sisyphus's palace. Her old dress had been removed while she slept, as though Sisyphus hoped her old love and life could be stripped away as easily.

Persephone spoke as she gently wrapped the broken wing with the cloth.

"Tell me about your life," she said, trying to distract them both from their present situation. "You said you were not always this way. Not always harpies."

The angry harpy's eyes had closed, resigning herself to Persephone's care.

"We were Amazons," the harpy shared. "We fifteen are the only ones left of our kind. Strong women are more of a danger than Ares himself. Apparently."

"What's your name?" Persephone asked.

"I no longer have a name. None of us do. We can't remember more than glimpses of our lives on earth. I see fleeting images of the fifteen of us, with strength and weapons and pride. And now we are here. We are this…"

Persephone felt the weight of the harpy's grief. She shared it.

"We are decaying," the harpy said. "Can you see it? Can you smell it? Our pain? Our suffering? We're rotting from the outside in."

"Not any longer, dear one." Persephone spoke through her

tears. She kept her voice strong, kept the pity out of it. "I will take care of you now. I can heal you. Let me," she begged.

The angry harpy bowed her head. Then she nodded.

Persephone sniffed, wiping her tears away before the harpy could open her eyes and see them.

"Nike," she said.

"What?" The harpy opened her eyes. "What's that? Nike?"

"That is your new name."

"Victory," the harpy said. "Nike means victory."

"Yes." Persephone sat back on her feet and surveyed the harpy, seeing the creature how she could be once she was healed and in her glory.

"Victory."

CHAPTER 28

Persephone stood at the edge of the sea. Her feet were bare, her dress worn away to nearly nothing, ragged as all the gods' clothing had become. Hades watched Persephone with fascination. He wondered what she could be thinking as she stared out at the vast, tumultuous water around Hephaistos's island. Her legs were soaking wet and coated in black sand. Her long hair was streaked with braids, interspersed with loose strands waving freely in the untamed wind.

Persephone wasn't staring at the sea. She wasn't mesmerized by the crashing, churning waves. She was looking up into the ever-dark sky. She watched the sky as though waiting for something. As though she believed there was something beyond the darkness that encompassed the gods' world, the gods' every day. It was what he also believed.

The other gods followed Hades because they wanted to overthrow Kronos. They wanted power and better lives. They despised the near-slavery of their lives under their father. The uselessness, the forlorn endlessness. The stench-filled darkness, aimlessness, and ugliness.

And so they believed in Hades and his plan because it was vastly better than their current reality. But not even Zeus believed to the degree that Hades did in what their world could become. The potential for goodness, beauty, and light. Hades had a vision so clear he ached to make it a reality. He could see it all in his mind—the richness of a world with color and art, and a people to grow and foster these ideas.

Hades looked at the emerald in his hand, the one Persephone had found in the cave. Hera had polished all the other gemstones that Persephone discovered, but Hades had kept this one for himself. It was still rough. Its sides were uneven and grooved. Parts of it were black rock, but the parts that weren't were a vibrant shade of green, a bright color unlike anything he'd ever seen.

He closed his hand around the stone and saw that Persephone hadn't moved. He felt protective of her. She was the youngest of the gods, a mere child, he told himself.

He watched her closely now, Hades assured himself, to make sure the wild water didn't reach out to grab her. She was such a slight little thing, and Kronos had never managed to make the sea submit to his demands.

Suddenly, Persephone turned her head. She looked directly at Hades. Hades froze in her gaze, stunned. And confused at being stunned. He managed only a slight nod before turning away.

Hades wanted to look back, to see her again, but he reminded himself that Hephaistos was ready to try the lightning bolt weapon. He walked away but felt a strange tug at his chest. He ignored the pull of her, though it felt as if his body was working against him. The black sand beach felt more like tar than sand. Every step away from Persephone was a struggle, and Hades wondered why he was fighting so hard against her.

CHAPTER 29

"You want to leave," Hades said quietly, staff in hand. "You want me to abandon her."

Hades looked at the ground, to where the ashes of Persephone's vines spread out like insignificant dust. In his other hand, he turned the raw emerald over and over.

"I understand." Hades's voice was solemn. "Kerberos can lead you back to the entrance where we came into the Underworld. You should be able to climb the tree and return to Olympus."

Zeus began to speak but Hades cut him off.

"I'm not going with you," Hades said firmly. "I'm not leaving without her."

Zeus felt diminished in the strange and terrifying Underworld. He'd never felt so unsure, so fearful, even in the great war against their father. He was afraid for his brother, more than for himself—the shades hadn't seemed to want to possess him.

"What if Persephone is trying to warn you?" Zeus asked, watching Hades tighten his fist around the precious stone. "What if she can't leave?"

Hades carefully put the emerald back into his armor. With steady, measured steps, he followed Kerberos' head as it backed out of the cavern. Zeus stood still, waiting.

"I will leave the Underworld," Hades vowed. "With Persephone."

Zeus bowed his head. He exhaled in frustration and his breath sprayed the ever-dark Underworld halls with frost. Kerberos whined.

"You're angry," Hades observed, sweeping the frost off the dog's face.

"Not angry so much as..." Zeus acknowledged. "Fearful."

"There's no need to be afraid." Hades paused and turned to look back at his brother.

"No need?" Zeus threw up his hands. "Hades, you're not thinking clearly. Even for us, this place reeks of danger..."

"But she's here," Hades argued. "And she's well. You found the vines yourself! We just need to reach to her."

Hades motioned for Kerberos to run ahead, and the Underworld hound bounded off, thrilled to be free from the enclosed space.

"You saw what happened to the plants. I know you saw it."

"It means nothing."

"Nothing?" Zeus sputtered. "They turned to ash!"

"Perhaps growing things can't be sustained here."

"Aren't we growing things?" Zeus shook his head. "Aren't we alive? For now, anyway."

Hades didn't hear his brother's aside. He was distracted by the area through which Kerberos was running around with puppy-like joy, his dragon tail wagging.

"What is this place? This doesn't look like the way we came," Zeus said, noting the foreignness of their surroundings for himself. "And yet it must be because there was no other way into that cavern..."

A vast, open plain, an underground prairie, spread out before the gods. It was a desolate and barren sight, as colorless and stark as the rest of the Underworld. But unfamiliar—the gods had not come this way, and yet it was the way they'd come.

In the distance stood a single, massive rock. It looked out of place amid the otherwise empty landscape. The rock was triangular, like a billowing sail. It was made of gray granite, like rocks on the surface, and therefore felt both familiar and foreign. It was solidly set upon the black cave floor, but the stark contrast of its color made it look as though it floated on a dark sea.

Zeus cursed, exasperated.

"It's changeable," Hades said grimly. "The Underworld."

"It changes as we walk through it." Zeus finished Hades's thought.

Hades's head swam. With each step he took towards Persephone, the Underworld hurled him back ten-fold. The Underworld dangled hope in front of him, then snatched it away more quickly than it had arrived, making him feel her loss again and again.

Hades knelt. He rubbed his fingers against his thumb, remembering the way the leaves had felt. They were real, he reminded himself. Persephone created them. She called them up out of the bare rock and darkness and stench.

She's real. And she's here. Somewhere. Hades slammed his fist into the ground.

For a moment, all was quiet. Then the ground trembled. The floor around Hades undulated, moving in expanding, concentric circles, like ripples on a pond spreading out from a dropped pebble.

Hades rose, balancing on the shifting earth like he was riding a wave. He heard a loud crack followed by a bone-jarring crunch. Hade and Zeus edged closer together. Something beneath them had been unleashed.

Something was breaking through the ground at their feet. From one end of the vast Underworld prairie to the other, rocks rose out of the fractured earth. They looked like trees made of stone. They rose until they were taller than the gods. As they grew, they sprouted arms like tree branches. Each rocky branch was filled with metal thorns. Before the gods could move, the prairie was transformed into a maze of spiny metal shards.

Kerberos howled and whimpered, frozen in place, too afraid to move. He was surrounded by spikes. Only his heads were above the menacing points.

Hades and Zeus stood back to back, preparing for battle, as they had so many times. Hades raised an arm. Whipping through the dank air, spikes flew from the nearest granite tree, heading straight for his arm.

Hades swung his staff with superhuman speed and knocked

the spikes to the ground. One spike dug into his foot, piercing his black armor. Hades glared at it.

Zeus growled and prepared to hurl his lightning bolt at the spikes, but Hades spoke quickly. "Wait! Let me think. Or we'll be covered in them."

Zeus held off, grunting. At the rumble of his grunt, twenty spikes flew and buried themselves in his knees. Zeus grimaced. But waited.

"All right." Hades whispered. "*Quietly*. Aim your thunderbolt at the spikes in your knees. Then send fire at them. Gently!"

"Of course I'll do it gently," Zeus retorted in the quietest whisper he could manage. "They are attached to my body."

With an uncharacteristically subtle twist of his fingers, Zeus tilted his thunderbolt and aimed it at the spikes buried in his knees. He took a deep breath.

"Here goes."

Zeus zapped the spikes. They smoked and then melted, dripping to the ground. Zeus moved his feet before the melting spikes landed on them and more spikes flew at him. Hades deflected them before they struck his brother in the arms.

"Good," Hades said, relieved.

"We burn them?" Zeus asked, his lip curled into a satisfied snarl.

"Yes. Light my staff. Then we go together."

Zeus slowly aimed his lightning bolt at Hades's forked staff. The staff lit up, fire lighting every part of the staff but where Hades's hand gripped it.

Hades nodded almost imperceptibly at Zeus.

"Now!"

Zeus's glowing lightning bolt and Hades's flaming staff became a blur of fire, flame, and destruction. Harnessing all the swiftness of their godliness, Hades and Zeus turned the vast prairie into a conflagration. Each stalagmite burst into flame and burned blue as the gods' fire struck it, an eerie blue forest among the spreading orange flames.

"Kerberos, come!" Hades commanded. The terrified hound

leapt over the flames, landing beside his master in a spot Hades had swept clear for him.

The spikes melted into a viscous metallic sap that oozed down the stone tree trunks onto the ground. The stone trees didn't melt. Instead, they remained upright, like crooked skeletons, naked, their defenses literally melted away.

The flames swept out of the cavern. The Underworld burned with the gods' fire. Smoke swept from room to room, infiltrating every portion of the Underworld with at least some residue of the sweeping blaze. Curious shades huddled together by the thousands. Drawn from their corners and caverns, some approached the flames, pulled by the heat and light.

Zeus and Hades lowered their weapons. The prairie was charred and blackened, a haunted and ruined forest.

The gods stomped through what looked like a battlefield, among the burned-out stone trees that resembled the shadows and ghosts left behind after a war. The ground was uneven and shiny, the melted spikes coating it like tangled strands of thread. The pungent smell of burning metal and earth filled the air.

Hades leapt up onto the ship-shaped rock. It glowed among the blackened ruins. He stood atop it as if he owned it. He pounded his chest and howled. He was telling the Underworld he had come. He challenged it to defy him and his wishes to find Persephone, daring it to stand between him and his love.

"Persephone!" he called. "Persephone!"

Zeus stood by Kerberos and looked on anxiously, understanding there was no going back. He would never drag Hades from the Underworld without Persephone.

CHAPTER 30

In the harpy den, Persephone looked up from where she watched over a sleeping Nike. Ashes floated into the room. They swirled around the harpy den like the lightest of snow.

Marveling, Persephone held out a hand. An ash landed on her fingertip. It was so light she barely felt it touch her skin. She pressed her thumb against the ash and felt an intense rush of familiar heat. Her eyes widened.

"Hades?" she whispered. She opened her hand.

A tear fell from Persephone's face onto the little pile of ash, which soon collected on her palm. As her tear hit the ashes, a wisp of steam rose from her hand. The steam turned pink and snaked up towards her face. Persephone waved it away. But as her breath hit the steam, it released the sound of Hades's voice. She heard his cry for her. His plea for her return.

"Persephone!" she heard his defiant call. "Persephone!"

"Hades?" Persephone called back, overwhelmed at hearing his voice so clear and so near. His voice surrounded her, enveloping her.

Nike woke to find Persephone quietly weeping. Wisps of pink steam encircled the goddess's head. They swirled around her dark hair, repeating Hades's cry over and over.

"Hades," she answered again and again, knowing he wouldn't hear.

Persephone wanted to say more. There was so much she wanted to tell him, about how she loved him, about how she'd always loved him. That the loss of him felt as though she'd been torn apart.

Days had turned into months since Persephone had arrived in the Underworld. Persephone knew that she should tell Hades to go. To leave her. That she'd sacrificed herself for his safety and his life and their dream of a beautiful world on the surface. But hearing his voice so near and real, she just wanted him to come find her and take her away with him. And so she begged him to come to her. Sadly, the more Persephone spoke, the more the steam dissipated, taking Hades's voice with it. Until it was gone.

Persephone bit her lip. Then she hung her head and sobbed.

Nike sat up. Persephone curled on the ground and wept uncontrollably, her body racked with despair. Nike spread her wings over Persephone's shivering body like a shield.

In time, the other harpies returned to the den. Persephone had moved them to the den, replacing the cell where Sisyphus had kept them for untold years. One by one, the harpies returned to find Nike holding her wings over the goddess. The harpies encircled their goddess, keeping silent vigil.

When Persephone cried all she could, she wiped her eyes and looked up at Nike. Nike drew her wings back and stood tall.

"Tell her," Nike quietly ordered the harpy Erato, her eyes not leaving Persephone's face.

After a short pause, Erato complied.

"I've seen him," the harpy said.

Persephone said nothing. Erato wasn't sure the goddess heard her.

"I've seen him," Erato said more loudly.

Still nothing. Nike gently nudged Persephone.

"Who have you seen?" Persephone asked dully, dutifully.

"Hades."

"We both have," Clio the harpy added, nodding.

"What?" Persephone shot up. "How close is he? How is he?"

"Hades is with Zeus. When we saw him, he was…sleeping," Erato answered with some hesitation.

"Sleeping?" the goddess asked, surprised and concerned, wiping her wet face with the back of her hand.

"They're in great danger, Persephone," Nike said, her voice grave. "They're tromping through the Underworld unaware, oblivious to its warnings and perils."

"It's true—" confirmed Clio. "Hades had the look of one who had encountered the shades."

"Shades, yes," Persephone sniffed. "I've seen them too. So many of them."

"No, this was different. They tried to take him."

"Take him?" Persephone raised her eyebrows. "Take him where? What do you mean?"

"He had the pale cast on his skin, like the shades tried to claim him as their leader. As their hope."

"Take me to him." Persephone rose. "Take me now."

Nike refused. "You can't go to him."

"What? Why not? You can fly me to him!"

"Sisyphus will know," Nike explained.

"I don't care!" Persephone stomped her foot. "He can do nothing to us once Hades and I are together. We'll be out of the Underworld before Sisyphus can worm his way to us."

"No." Nike shook her head. "You won't. I hate Sisyphus. You know I despise him. I want to claw out his eyes and tear his body until what remains of it is only shreds of flesh. But, he was right." She shook her eagle head. "You cannot leave the Underworld. And you know it. To go to Hades would be to destroy him."

"But he's already being destroyed!" Persephone cried. "He cannot be without me!"

"He will have to try," Nike said coolly.

"But he's so close," Persephone pleaded. "I've changed my mind. I can't let him go. He's nearly here! He braved the Underworld. He broke what we gods believed was an unbreakable barrier. For me! He risked everything. He's risking it still! I can't turn him away." Persephone wrung her hands. "Don't you understand? I thought I could turn him back, but now...he's so close...I can't do it. I have to go to him!"

"You asked us to make a map," Calliope interjected quietly.

"We've begun it. Here."

She pointed to one wall of the brightly-lit den. Calliope, the harpy with white-tipped wings, spread those wings and took a short, graceful hop to the other side of the den. She waited for Persephone to join her, which the goddess reluctantly did, after directing a withering look at Nike. Nike stood firm, unmoving, letting Persephone listen.

"This is where we are," Clio said, touching a wing tip to the wall. "And this is where we saw him."

"By all the gods," Persephone swore. "He's closer than I imagined. And yet..."

She caressed the drawings of two figures, where the harpies had marked the place they'd seen Hades and Zeus. The figures looked so small on the sprawling map that, thus far, filled one wall of the large den.

"He won't give up," she said softly, pressing her fingers to the wall, to his reclined figure. "He'll never abandon me."

The den wall was made of red clay. When the harpies carved into it with their claws, they made white marks, scraping away the surface clay. In that clay, the harpies had carved the hiding and wandering places of shades, the waterfall, pools of lava, towering rocks that curved to the roof of the Underworld. Persephone saw drawings that represented giants and other terrifying creatures who hid in the dark. She saw a tree atop the earth that she didn't know had been created when Ares killed her. She noted its roots, and the hole to which it led, where Zeus and Hades had dived through.

She saw Kerberos at the base of the hole, guarding the entrance, and shivered at the memory of the terrifying beast. The Styx, the tangle of caves, the marks that designated the morphing areas, the desolate barren hopelessness of it.

The harpies had drawn Olympus, too. It towered above the Underworld. It looked so far away. It seemed unfathomably remote. Persephone thought back to being there herself, and it felt like that must have been someone else's life.

She looked at the harpies, looked into their eyes, one by one.

She saw pity and kindness, fear and strength. She looked at how well Nike's wing was healing. How the claws and beaks of the harpies had regained a measure of shine, and stopped peeling under Persephone's care. She thought of how her healing plants grew in a hanging garden above the palace walls.

"This tree." Persephone pointed to the laurel tree on the map, the one that grew when Ares killed her. "I don't remember this tree, but I know this place. This is where…"

"Yes," Nike answered, cutting her off. "It's where Ares took your life."

Persephone shook her head as if she could rattle out the memory of what happened in that place. But she could still vividly see her friends gathered around her, laughing, on that beautiful, bright day. Just before Ares arrived. She could feel the flowers she'd gathered in her hands. She could hear the laughter of her friends…

Persephone closed her eyes and shook her head again, vanquishing the memories, opening her eyes to the present.

"But, how have you seen that place? That tree?" Persephone asked, puzzled, the question rooting her to the present. She inhaled sharply. "Can you go to the surface?"

"Since you healed us, we can," Melete said, her kind eyes beaming. "Our strength has returned and even multiplied in the months you've been with us. We can make the journey. Sisyphus doesn't know we are capable of it. He still thinks we live in fear of him and his arachnid minions."

The harpies all nodded and murmured in agreement.

"Does time here pass in the same way as time in other parts of the Underworld? At the same speed?" Persephone asked, her hand still pressed to the image of Hades, wondering how long he felt they had been apart.

"I don't know, my lady," Melete said.

"And on the surface? How does time pass there?"

"I think time passes faster on the surface. And I think the passage of time changes down here, the way the landscape in parts of the Underworld shifts and moans and moves," said

Melpomene, a harpy with deep brown eyes and a beak streaked with blood-red.

Melete glanced at the markings on the wall, where Philos counted the days for Persephone. Philos placed the tally of marks in the darkest corner of the den, near the floor. None of the creatures wanted Persephone to focus on the tally, a count of her time away from Hades and her mother, but the goddess looked at it every day.

Persephone shook her head. "Then you can leave this place! For good! All of you!"

"We cannot," Nike denied.

"But why? What holds you here?"

"You," Nike said proudly. "We will not leave you."

Persephone was speechless, moved by the harpies' devotion.

"We will serve you until our dying day."

Persephone hung her head. She was ashamed of herself, of how selfish she was being. She had vowed to protect the harpies. She'd named them. She loved them.

She thought, too, of the shades, of the countless souls wandering aimless in the vast expanse of the bowels of the earth. She sensed she could give them comfort, that she should give them comfort.

Yet more than anything she wanted to flee. She wanted Hades to swoop in and lift her up and fly her away.

She closed her eyes. She put her hand on her chest. She felt for the mark: the mark Ares's spear left when it pierced her chest and sent her to the Underworld. It was an indentation the size of her fist, and it marred her seamless skin.

Hades had not seen the mark. He hadn't felt it. She knew he would weep when he saw it, not because it was an imperfection, but because it had caused her pain.

Her separation from Hades caused her as much pain as Ares's spear. It left its own kind of mark on her, changing her, leaving its own gaping wound.

Persephone sank down to the ground, feeling hopeless and lost. Not knowing what was right and, even more deeply, not caring what was right. She wanted Hades and she wanted to make her way back to him. If that was weak and selfish, she decided, then she would be weak and selfish.

But then, she looked into Nike's round, concerned eyes and saw her reflection there. She saw the girl Hades loved and the woman Nike respected. And she knew what she had to do. She spoke softly.

"You're right. To want him is to lead him to his destruction," Persephone said sadly. "He can't be here. In the Underworld. He has to leave—or this place will ruin him. I can't let that happen. I have to make him leave me behind." She exhaled, shaking her head. "I just don't know if I can do it myself."

Nike nodded once. She turned to Melete, the kind harpy, and together the two harpies flew off to do what Persephone wished, but couldn't bring herself to ask.

CHAPTER 31

ike and Melete followed the blistering smoke and telltale burning smell until they found the intruding gods.

Seeing them approach, Hades leapt off Ship Rock. His forked staff aglow with flames, his noble face was focused and determined, like an eagle hunting prey. His black armor blended into the blackened forest of burned and melted rock and metal, leaving only his handsome face beaming out from the darkness.

Zeus, broad and grimacing, a thick dark beard grown on his face, wielded his humming lightning bolt. His brilliant golden armor was tarnished and blackened from the fire. He hovered near Hades protectively.

The harpies screeched and swooped around the two gods, circling them, careful to stay out of reach of Kerberos' gnashing teeth and whipping spiked tail. Their ear-piercing screeches echoed in the expansive room.

"You should not be here!" Nike berated, then swooped in closer. "You do not belong here," she screeched in Hades's ear, leaving him temporarily dazed.

"Get out!" she screeched at the top of her lungs. She and Melete dove and circled the gods, who held their ears, attempting to block out the painful and paralyzing cries.

The harpies flew around Hades and Zeus in a dizzying dance, their wings lifting dust and ash until it swirled like a cyclone.

Hades and Zeus coughed violently. The thick fog of dust and ash filled their eyes, ears and mouths, choking and blinding them. The gods fell to their knees. Their weapons dropped to the ground.

When she saw the weapons fall, Nike signaled Melete to pause. The harpies hovered above the weakened gods. Kerberos cowed nearby, his ears ringing with the harpy screams, which could shatter fortress walls.

Nike stretched her neck until her shining yellow beak nearly touched Hades's pained face.

"Turn around," Nike commanded quietly, silently pitying Hades.

Hades struggled to regain his composure. "Where is Persephone?"

"It doesn't matter to you. She doesn't want you here."

Hades shook his head, his face contorted in pain. "I don't believe you."

"Persephone will be Queen. She has a new life here."

"I don't believe you," Hades repeated through gritted teeth.

"It's the truth."

"No," Hades uttered, on his hands and knees as he struggled to stand.

Melete had to turn away. She was too full of pity for this man, who loved her beloved Persephone. She couldn't bear to watch Nike break his heart. Zeus watched Melete with interest.

Hades regained some strength and composure. "Take me to her," he asked. "Please."

"If I do, it would be the death of you. And for that, she would never forgive me," Nike answered.

Melete snatched up the gods' weapons before Zeus could grab them. She soared away. Zeus howled in fury and stumbled after her.

"Leave this place," Nike commanded Hades again. "Return to the Styx. Your hound will guide you. Cross to the other side. Then climb back up to the surface, to the tree, and never return."

"No." Hades shook his head slowly as he rose to his feet, his dark eyes not moving from Nike's face.

"She's going to be married," Nike said.

"What?" Hades looked stricken, as if Nike had slapped him across the face.

"She's getting married."

Hades shook his head, disbelieving, swaying like a windblown leaf. Zeus ran to support him before Hades fell. He put his arm beneath his brother to hold him up.

"Go," Nike said with a trace of kindness in her voice. "Return to the surface and think no more of Persephone."

Melete exchanged a pitiful glance with Zeus. Then she turned and flew after Nike, leaving Hades in more devastation than they'd found him.

. . .

Hades was stunned. He felt battered and bruised, as if someone had thrown him to the ground from the peak of Olympus. He leaned on Zeus's arm, his mind reeling.

Persephone was getting married?

She truly wanted him to leave?

Zeus glanced at Ship Rock, where the harpy had left their weapons. He reached his arm out to call his lightning bolt to him, and Hades did the same with his still-flaming staff. The red-hot weapons whistled through the air as they sped to their masters, who caught them in outstretched hands.

With his staff in hand, Hades stepped away from Zeus's support. He swayed, and Kerberos steadied him with a nose. Then, in a blur of swift fury, Hades leapt over Kerberos's head to land astride the hound.

Hades stood atop the animal, and shouted in a voice that echoed throughout the Underworld like a wounded beast's.

"I have bested my father! I dominated him and then I tamed the world! You can neither scare nor outsmart me!"

He clenched his hand into a fist that shook with power and rage. As his fist shook, so too shook the entire prairie. Ship Rock cracked.

"Persephone would never betray me."

Hades swore, and the deep rumble of his voice made the tremoring rock crumble. It collapsed into a pile of rubble.

"She would never choose another over me," Hades said. "I will not leave her here with your monsters and darkness and lies."

Hades paused. He continued in soft, measured tones that were more threatening than his shouting.

"I created a new world from the ashes I made of the old. I'm here—in the place everyone told me I could not go. Yet here I stand. I won't be denied what I've come to find, no matter how ancient this place, no matter what terrors and lies it throws at me."

Hades commanded Kerberos gravely again. "Find Persephone. Follow the scent of those creatures. They'll lead us to her."

The hound howled, and bounded off with Hades on his back and Zeus close behind.

CHAPTER 32

"How is he?"

Persephone sprang to her feet when the harpies returned, her voice a raw whisper. She wrung her hands, kneading and twisting her dress, her expression expectant but hesitant.

"Will he go?" she forced herself to ask.

The other harpies stood single file at her back, awaiting the news, the wings of each folded at their sides. Melete landed and took her place in the line. Nike paced back and forth in front of the harpies, her claws scraping the den floor in a rhythmic pattern.

"He is stubborn," Nike answered with reluctant respect, her wings behind her back.

"And strong and handsome and full of love for you," Melete added. Nike shot her a withering look.

"I don't know if he'll leave or not," Nike answered truthfully. "He looked as though he might give up when he learned you were to be married."

Persephone hung her head. "He must feel so betrayed…"

"It had to be done," Nike assured her. "He had to be told. That may be the only thing that will drive him away. That will save him."

Persephone could only nod weakly.

CHAPTER 33

Hades and Zeus thundered through the Underworld, with Kerberos on the harpies' scent. The hound stopped sharply when he reached the end of a crevasse. On the other side of the deep gash in the earth was an expansive space dotted with mesas, each flat-topped formation a significant distance from the next.

Hades dismounted. The air was thick with the pungent smell of sulfur, wafting up from the deepest recesses of the Underworld.

"We'll have to jump."

"Easy," Zeus said eagerly.

They leapt across the crevasse and landed on the nearest mesa. A deep rumble shook the ground once their feet hit land.

"Not again," Zeus sighed.

The gods stumbled as the earth beneath them stirred and shook. Hades looked around. The mesas were shifting. Some grew taller, others shrank lower. Still others moved forward or back, trading places with one another.

"We have to jump fast," Zeus remarked. "Will Kerberos lose the scent?"

Hades shook his head. "I don't think so."

Kerberos barked, his three heads nodding in unison, and jumped to the next mesa to show Hades he was still on harpies' trail. As that mesa moved again in its grim Underworld dance,

Kerberos was shifted farther away from the gods.

"Good boy," Hades praised with a grin, not taking his eyes off the hound.

"Let's follow." Zeus was about to leap when Hades put a hand on his shoulder.

"Wait." Hades said. "Did you hear that?"

"Persephone again?"

Hades shook his head. "No." He watched Kerberos get ever farther away as their mesa shifted. "It sounded like muttering, like a crowd of people."

Zeus cocked his head. "I do hear it."

It immediately brought the shades to Zeus's mind. Something about the hopelessness of the sound chilled Zeus to the bone, reminiscent of their earlier encounter with the dead.

"Let's go," Zeus encouraged, not wanting to linger long enough to run into the shades again.

"It's getting louder."

Hades was mesmerized, as if the sound was putting him in a trance. His view of Kerberos was blocked as a mesa rose in front of them, but he didn't seem to care.

As the mesa rose higher and higher, Hades stared at it. The wall of the mesa rose and its sides became exposed, revealing a secret.

"Zeus," Hades whispered. "Look."

"Hades, we can't linger." Zeus pulled at Hades's arm, urging him on. His gaze was on the opposite side, at the way out. "Let's go. We can't see the filthy hound! We need to move!"

"I can hear him breathing. Leave him—just look!"

Zeus exhaled in frustration, then turned to see what had Hades distracted.

"What is that?" Zeus asked, astounded, when he saw what had captivated Hades. "Is that where the sound is coming from? Is it a message?"

The rising wall was covered in drawings. Thousands of simple stick figures of men, women and children had been carved into the rock. As the mass of land rose, the drawings of the figures kept coming, endlessly. The cacophony of voices grew louder, although the sound was still a jumble, an undiscernible, hushed roar. Haphazardly placed among the mass of figures, Hades and Zeus saw detailed drawings of faces. Their expressions were haunted, pleading.

"I think it's a cry for help," Hades said.

Then, suddenly, the mesa tilted forward, towards them. All the other mesas lost their balance or came to life, and became bent on destruction. Their dance became crazed, the land masses moving and shifting and crashing into one another. Hades and Zeus exchanged a glance and jumped, just before the carved mesa tumbled down in front of them with a rumbling crash. It smashed the carvings and the mesas it landed on. Quiet screams replaced the murmurs, the noise of panicked thousands. Hades and Zeus were shocked and unsettled by the sound.

"These aren't alive, are they?" Zeus asked, bewildered, picking up a fragment of carved rock that fell near his feet. He traced the figure of a little girl with his large fingers.

"I don't think so…I don't…I don't know…"

"Zeus!" Hades shouted. "Look out!"

Zeus looked up to see a storm of rock descending. Boulders showered down on them like hail. Zeus threw the fragment aside. He and Hades pulverized the falling rocks with their weapons and their fists before the stones could hit them. Then they fled, crashing though incoming mesas, leaving gaping holes in the stone as they escaped the worsening destruction.

Kerberos howled and leapt and was soon out of sight. As the unstable ground beneath them continued to shake, Hades and Zeus relentlessly smashed and leapt and ran. Hades could see the end of the mesa-filled room just beyond where they stood, but before they could get there, they lost their footing. The ground suddenly slanted vertically, and the brothers slid down towards the bottomless crevasse. The young gods dug their fingers into the rock. Zeus stopped his descent, Hades stopping himself soon after.

"Now!" Zeus shouted and propelled himself up out of the crevasse.

Hades tried to propel himself at the same time, but as he pushed against the rock, it held firm: he was stuck to the stone. The rock had grown over his fingers, encasing them in the stone, making Hades part of the mesa itself.

"Zeus!"

Hades called for help when he realized he couldn't break through the stone. Instead, it spread. The rock now covered his entire hands, and was moving up his arm.

"Zeus!" Hades called again. He planted his feet on the stone and pushed away with all his strength, but his hands didn't budge. The rock crept past his elbows.

Hades kept pushing against the rock, desperation seeping into his mind. He tampered down the desperate feelings with the conviction that he would free himself—and find Persephone, if he had to tear his arms off to do so.

Gravel slid down the vertical rock, colliding with his face and arms, and making it harder for Hades to get a firm footing to press against the rock. His feet slid but he kept fighting. He would fight the Underworld until there was nothing left of him.

Hades glared at the rock with an intense stare that made grown men cower. Then he heard Zeus's voice.

"Dive!" Zeus ordered. "You mangy hound, dive!"

Hades looked up to see Kerberos's three massive heads plummeting towards him. Hades hugged the rock to avoid being crushed by the dragon-tailed hound but, as he did so, the rock grabbed his feet and began to encase them, too.

Hades whistled for the hound. Soon Kerberos came up out of the abyss with Hades's flaming staff in one of his mouths. The other mouth growled, while the third licked Hades's back.

Kerberos' claws dug into the rock and he ran up it, as though the wall was the ground. Then he clung to it, hovering over where Hades was trapped. With an angry yowl, Zeus came flying down from above. He landed on Kerberos' back and took hold of

Hades's staff. Balancing on the back of the hound, Zeus pointed his thunderbolt at Hades's hands and the staff at Hades's feet.

"Release him!" the god of the sun thundered. "I demand you release him!"

Light burst forth from the weapons and Hades pulled away from the rock. He felt intense heat at his hands and feet, and felt the rock weakening. With one final pull, he was free.

He plummeted down towards the abyss until Kerberos caught him in his teeth. The dog bounded up the wall with Hades in his mouth and Zeus on his back.

Kerberos didn't stop running until they were far away from the collapsing and destroyed mesas, and back on the scent towards Persephone.

CHAPTER 34

Sisyphus came to the harpy den looking for Persephone.

He barked orders to her harpies. He insulted the way they looked, the way they flew, and the way they thought. Sisyphus took Persephone by the arm and pulled her along the halls. They walked through the palace, and he talked and talked and talked.

She heard none of it. His words were just noise. She was living in her mind. For her mind was full of Hades. She knew she had work to do. She knew she had resources and power, but she fled into her thoughts and memories of Hades. Everything going on around her was irrelevant. It was as if she'd become a shade herself when she'd made the decision to turn Hades away from her after discovering he was so close.

She didn't care that Sisyphus was rubbing her back. She didn't care that he was gliding a bare finger along her neck, as if she belonged to him. Words like Marry. Rule. Queen. Mine. They all swept past her. They couldn't touch her while she was in paradise with Hades.

Sisyphus had slave shades flitting around her. They fitted her with cloth, jewels, and a crown.

"Wedding," the shades said in hushed tones when they thought she couldn't hear. "Lovely. Tragic. Sad. Terror," they said, shaking their heads. "Monster."

Persephone simply stood there, a dreamy look on her face, for she was content and far away.

"My lady." Philos approached with a deep bow.

The shades flitted away with their measurements and their assignments. Sisyphus had left. He had told her where he was going and what he planned to do, but she hadn't listened because she didn't care.

"Persephone," Philos said quietly. He touched her arm. She lifted her other arm to place a hand on his shoulder. Her arm felt like it was floating, like it didn't belong to her. She stared at it, confused at the intrusion of reality into her beautifully perfect fiction.

"Persephone," Philos repeated.

"What!" she snapped.

"Apologies," Philos whispered. He bowed again. "You asked me to find out how Ares comes back and forth into the Underworld?"

"Yes," Persephone answered, remembering, reluctantly dragged back into the present. Hades's face was still vivid and bright in her mind. She clung to it as she clung to breath itself.

"He is here," Philos said. "Ares. He has come back. Look."

Philos pointed and Persephone turned, gliding gracefully, slowly, as though she was underwater. Then she saw him. Hades's face shrank in her mind, getting smaller and smaller, escaping Persephone's fervent grasp. It was replaced by another face.

Ares.

The god of war towered over Sisyphus. Sisyphus nodded and spoke to him ingratiatingly. Anger rose in Persephone—unbeckoned, unwanted—but it rose nonetheless. She hadn't wanted to feel anything, but fury slapped her safe, dreamy lie until it shattered and she could no longer hide behind it.

"You can watch him when he goes," Philos whispered to Persephone. "See how he returns to the surface."

"Yes," she said, the fog of memory cracked and shattered at her feet. She inhaled, regathering her strength. "Yes. Thank you, Philos. I will."

Philos scribbled on his ever-present tablet. He showed Persephone a hasty sketch. "Sisyphus took him to view the most recently mined metal here," he pointed. "And the weapon, the one I told you about—it's nearly finished. Now Ares will return to the surface."

Persephone nodded. "Well done, Philos. Thank you." Then she returned her gaze to Ares and Philos shuffled away.

. . .

Ares's blood-red armor was now so full of spikes it looked like a weapon of death itself. His teeth had morphed to mirror the spikes, sharpening as if he'd filed them into tiny daggers.

Persephone gave a quick wave with her hand. Urania and Terpsichore swooped down and silently landed in front of her, their wings folded, their eyes on hers.

"Follow Ares," Persephone instructed her harpies. "Find out how he comes and goes from the Underworld. The entrance at the tree is too new—it grew only after I died."

Persephone was surprised to find that saying those words didn't hurt; rather, she felt nothing as she said them.

"Ares must use another way to come here," she went on. "I want to know what it is."

The harpies saluted.

"Be discreet," Persephone warned. "Be sure Ares doesn't see you. He's dangerous and not entirely stupid."

The two harpies nodded as one and noiselessly flew off.

"But before he goes," Persephone said to herself, "I will have a talk with the god of war."

As Persephone walked towards him, she realized she was trembling with anger, her shaking growing more intense the closer she got to Ares. She was suddenly so full of fury she didn't know what to do with the feeling. She called Hades to mind, but that only made her more angry as she raged at the loss of him.

The warmth she felt in her fingertips, the humming power

that she'd restrained when she'd first decided to stay docile to learn Sisyphus's plan, she could no longer control. The power spread from her fingers up her arms and throughout her body. Seeing Ares so soon after she had just let Hades go, enraged her. She was a leader of her own band now, of her own warriors. She had healed them. They respected her. Her Amazons. They saw her as a warrior too.

Persephone balled her hands into fists. Her heart pounded. Her heart had been beating more steadily recently. Now it thundered so loudly she thought it would give away the intensity of her anger, and perhaps the extent of her burgeoning desire to defeat Ares.

The idea had begun as a whisper in her mind: fleeting, impossible. A tiny wish. Seeing Ares again, it returned as a gale force. Persephone wanted to bring the god of war to his bloody knees.

She was at the doorway of the island palace now. Ares and Sisyphus stood on the narrow spit of land ahead of her, on the pathway over the lava. Persephone remembered that was where they'd stood when Ares told her he had sent her to the Underworld. That he had killed her.

He had said it with no remorse. No guilt. No sympathy. As if she didn't matter at all. As if her life had no value compared to his. Not just his life. His ambition.

He had told her he killed her, ruined her life, and he said it with pride.

But she would not be invisible. She would not be a game piece in his war play. She would be a player. And she would master him.

Persephone's gaze moved to the roaring waterfall behind the two men. She narrowed her eyes and stepped out of the doorway. She slammed her fist into the palace wall. The wall disintegrated into fine, floating dust. She flung her other hand at the vanished wall, and, from the dust, a new wall made itself.

The new wall was solid glass. It appeared soundlessly, the billions of dust particles remaking themselves at Persephone's unspoken command.

The wall was as thick as a man's body. It was no single color. It was iridescent, colorless, but reflecting every color of the rainbow. The glow of the lava sea beneath the palace's island reflected up, and the wall shimmered.

Born from Persephone's anger, the wall was textured like the prickly lettuce plant. She wasn't surprised to see that pattern in the glass. She'd created prickly lettuce for one of Aphrodite's lovers after he'd been slain by a boar. Persephone had cradled his fall with the tall stalks and feathery seeds of the lettuce. To her, that plant symbolized the death of love.

"What in Kronos?" Ares swore as the wall materialized, taller than the tallest spire of the palace.

"Ares," Persephone began as she strode towards him.

Her anger subdued, dispersed, and then held firm by the glass wall, she spoke coolly as she approached the two figures, "You smell vile. Is that vomit?"

"What?" Ares tore his gaze from the impressive wall and looked to Persephone in surprise.

"Beneath your feet." Persephone pointed, her nose upturned in a look reminiscent of Hera.

Ares lifted his foot. In the large footprint was a pool of vomit, blood, and urine.

"Ah, yes," he nodded. "Remnants of battle. Nothing a woman is capable of handling." He lowered his foot with a thud and a disgusting splash.

"No woman except Athena, I'm sure you mean," Persephone said innocently.

"Who said Athena is a woman?" Ares joked, and Sisyphus snickered.

"How is your plan going? Are you the new king of the gods yet?" Persephone's tone was mocking. "You're having some trouble, aren't you? Athena is more of a match for you than you thought, I presume, though I don't know why you would ever challenge her. You're no match for her—and never have been. You'd need a god or two on your side to even stand a chance against her, and what god would side with you against her?"

Ares shifted from one foot to the other, the revolting contents of the puddles beneath his feet splattering onto Persephone's gown. She couldn't have cared less.

"You know nothing of what's happening above. Don't pretend otherwise," Ares answered defensively.

"I know that war requires strategy. And I know you will never outsmart Athena."

Ares snarled. He knew he was no match for Athena—it was a fact that always rankled him, being considered a lesser of the Olympians. Persephone wanted to make him angry. She needed him, a god it was easy to antagonize, to stomp petulantly back to Olympus because her harpies were watching, ready to follow him.

Sisyphus caught his breath, shocked by her boldness. Ares's snarl turned into a wolfish smile. Then he threw his head back and laughed. Piercing screams accompanied Ares's laughter. Persephone covered her ears to shut it out, but the screaming only stopped when his laughter died down.

"You know nothing," Ares scoffed. "So, stop talking. This is a time for the men now."

Persephone was shaken by the terrifying sound, the horror of the screams. It was the sound of battle, of war. She had heard it before. If the gods were fighting, she knew, everyone and everything suffered.

Ares leaned close to Persephone, his cold eyes and his dagger-like teeth like those of a wild animal.

"Athena will bow to me. She thinks she has won but she hasn't. Poseidon is joining me. He, too, thought Hades was the wrong choice to be king. Athena cannot fight the two of us. She will kneel and beg me for mercy. If I choose to grant it, fine. If not, she may soon join you here."

Ares waved his hand to indicate the Underworld. Then he turned and strutted down the walkway towards the waterfall. He leapt up into it and vanished.

Persephone saw a faint flicker behind the falls, and knew her harpies were following him.

. . .

When they were alone, Sisyphus began it.

"You need to take more care, my darling," Sisyphus cooed as Persephone allowed him to take her arm and turn her towards the palace. Her mind was thrumming, building a plan. Sisyphus and Ares still underestimated her; she would use that to her advantage. "You are accustomed to a special position in the cadre of gods, the doted upon and beloved youngest god. But your circumstances have changed, something I know I don't need to remind you of. You are no longer special in the same way. Challenging Ares like you did can be very dangerous. You're special to me, of course. But I am your only protector. You don't yet know how bad the Underworld can be. I've been sheltering you. I've been giving you special treatment. Things could be much worse for you if you don't watch yourself, my darling. As you now know, death is not the end..."

Sisyphus put his skeletal hand on his empty chest and looked at Persephone with false sympathy. Then he grinned.

"Remember, you will be Queen here, Queen of all you see. But, well... I wasn't sure when to tell you this, but now is as good a time as any."

Persephone couldn't hold in her irritated sigh.

Sisyphus didn't hear it. He stopped walking.

He lowered his voice as if about to confide a great secret. "Hades has turned back. He has left you, my dear. I know that's what you wanted. It's what we agreed upon. But I also know it may be hard for you to face. That he abandoned you so quickly. With such little...fight."

Persephone didn't know whether she believed what Sisyphus said or not. She didn't know whether she wanted to believe him or not. She couldn't deny that the thought of Hades no longer searching for her, no longer relentlessly challenging the Underworld to come for her, left her feeling empty and alone.

But the greater part of her felt relief. He and their world would be saved.

"I'm surprised he turned away from you this quickly." Sisyphus was unrelenting in his attack, his war to wear down her confidence in full swing. "But then, he is king of the gods. The entire world sits at his feet up above. You're valuable to me, my darling, but you're no match for that."

Persephone let Sisyphus talk. She was plotting. He kept talking, the sound of his own voice almost as dear to him as his pride. She let his words wash over her as if she was an immovable stone and his words were simply water moving around her.

"Ares wanted Hades to stay here, you recall," Sisyphus reminded her. "He wanted me to keep Hades trapped in the Underworld. But he reconsidered. Ares doesn't fear Hades and Zeus. He's confident he can defeat them. With Poseidon and our vast number of weapons and arms, Ares is poised to beat them."

Sisyphus continued, undeterred, in the face of Persephone's silence. They had reached the palace doorway. Sisyphus snapped his fingers, and a guard lowered the massive gate that blocked the entrance to the island haven. It hit the ground with a heavy clang, shutting Persephone inside.

"I have seen the changes you've undergone since you arrived here," Sisyphus whispered conspiratorially, leaning in and speaking into her ear. "I think Hades wouldn't mind them after he got used to them. Your cheeks are getting a little pink and I believe you stand taller. Gangly. It doesn't bother me. I will love you regardless, my dearest. But maybe you could use some rest. Or a bite to eat. It's probably for the best that Hades doesn't see you. That way he can remember you in your glory."

This she didn't ignore. Persephone put her hands to her cheeks. They felt warm and flushed. She moved her hand to her now-beating heart. She had changed since she came to the Underworld. But for worse or better?

"This is marvelous, my darling," Sisyphus praised, the fingers of his good hand poised beside Persephone's towering glass wall.

He pressed his hand onto the wall, then howled and yanked his hand away. His skin sizzled. Shocked, he held up his hand. Every part of his flesh that had touched the wall was red and blistered.

"How could it—how did it—" He sputtered, cradling his throbbing hand. "What did you do?"

Persephone glared at him. He'd been trying to weaken her. It would be a more difficult task than he anticipated.

"Oh my." Persephone's voice dripped with false concern, and was laced with venom. "And that's your good hand! You need to take more care, my *darling*." She spat out the word. "The Underworld can be a dangerous place."

Sisyphus leaned away from her, his face betraying true shock.

Persephone opened her eyes wide and tilted her head. She wore an innocent look on her face, but her eyes glowed, ferocious.

She willed herself to stay strong. If only until she destroyed him. Her head held high, she left him stunned and silent.

CHAPTER 35

Persephone tended to the plants she'd been growing in the Underworld. She had built a hanging garden at the top of the palace's tallest tower. The garden was the only place Persephone had found any measure of peace on her island prison, other than in the harpy den. The plants, all of them new and unique to the Underworld, grew until they covered the tower completely. They climbed, spreading to the tip of the tower's spire, turning that part of the structure a vibrant, pulsating green.

Sisyphus was eager to be generous when it didn't inconvenience or irritate him, so he gladly allowed Persephone to take over the tower as her own. She wanted the plants to have the heat of the lava, but not the full intensity of its warmth. Most of the plants grew without dirt or soil, which was a rarity in the rocky Underworld.

Persephone knelt and watered her newest creation. It had just sprouted from the rocky ground at the base of the tower. She stroked its leaves and gently lifted one of its tiny purple-blue buds.

"Akoniton," she named it.

At the sound of her voice, the akoniton swayed slightly and grew a little taller.

"Tell me," Persephone said, turning to face her returning harpy scouts, who had just landed and were silently awaiting her acknowledgement. "What did you discover? How does Ares come and go from this place?"

"You were right, my lady," Terpsichore reported. "Ares has an entrance much closer than the one Kerberos guards." She turned her head, her sharp beak pointing at the waterfall. "Ares's entrance is closer than you might think."

"The waterfall." Persephone guessed, following the harpy's gaze.

"Yes."

"I saw Ares dive into the lava the first time I watched him leave the Underworld," Persephone remembered. "But today, he leapt directly into the waterfall."

The other harpy stepped forward, her wings crossed behind her in a dignified manner.

"We think the two are connected," Urania said. "We believe Ares can dive into the lava and come out at the waterfall. From there he flies up the water. Or, like today, he can simply leap up into the falls."

"He leaps up into the falls," Persephone mused. She leaned forward, resting her elbows on the waist-high ivory-colored wall that encircled the tower. She looked longingly at the waterfall. "I must try that myself," she said quietly.

"I'm sorry. What did you say, Persephone?" Urania asked, tilting her sharp eagle's face.

The lava bubbled and flowed far beneath them.

"Just thinking aloud," Persephone answered, unwilling to tell her harpies of her desire to try to climb the waterfall. The desire to see her mother, to see Hades one more time—she didn't know if it would ever leave her. She sensed her harpies wouldn't want her to try it, and she didn't want them to try to talk her out of it. Or—worse—tell Nike her thoughts.

"The lava doesn't harm Ares." Persephone changed the subject and began circling the tower balcony, the two harpies trailing behind her. "Yet it burned my dress, and I felt the intensity of the heat more than anything in Hephaistos' volcano. Ares's armor turned red after he emerged from it. Was that change caused by the lava, or was it the armor changing to match Ares's darkening mind?"

Persephone stopped walking and the harpies, matching footstep for footstep, immediately stopped too.

"Did you follow him all the way to the surface?" she asked, hopeful.

"We did," they answered. Persephone caught her breath.

Persephone turned. She reached a quivering hand towards Urania's light brown wing. She wanted to feel it, to touch it, to be close to something that had been so recently up above. In the light. In the fresh air. In the sun. Persephone touched her wing. She felt the warm glow of the sun on her fingertips. She smelled the freshness of the earth after a rainstorm. She smiled, wistful.

"How does it look? Above? How does Athena fare? Does she know about Poseidon joining Ares? Does she have enough weapons? How is my mother?"

The harpies exchanged glances.

"The earth is… suffering," Urania said.

Persephone bowed her head. Her mother was still grieving. She had to send her a message. She had to tell her she was—she would be—all right.

"We can go back and scout to see how Athena fares and what her supplies are."

Persephone nodded. "Yes, you will need to."

"We flew in Ares's wake," Terpsichore said. "We followed him all the way to the waterfall's source. It's a spring in a small village near the sea. The town is called Nesos and the people are building a sanctuary at the spring."

"But the humans don't know the spring's purpose."

"No, and they'll never discover it. It's too well disguised."

"Clearly. If we gods didn't even know of its existence. Except Ares…"

"When we emerged from the water, Persephone, we felt different," Terpsichore shared. "We felt—renewed. Cleansed. As though the water washed us clean."

Urania had a hopeful look on her intelligent face and Persephone read her thoughts. She looked at both harpies sympathetically.

"You can be washed clean, my majestic warriors. But you'll never truly go back."

Persephone caressed their cheeks.

The harpies bowed their heads. Persephone knew they harbored hope that they could be women once more, women and not monsters.

"You can never be the same way you once were." Persephone felt the hole in her chest and quietly sighed. "None of us can."

· · ·

Later, Persephone sat on the floor in the harpy den. Her gown fanned out around her, and the faraway look that was often in her eyes was gone. It had been replaced with a focused intensity. Nike took note of the change.

"What's on your mind?" Nike asked, narrowing her eyes. "If you're devising a plan, share it with me."

"I think you forget who is mistress here and who is indebted to her," Persephone replied haughtily.

Nike looked at Persephone expectantly. Waiting.

Persephone gave in. "All right, I'll tell you. I was thinking, what would happen if I tried? If I went to the falls and tried to rise up them? Like Ares."

"I knew that's what you were thinking," Nike chided. "And I don't know what would happen, but the thought frightens me."

"I thought nothing frightened you."

"Nothing does," Nike agreed. "Nearly."

Persephone smiled warmly at her.

Nike and Persephone stood and walked across the harpy den to the sprawling map the harpies had carved into the wall, which tallied the weapons Sisyphus had stored for Ares. More details were added to the map each time the harpies returned from exploring the vast recesses of the Underworld. Persephone traced her fingers over roving packs of fanged mongrels, Sisyphus's mine, the cavern of the Fates, and huge, empty, cold halls where the numberless shades flitted in and out aimlessly.

A slave shade wafted into the harpy den. She held up a tray made of solid gold. Persephone saw her and wondered if she would ever get used to seeing the shades. They still possessed the images of their faces and bodies, but they were transparent. Persephone could look at the girl and see Nike right through her. The shades who were slaves in the palace were told to keep their feet touching the ground, but it was an illusion—the shades were weightless. They were insubstantial. They naturally floated like dry leaves torn free from a tree.

"For you, my lady," the girl said. She held the tray up in front of Persephone, bowed her head and waited. Shades could be taught to make themselves solid, to hold or move things.

"No, Helene," Persephone refused kindly. "Thank you but I'm not hungry. I have things on my mind that distract me from food."

"Philos sent it for you," the shade persisted, her lips curling into a shy smile. She lifted the gold lid to show Persephone the gloriously colored fruit beneath it.

When Persephone saw the fruit and smelled its sweetness, she changed her mind. She reached out for the fruit hungrily. She hadn't noticed that she was famished.

"Thank you, Helene," Persephone said. Nike nodded at the shade and Helene knew she was dismissed. Helene left the tray with Persephone and floated out. Neither Persephone nor Nike saw that the young shade paused just outside the doorway.

"How can I not attempt it?" Persephone asked Nike as she turned a fig in her hand. "Someday. When it's a way out? The chance to let my mother know I'm all right? To, just for a moment, feel the sun? To see Hades's face?"

Helene's eyes widened. She listened intently as Persephone repeated everything she knew about the waterfall passageway to a silent but disapproving Nike. Then Helene quietly slipped away. She left the lid of the gold tray on the floor outside the den's door, but no one noticed.

CHAPTER 36

Hades and Hermes were among the humans once again.

Fair Hermes was slightly shorter than the dark-haired and darkly-cloaked Hades, but had a similar lanky build. Hades, all stiff-backed grace, strode confidently beside the languidly moving Hermes. Hermes had been given the task of being the messenger god, and Hades had begun taking the god with him when he wandered among men and women to ensure they were doing well and that they were being fairly ruled. And fair to one another.

"What shall it be this time?" justice-loving Hades asked the enthusiastic young god. "Merchants? Shepherds? Farmers?"

Hermes' mischievous eyes sparkled. "Beggars," he answered.

"You want to challenge them," Hades said, eyebrows raised in amusement.

"We will be travelers looking for hospitality as we make a long journey home," Hermes elaborated, the wings on his golden sandals flitting in eager anticipation.

Hades eyed the sandals. "Don't make me regret having Hephaistos make those for you."

"Right," Hermes said. "Sorry."

He quieted the buzzing wings. They got noisy when he didn't contain his excitement, and their hum had given the gods away on more than one occasion.

Hades nodded briefly. Then he swept his cloak over his face. When he removed it a few seconds later, he had shrunken and aged into a stooped old man. His hair was white and mostly gone. His stunning face was unrecognizable, lined with fatigue and age. He leaned on a gnarled old stick, in place of his thunderbolt. He smelled of rotten fish and the sea.

Hermes looked at him in awe. "That is well done," he said approvingly.

"Thank you," Hades answered with a trace of sarcasm.

Hermes flushed and then spun around with a flourish. When he stilled, he was a younger version of Hades's beggar. He had filthy, matted hair crawling with lice and other disgusting critters. His face was spotted with crusted sores. His cloak had holes in it, and he wore no shoes on his feet.

Hades proudly patted Hermes on the back.

"I'm almost afraid to touch you," he laughed.

"That's what I was aiming for," Hermes said.

Hades leaned his old man's body against Hermes and pointed to a house in the distance.

"There," Hades directed. Then he threw his disguised thunderbolt into the sky, and a clap of thunder erupted. From Olympus, Zeus nodded, and rain began to pour down on them. Hades caught his thunderbolt and leaned on it again.

"Nice!" Hermes enthused.

Hades smiled and shook his head. He held out his arm. "On we go."

Soaked through, but not feeling it, Hades and Hermes trembled in their disguises, for humans would be cold and suffering in such a storm.

They shuffled up to the simple house with a red-tile roof. Hermes knocked on the door.

A few moments later, a small child peeked out. She was so little she could hardly open the heavy door. She managed to open it just enough to poke her face out at the wet visitors. The little girl had a round face and long, smoothly combed hair. The house was dilapidated on the outside, with cracks and crevices in the cream-colored stone, but the girl was clean and looked well cared for.

The child looked from Hades to Hermes and squinted her eyes. She puckered up her mouth and then whispered, "You're playing hide and seek?"

Hermes turned to Hades, confused.

Hades knelt with an ease that betrayed his disguise and put his finger to his lips. He looked the little girl in the eyes.

"Yes, we are."

The girl nodded, understanding.

"Grandpa told me you gods do that sometimes."

"He was right," Hades whispered back, unfazed that he and Hermes had been discovered. "So, will you let us play our game?"

The girl tilted her head, thinking.

Eventually, she answered. "Yes. I'll get my grandmother. I won't tell on you."

"Thank you," Hades said generously.

The girl scampered off. She returned shortly after, pulling a grey-haired woman along behind her.

"Come in," the woman urged immediately, upon seeing the drenched and filthy strangers. Reaching her arms out, she said in a voice that was a combination of concern and authority, "Come in out of the rain."

She gently took Hades by the arm and nodded for Hermes to follow. She led the elderly-looking Hades to a chair and settled him in it while instructing, "Daphne, bring the other chair over here. By the fire."

Accustomed to following her grandmother's instructions to the letter, the girl dragged the chair across the room and set it beside Hades's chair, leaving behind faint tracks on the packed-dirt floor.

A round hearth in the center of the room dominated the small space. A large pot was poised just above the flames, hanging by a chain from the ceiling. On the other side of the room was a table. Food and terra cotta pots were neatly arranged upon the shelves that lined the walls above it.

"Thank you, Daphne," her grandmother said. "Now, go back to your mother."

Daphne hesitated, not wanting to miss out on what the disguised gods were going to do. Hermes gave her a wink. The girl squealed and ran out of the room.

"Silly girl," her grandmother said fondly, smiling as she covered the two strangers in the rickety old chairs with warm blankets. "Silly, but good. The joy of my life, that girl. Now." The grandmother assessed the forlorn-looking strangers with a well-practiced eye. "You two are in quite a state! Don't worry, we'll take good care of you. You will eat and then you can stay the night. You'll not want to go back out there in this storm."

She filled two cups with well-watered wine and handed them to the disguised gods.

"This will warm you," she said knowingly. Then she put her hands on her hips. "My dear boy!" She exclaimed at the sight of Hermes' bare, scraped feet. "Look at your feet!"

The woman muttered a few words to herself, then took a wide bowl from a shelf and poured warm water into it from the pot above the fire. She knelt at Hermes' feet and gently washed them.

Hades was filled with pride.

"You're a good woman," he said, clasping his walking-stick thunderbolt in one trembling hand and the wine in the other.

"I'm no more than what the gods expect of us," she replied simply. "Hades and Zeus ask us to show hospitality to those who come to our door. And so we do. We share what we have."

"Still," Hades said in his quivering elderly voice. "We thank you."

The grandmother nodded curtly. She dried Hermes' feet and tucked them under the blanket. Then she walked around the hearth and knelt on the hard, uneven floor before a chest that sat inconspicuously in the corner. Hades and Hermes watched her open the chest and move a few items aside. She pulled out a pair of leather sandals, clasping them to her chest briefly before closing the box.

"These were my husband's," she said, rising gingerly and walking back to Hermes. She held the sandals out to the young god. "Take them. They're yours now."

"These are good sturdy sandals," Hades said, his hand out, indicating that Hermes was not to take the gift. "Are you sure your husband won't want them still?"

"He's passed into the Underworld," the grandmother answered matter-of-factly. "He needs nothing now."

Hades lowered his eyes in respect and acknowledgement.

"Thank you, kind lady," Hades said in his own godly voice.

Hermes took the sandals. The instant his immortal fingertips touched the leather, both gods shed their disguises. The grandmother flew back in shock at the sight. Before she fell onto the hearth, Hermes had her in his arms and the two of them hovered above the ground, his winged sandals humming.

Hades stood tall, his glorious form looming luminously inside the little home.

"I am proud of you," he said, grasping the shocked woman's trembling hands.

"Hades?" she asked meekly. "Is it you?"

Hades smiled.

"You are what I hoped humans could be..."

Hermes lowered the woman until her feet touched the ground again. She held firm to Hades's hands and gazed up into his dark, far-seeing eyes.

The rain had stopped. The sky was clear, both land and sky washed clean and left pristine. The fresh earth and fresh air filled Hades with the promise of a bright, limitless future.

Hades slid a hand from the grandmother's grasp and pointed towards the window. Two large black hounds sat at the gate—their eyes drooping, chests and hind legs powerful.

"Look there," he said. "The Molossians—those dogs are my gift to you. They will hunt for you and guard your home. And you'll find sheep and goats in the courtyard. And olive trees now line your hilltop in neat rows."

The grandmother fell to her knees. "Thank you," she wept, overwhelmed.

Hades lifted her to her feet and wiped her cheeks with his hands.

"Your granddaughter is clever," he told her. "Listen to her when she tells you what she thinks. And prosper." Hades smiled. "Until you're reunited with your husband in the Underworld."

Hermes placed the sandals back into the woman's hands. As she looked at them, the hearth and floor in her home were transformed into elegant green and white marble.

And then the gods were gone.

• • •

Hades and Hermes stood atop the nearest hill and watched the grandmother run like a young girl, showing her family their new riches. Daphne rode atop the back of one of the large dogs. The other one licked the grandmother's face. The family embraced each other, wept with joy, and then they killed a sheep to fill their empty bellies. They poured out wine and gave the sheep's entrails to the gods.

"Why do we get the bones and entrails, and not the best part of the animal?" Hermes asked as he picked dried dirt out of his winged sandal.

"Do we eat what they give us?" Hades asked in return.

Hermes wrinkled his nose. "We don't eat that food."

"Then why ask it of them at all?" Hades asked, his gaze still on the family. The little girl turned towards the gods. Her arm around one of the hounds, she looked at Hades even though he was almost indistinguishable in the far distance.

Hermes stood shoulder to shoulder with Hades and tilted his head.

"Why do we ask it of humans?" Hermes repeated, perplexed, smoothing down his shining, fair hair.

"It's a token," Hades answered, turning to Hermes. "So humans will think of us when they fulfill their most basic need. Their needs and our powers must be entwined. Their gratitude is the key to our power over them. And, the offering is important to Zeus."

"But you prefer that humans create beautiful things to honor us," Hermes said.

"I do," Hades acknowledged. "Beauty and art make our existence worthwhile. It's the same for men and women."

Hermes nodded. Hades furrowed his brow, a predatory expression coming over his face.

"What is it?" Hermes asked.

Hades closed his eyes, listening. A grim look came over his face. He opened his eyes and stole a last glance at Daphne, who was still watching him. The dog had lain down and she'd snuggled into the curve of its body.

The dog's ears suddenly perked up. Hades saw this and signaled to the dog to be at ease, so the Malossian lay his big head back down. Daphne put her head on top of his and Hades exhaled.

"If they could all be like you," Hades said softly. His breath soon reached her and put her into a sweet sleep. "If…"

Then, in a flash, Hades swooped into the air, his lightning bolt flashing, Hermes at his heels.

CHAPTER 37

"Stop!" Hades commanded.

He yanked on Kerberos' fur as they bounded towards the entrance of yet another vast, cavernous room. The beast bucked, then skidded to a halt before they passed through the uneven doorway.

"By Kronos." Hades swore softly, patting the great beast's fur to calm them both. He shook his head. "There are so many. I thought we were coming upon a fog. But it's—it's them."

The gods had nearly rushed headlong into a sea of shades.

Hades felt a stab of hopelessness. Zeus tightened his grip on his thunderbolt. The aimless shades were all they could see. They hovered and floated in an unknowable number before them, like the uncountable stars in the sky.

The shades glided, weightless, but looked anything but. Their shoulders drooped and slouched as if, like Atlas, they bore the weight of the world. Their wan, colorless faces were fixed on the ground, as if their necks no longer cared to support their heads. They made no sound. Hades would have preferred that the shades make some noise—even rage or wails of sorrow—but there was nothing. The space around each shade was a void, a vacuum of sound.

Hades lifted his hand. There was a thickness, a stickiness, to the air around the shades. A tactile reminder that they were trapped in the malaise of the afterlife.

A few bold shades approached the gods, reaching for them with outstretched fingers. A low growl from Kerberos was enough to send the shades scurrying for cover. With Kerberos at his side, Hades didn't feel in danger from the shades. He dismounted from the huge hound and stood at the precipice of the cavern, like a man at the edge of a roiling sea.

"I know that man."

Hades pointed to the shade of man with a face resembling a fish. Hades furrowed his brow as the shade went gliding past him. "He was a thief. And a murderer. Hermes and I sent him here."

Zeus grunted, acknowledging that he heard his brother, but he wasn't really listening. He was looking for a way out that didn't take them into the swarm of shades. Hades had more confidence that Kerberos would keep them safe than Zeus did.

Zeus spun around to find shades blocking the way they'd come in. Walking, floating, and hovering, they closed in around the gods and the hound. Kerberos swished his dragon tail and the shades flew back. But they didn't go away. They grew bolder the longer Hades was there.

"And I know that woman," Hades said, seemingly unaware of the other shades closing in around them.

Hades pointed to a grandmotherly-looking woman. He stepped towards her, two of Kerberos' heads trailing close behind him and baring their teeth. The shade of Daphne's grandmother shrank back from the hound, terrified. Hades reached out to her.

"Wait," he called. "It's all right. Don't fear him."

Kerberos growled again. In unison, all the nearby shades whisked themselves away to the far side of the cavern, with Daphne's grandmother caught up among them.

"Wait!"

"Good dog," Zeus praised Kerberos and leapt onto one of his necks. "Come on, Hades! Your pup cleared our way. Let's go!"

But Hades didn't move. His focus was set on the good woman, who was now among the tangle of shades. It was a stew of good and evil people, kind and wicked, fair and treacherous.

"Why," Hades said to himself. "Why is that good woman in the same place, in the same condition, as that killer? One shade's existence is the same as the other. Why?"

"That's nothing to us," Zeus answered impatiently from Kerberos' back. "Who knows how the Underworld works? And who cares? It's not why we're here. We aren't here to bend this place to your will and instill order." Zeus dismissed Hades's concerns, knowing his brother's mind. "We're here to find Persephone and get out. As quickly as we can. Come, Hades," Zeus implored, waving, willing Hades forward. "Let's not lose Persephone's trail."

Hades started to turn away from the shades, but the memory of Daphne's grandmother made him pause. She had welcomed the two ragged and helpless strangers into her home. She had given Hermes the sandals that belonged to her beloved husband. She washed Hermes' bare, festering feet with her own hands. The selflessness by which she lived her life meant something to Hades while she was alive. Why should it not have meaning after she died?

"There is no justice here," Hades said angrily. "This realm has no ruler and no laws."

"It's a wasteland. It's not meant to."

"But it should."

"Of course, you want justice—but who will dispense it, brother? Who could tame this wilderness?" Zeus threw up his arms, indicating the bleak Underworld cavern, one among an untold number of bleak Underworld caverns. "Who would want to?"

Hades shook his head. He looked at the fish-faced man he'd labeled a murderer. "That man killed once, and he was trying to kill again. So, I threw my thunderbolt and sent him here."

Zeus nodded approvingly. "Good," he said. "You ended his life. And isn't life the most precious thing humans have? Isn't that the greatest gift we gave them? You took that away from him. Isn't that justice?"

"I thought so, yes. But now. Seeing them here…" Hades shook his head. "Seeing that the Underworld is the same for both. I cannot let it stand."

"Fine." Zeus gave in, anxiously watching the shades regain confidence and inch closer to Hades. "Just hurry."

Hades stepped again to the edge of the precipice. He held his flaming bronze staff down by his side.

"Keep watch on the shades," Zeus instructed Kerberos, as the dog stretched his necks and reached his faces near Hades. "They want your master for themselves."

Kerberos bared his teeth and Zeus's legs vibrated with the low growl.

"Good," Zeus praised the smelly beast. "Good...um...dog."

• • •

Hades wordlessly called to Daphne's grandmother. She peered out from the tangle of shades, and slid her insubstantial form in between the others until she hovered in front of him. Kerberos' great heads were lowered in submission behind Hades, so he wouldn't frighten her.

Hades reached out and took her hand, which became substantial at his touch. Together they rose, floating above the great dark space. Hades towered over her in both height and power, but there was a soothing gentleness and reassuring empathy in his strength. She did not fear him. Rather, she, like the other shades, was drawn to him.

Hades looked into the woman's eyes. He was looking at the grandmother's essence, her bare soul—what had once made her physical body vibrant with life.

That's what the shades are, Hades realized. They are humans still, just without their bodies. In the Underworld, their bodies are a mere shade, a reflection of what they were up above, but the soul is firmly in place. Held in a kind of resting state for most of them, like a dreamy fog.

Hades touched the grandmother's cheek. Color returned to her face. Her dress turned a soft shade of purple. Hades led her to the opening they had just come from, which Kerberos had cleared of shades. Hades waved his hand, and the darkness ebbed a little in the vast open space. A large round hearth sprung up out of the earth. And a stone chair beside it. Hades led her to the hearth and sat her down, the way she once had done for him.

"I see a great field here," Hades told Daphne's grandmother in his rich, warm voice. "Do you see it?" He knelt beside her, creating a vision in her mind for her. "The grain flows in the wind like water. Daphne plays with the dogs in the orchard. When she grows into a woman, she will take care of you."

The grandmother smiled.

"Sit here," Hades instructed. "And be calm. She will come to you."

She folded her hands in her lap, immersed in the image Hades created for her.

Hades had a clear vision of the field he'd imagined. He saw in place of the emptiness of the cavern, a field of golden grain, where the worthy could find solace and peace in the afterlife. Persephone could grow such a field here for the deserving shades, he thought. She could make something beautiful here…

"Where is your husband?" he asked, as he rose. He glanced back at the cavern they'd just left, the one still thick with shades. "Could you not find one another? You said he was here, in the Underworld."

"Can we go now?" Zeus barked, having ridden Kerberos into the room to follow Hades.

"Not yet." Hades rose, his face fearsome as he left the grandmother's side. "Not just yet."

"Ah, right," Zeus remembered. "Fishface. Well, let's get to it."

Zeus smacked Kerberos's haunches and the dog bounded over to a web of shades. The shades dispersed when they saw him heading their way, but the hound was too fast, and a few seconds later he proudly pranced over to Hades with the fish-faced man held in between his teeth.

"I have something else in mind for you," Hades told the man dangling from Kerberos' drooling mouth. "Something quite different."

The man scowled and Hades nodded.

"You're most deserving of it. You took advantage of the weak in your lifetime," Hades said calmly. "Of the small and the young. Now, you'll feel what it is to be small and weak."

Hades took his staff, and, in a sweeping motion, he carved out a pit the size of the man's body. Kerberos dropped the man into the pit, and then Hades filled it with rocks until only the man's head was free.

"Here you will remain," Hades said to the man, whose full fish-like lips were curled in useless rage. "To be stepped over, or on. As small a creature as you made your victims feel."

The man opened his mouth to speak, but Hades held up a hand and no sound came out. The man's face reddened, his shade now beet-red, the way it would remain for the rest of time. Silent, red, helpless.

"Can we go now?" Zeus prodded.

"Yes," Hades said, satisfied. "Let's go."

He turned his back on the man and walked away, his stiff-backed walk purposeful.

"I just don't care for them the way you do," Zeus said, glancing back at the now-silent shade. "Humans."

"I know," Hades replied, walking beside Kerberos, who was sniffing the air, back on the harpies' scent, back on the trail to Persephone.

"Why do you care about them so much?"

Hades paused. "I feel responsible for them."

"Why?"

"We created them."

"That doesn't make me feel like I have to take care of them. Or care about them. So, why do you feel that way?"

"I don't know. I love them. Persephone does too."

"I know," Zeus said, chastened. "Let's go find her."

Hades leaped onto Kerberos' back and the hound bounded ahead, leaving the countless shades behind them.

CHAPTER 38

Philos closed Persephone's door behind him. Sisyphus had gone to meet the new shades arriving from above and Philos was joining him there.

The massive door clicked loudly as it shut, but the sound didn't ring with the same finality for Persephone that it once had. It no longer made her chest constrict as though the breath was being squeezed from her lungs. Once Philos's determined shuffle had faded, Persephone grasped the carnelian handle and heaved the door open.

She glided quietly through the palace until she reached the front gate. Made of bronze as thick as her body, Persephone paused at the gate, then stepped forward and walked through it.

She took a few steps along the narrow causeway, and then knelt at its edge. She stared at the bubbling lava, wondering. She held her hand just above the lava and felt its intense heat radiate onto her skin. She thought again about how Ares dove into the lava. She took a deep breath, then dipped her fingertip into it.

Persephone raised her eyebrows. The lava felt soft, like warm mud. It didn't burn. Her face lit up. Maybe she would see her mother again very soon. And Hades. She could tell them herself about Ares's plan and Poseidon's treachery.

Out of the corner of her eye, Persephone saw a shape move swiftly past her. She turned to see Helene. The shade was heading straight for the waterfall.

"Wait!" Persephone cried, immediately knowing what the shade planned to do. She jumped to her feet and ran after the girl.

"Helene!" she called. "Stop!"

The girl didn't hesitate. As Persephone chased after her, the shade half-ran, half-floated, at a desperate pace.

"Stop!" Persephone yelled. "Don't!"

Helene paused when she arrived at the waterfall. She turned back to Persephone for a moment, her eyes alight as if she were alive again. Then she stepped into the falls.

Helene stood there, letting the water stream over her.

"No!" Persephone shouted, approaching the falls as the girl's feet lifted off the ground. "Stop!"

The frantic goddess reached into the falls for the shade, then followed her, getting soaked in the torrent of falling water. Helene rose higher, as if she was being lifted by an invisible hand against the current of the rushing water. Persephone grasped at the shade with one hand, shielding her eyes from the piercing water with the other. But she couldn't get a hold on her; Helene was soon beyond her reach.

Ever so briefly, Persephone brightened. She held her hands over her eyes and watched. She thought for a moment that the girl would make it, that she would keep rising like Ares and return above. But then, Helene began to fade. Her image flickered and faded until she disintegrated into the mist. She never looked back down at Persephone. She just called her lover's name in joy and release.

And was gone. She became the spray, disappearing forever.

"No!" Persephone cried as someone yanked her out of the waterfall. She buried her face in Nike's feathered chest.

"I thought it might work," Persephone cried, fruitlessly beating her fists into Nike's strong body. "I thought it would work! For a moment, it seemed like she was rising back to the surface. She thought so, too. I saw the hope in her eyes."

"But the water claimed her," Nike said softly.

"The dead cannot leave this place." Persephone's voice was resigned. Her arms fell to her sides. "They remain here. Or they are nowhere. They are either here or they do not exist at all."

Nike had no response. Persephone turned away from her. Tears streamed down her face.

"It's my fault, Nike! She heard me talk about the waterfall. About how Ares used it and how I planned to try it myself."

"She knew the risk. She must have heard you speak of that as well."

Persephone turned back to the waterfall. She reached her hand out and felt the spray of water. "But I'm more responsible than you know. You see, I showed her...her..."

"Her what?"

"Her family. I showed her her family. Her lover. Nike, when I touch the shades, I reconnect them to the living. I make them remember their life above. I'm like a conduit through which their memories travel. The people they loved and who loved them in life are brought back to them, in vivid color. I did that for her once. I showed Helene..." Persephone paused, choking up, tripping over the girl's name, over her memory.

"I showed Helene her lover and her family," Persephone went on. "She knew they loved her, that they honored her and missed her. I thought that would help her...but I was wrong." She stared down at her hands. "I was all wrong..."

"You weren't wrong," Nike reassured her. "It did help Helene."

"No, it didn't! She risked her existence to leave this place!"

"That proves it helped her. She remembered what she'd lost. And that made it both easier and harder for her to remain here."

Persephone shook her head at Nike, utterly perplexed. "I don't know what I should do."

Persephone sat, frustrated and hopeless. Nike whisked the bottom of the goddess's dress out of the lava with a claw, and stomped out the burgeoning fire that had emerged on the fabric.

"I wanted to make things better for her, for the shades," Persephone mused. "But my help only makes it worse."

"Persephone," Nike began. "The shades are slaves. I've been a slave. It's a hopeless existence. And here, it's one without end. She is better off being nothing."

Persephone looked up at Nike's noble face, horrified. "Can you really mean that?"

Nike nodded. "Persephone, as a slave, you don't exist anyway. Not really. It's almost worse than not existing because you have no rights, no power. You're not really a person. You're an object, but one who can think, and who longs for freedom."

"So," Persephone struggled to understand. "All of these shades, the ones who are slaves, feel as desperate as she did?"

"Yes. And the ones who aren't slaves feel a different kind of hopelessness and helplessness that is almost as terrible. For they have no memories, no purpose, no past or future. They may as well not exist."

"It's horrible."

"It is."

"But, what can I do about it?"

"I don't know. What can you do?"

Persephone rose.

"Bring Philos to me," she said. "And send for the other harpies. It's time we put our plans in motion."

"I presume this is the end to your thoughts of climbing out through the waterfall?" Nike ventured.

Persephone didn't respond. Nike flew off to do her bidding.

. . .

"Philos," Persephone began. He was the first to come to her where she waited with her back to the waterfall.

"What's wrong?" Persephone asked when she saw him. The old philosopher was clearly distressed. He muttered to himself more than usual and, every few steps he took, he stopped looking down at his tablet to look up and shake his fists.

"My wife," he mumbled. "My wife."

Persephone held his quaking arms still. "What about your wife?"

"She's here! She's here…"

"You saw her?"

"Charon brought his boat. The shades stepped out and there she was. My beloved. She was here. She is here…"

"Did you go to her? Did she know you?"

"Sisyphus wouldn't allow it. She was swept away, like refuse! Like trash! And now I don't know where she is! She wanders lost and alone. And not knowing that I'm here, that I've been waiting for her…"

Philos tore at the few strands of hair on his head. Persephone wrapped her arms around his shoulders, soothing him.

"We will find her. Hush now. I promise. I will find her."

Persephone looked up when she heard two of her harpies approach.

"Take him," she instructed Erato and Urania. "Go with him to the armory. Take stock of the weapons. Take bows for yourselves and bring me arrows. As many as you can without making it obvious that they're gone. Bring them to the tower."

Persephone held Philos' worried face in her hands.

"Show them all the weapons Sisyphus has stored for Ares. I will find your wife," she told him. "I will bring her to you."

Philos couldn't bring himself to acknowledge her, he was so upset. He huddled over his scribble-filled tablet, bent over more than usual. Persephone knelt and looked up into his eyes.

"Trust in me, Philos. I will reunite you with your wife. Now go," she ordered. "Show them what they need to see."

Erato nudged Philos onto her back, and she and Urania flew off.

Three harpies flew past them on their way to Persephone. Persephone reached her arms up. Thalia swooped beneath her, lifting Persephone into the air and onto her back. They soared up past the waterfall and Persephone's glass wall. They circled the island palace with its glowing lava moat, until they reached Persephone's lush green tower, now thick with foliage.

Persephone climbed off the harpy's back and stood upon the wall. Her toes hung over the edge as she looked across to the waterfall, thinking of what was on its other side, what was above it and beyond. Then she thought of Hades. He would approve of her plan. She drew her shoulders back and exhaled, allowing herself a small smile.

A harpy on either side of her, Persephone turned and held the tips of their outstretched wings as she stepped down from the wall. She crossed the balcony and knelt beside her akoniton plant. She pulled a handful of the akoniton out by the roots, collecting them in her lap.

Moving with silent purpose, she ground the leaves and roots into a fine powder. Then she added the powder to a large bowl of bubbling lava. Once the powder touched the lava, the concoction steamed. It turned green and then black, and a rancid smell wafted up from the bowl. Persephone nodded in satisfaction.

All her harpies had arrived. Erato and Urania had baskets full of arrows and bows for each harpy. Persephone took the arrows, and dipped them one by one into the akoniton.

"It's time we armed you, my former Amazons, my magnificent harpies," she proclaimed.

She gave the first six arrows to Nike.

"These are now tipped with poison. Any living creature pieced by one of these arrows will die."

Nike nodded.

"Now go," Persephone told Nike. "Fly up to Olympus. Find Athena. Tell her that Poseidon has joined Ares."

Persephone turned to Erato.

"You've taken a count of the weapons. Tell Athena what you found. Tell her of Ares's Underworld armory. Stay if she needs you. I want ten of you to go above with Nike. Urania, you report to me of what Athena said, what she needs. Melete." Persephone turned to the kind harpy. Her voice softened. "I have a different errand for you."

Persephone took the wreath of flowers off her head. It was a wreath made from the first plants she had created in the Underworld.

"Take this." She placed it on Melete's head. "It's a message for my mother. Tell Demeter I'm well. Tell her that I flourish. This is my gift to her. Tell her that I love and miss her."

Melete bowed her head.

"I will," she said quietly.

"Keep your sharp eyes on watch for Ares," Persephone told her harpies. "We don't want him to know we're making Athena aware of his plans. Or that we're going to help her defeat him."

Nike nodded curtly and led the harpies as they flew away from the tower in an arrow formation.

Before she flew off, Persephone pulled Melete aside. "And please, find out if Hades is up above. If he made his way safely back? I need to know."

"I will, my lady." Melete assured her. "I will."

Persephone smiled weakly, and Melete turned and flew to catch up to the harpies making their way to the world above.

Persephone stood with the remaining harpies, and they watched the others until they were out of sight. Once they disappeared into the waterfall, Persephone said to the remaining five harpies, "We need to find Philos's wife."

"Persephone!" Sisyphus called.

Persephone looked over her shoulder, at the closed door that Sisyphus would soon be coming through.

"I'll deal with him. You five go. Find Philos's wife. Bring her to me."

The harpies flew off, the wind from their swiftly beating wings blowing Persephone's hair all around, making her almost feel as if she was flying with them.

Persephone looked out over the waist-high wall around her tower and waited for Sisyphus to come to her.

Moments later, the thick door swung open, and Sisyphus sidled through it. A look of immense pride and satisfaction came over his sharp-chinned face when he saw the goddess standing there. Waiting for him.

"This is nicely done, Persephone," he complimented falsely as he looked for the first time at the thick foliage on the tower. He pulled at a vine and yanked it from the wall. "I'm glad you've made yourself a cozy little haven here."

Sisyphus liked to speak to Persephone as though she were a child. He harbored hopes that she would come to need him, to rely on him. That he would be her authority figure. He would discipline her once they were married. Once she was his wife, Sisyphus believed, he would control her completely.

"Someday," he said as the harpies flew away, "I may let you explore the Underworld on your own. Right now, it's too dangerous. And, I admit, I like knowing where you are. I can find you whenever I want you. And I know you're safe."

Persephone held the bowl of the akoniton against her waist and turned to look into Sisyphus's sinister eyes.

"Your words," she began, setting the steaming, stinking bowl on the wall. "They are empty of any truth or goodness. Like your soul."

An amused look came over Sisyphus's face, as if Persephone was a gnat attacking a lion.

"You could help the shades here," she went on. "You could make their existence more tolerable. But you choose not to. Instead, you enrich yourself, work to empower the most wicked of all the gods, and doom these souls to a listless, wasted eternity."

"If even one of these shades were as clever as me," Sisyphus sneered, "he could have done the same. But not a single one of them is. So, I rule them. They do what I want. It's the way of the world. And so, it's the way of the Underworld, too."

"I will change it."

Sisyphus chuckled, attempting to cover his grin, his delight.

"Well, you radiant creature, you certainly possess more fire than I anticipated. I like it."

He traced his fingers along Persephone's bare collarbone and leaned to whisper in her ear.

"I will let you know when I tire of it."

Persephone fought to keep herself from glancing at the poison in the bowl. She didn't know what effect it would have on a shade.

But she couldn't keep herself from looking at the waterfall.

Sisyphus followed her gaze.

"Ah, yes. You found Ares's doorway. Oh," his bone-hand went to his chest as he feigned dismay. "You didn't know! I have spies everywhere. I know every move you make."

Persephone shook. Sisyphus thought it was from fear, but it was anger.

Sisyphus touched her again and Persephone flew into a rage. The plants that encircled the tower responded to her anger, and tore themselves from the wall. They swarmed and encircled Sisyphus, wrapping him like a mummy, ensnaring his limbs, covering his eyes and mouth. He was blind and motionless. He dropped to the ground at Persephone's feet.

Surprised, Persephone watched in triumph as he writhed and wriggled in a failed attempt to free himself. Too soon, the door came smashing down, crashing onto the ground and nearly flattening Sisyphus. His hulking, spiderlike guards came in and cut their master free with their pincer-like masks.

Sisyphus sputtered and stumbled, embarrassed and angry. He looked up at a defiant Persephone, who stood with an unconcerned look on her face.

"Again. You forget that I am a goddess," she said. "It seems I have some power over the shades. And you—are a shade."

Sisyphus glowered. He rose to his full height, which was below Persephone's, and soon Persephone's tower was overrun with spider guards.

"Release the wolves!" Sisyphus stomped and commanded, like a petulant child who was denied what he wanted. "I want Hades torn limb from limb."

"What? Hades is still here?"

"Of course he's still here!"

Sisyphus plucked from his skeleton chest a vine that had become lodged in between his ribs.

"He thinks anything he wants can be his. I will show him that he's wrong. You're mine now! I will bring you his head and then we will marry. And you will submit to me. In everything.”

“I agreed to marry you if Hades was free. If he was led back above and safe!”

Sisyphus spat. His eyes narrowed in anger.

“I was going to let the Underworld take them out,” Sisyphus simmered. “But I cannot have Hades and Zeus stomping around the Underworld for eternity. I see that now. It’s too dangerous. Hades won’t stop searching for you until he finds you. And I need to bring you to heel, which I see is impossible if you’re encouraged by his mere existence.”

“I won’t do it! I won’t marry you if you hurt him!”

Sisyphus paused in the tower doorway. He stood on top of the felled door.

“I’ve re-thought,” he said, eerily calm. “I don’t need your permission. But I know now I have to rid this world of Hades before you will submit to me.

“I will kill him. No, that’s not quite right. I will destroy him. And that will break you.” Sisyphus’s mouth curled into a terrifying grin. “I will break you, Persephone. And remake you as my wife.”

Sisyphus stormed off, his spider henchmen trailing him. He left the two largest, grotesque creatures in the doorway, blocking Persephone’s exit.

CHAPTER 39

Hades's flaming staff and Zeus's glowing thunderbolt lit the way as Kerberos bounded through the Underworld, following the harpies' trail towards Persephone.

The hound reached a fork in the mangled maze of tunnels and stopped. Two distinct tunnels lay open in front of the beast. His left head leaned towards the left tunnel, its nostrils flaring with the scent of the harpies. The hound's right head leaned into the tunnel on the right, its nostrils sniffing the scent as well. The middle head howled—they had to choose one.

"Which scent is the most recent?" Hades asked the beast.

The heads on the right and left snarled and snapped at each other.

"I don't think they know," murmured Zeus, on edge. It was a narrow pass, with darkness on all sides.

"Do you hear that sound?" Hades asked, cocking his head.

He slid off Kerberos. The hound's center head sniffed and snarled at his other heads, arguing over which way they should go.

First came the rats. Squealing and scratching, rats rushed by the thousands, with tremendous speed, towards the gods and their hound. The rodents were as dark as the Underworld, except for their bright red eyes. They were the size of Hades's foot, with chomping teeth and long, squirming tails. The sound of their claws scraping rock was like a ceaseless, eerie chatter.

"It's just rats," Zeus said in relief. He raised his thunderbolt, clearing a space on the path in front of him so the rats had to go around him. And they did. They ran on all sides of the cave, like water following the path of least resistance.

"The rats aren't what I hear," Hades said grimly as the rats scurried past them like a wave. The rats ran with such urgency that Hades knew they were running away from something. He readied himself for a fight. Zeus did the same.

Next came the wolves. With their bronze-tipped claws gleaming, Sisyphus's wolves howled and sprang out of both tunnels. They knocked Kerberos to the ground. The hound and the wolves rolled and fought and slashed at one another. Kerberos swung his dragon tail and knocked two of them down.

Hades and Zeus also fought the hybrid wolves. But the gods were limited in their movements by the relatively narrow space in which they were caught. The wolves were relentless. The gods couldn't wield their weapons and swing them how they liked. Zeus smashed the cave walls with his thunderbolt to make more space, while Hades hurled his staff at a wolf who tore at Kerberos' throat. The wolf slid off the hound, and Hades turned to find another wolf leaping at his back.

Hades wrestled the wolf to the ground, but another sprung onto his back. It held onto Hades's armor with piercing bronze claws. Hades reached back and yanked the wolf off his armor. Its claws left deep gashes in the metal.

"What are these beasts?" he shouted, mystified by the combination of metal and animal flesh. He spun around and threw the wolf, smashing it into the cave wall, where it slid down until it hit the ground. It shook its head and slowly stood back up.

Hades and Zeus stood back to back, with a growling Kerberos by their side.

Gnashing wolves surrounded them on all sides. Sisyphus's wolves took measured steps in unison, closing in on the gods—until ear-piercing screeches had them covering their ears with their paws and howling in pain.

Hades and Zeus covered their own ears and fell to their knees.

Harpies emerged from both tunnels, bows cocked, arrows nocked. The harpies dove at the cowering wolves, knocking half of them on their backs. Then the largest wolf raised his head and howled. The other wolves howled in response. Together, their voices drowned out the harpies, allowing the wolves to regain their footing.

The harpies couldn't fully spread their wings in the confined space, so they kept their wings close at their sides, moving with the speed of diving falcons. The wolves growled and bared their bronze teeth at the harpies.

Two harpies shot arrows at the wolves, and Sisyphus's beasts instantly fell. The animals squirmed and smoked, until there was nothing left of them but bronze claws and teeth.

Hades and Zeus fought off the attacking wolves, whose organized attack gained momentum and intensity with the arrival of the harpies. The harpies let their arrows fly, and three more wolves went down. But one harpy flew too close, and a wolf rose on its hind legs. The wolf tore at her chest. Aiode screeched and tumbled down to the cave floor.

Hades felled the attacking wolf with a vicious backhand, and the animal was flattened against the far wall with a yelp. More wolves came barreling out of the two tunnels. Zeus smashed them beneath his thunderbolt in one hand and his fist in the other. More arrows flew and more wolves vanished, leaving only their metal teeth and claws behind them.

"Get on!" a harpy yelled as the wolves kept coming.

Two harpies swooped down beside the gods. Hades and Zeus swung up onto their backs and, in moments, the harpies were in the air again.

The gods and harpies fled, the harpies flying as fast as they could, leaving the remaining wolves howling after them. Kerberos chased them, the Underworld hound outrunning them with his huge strides.

The harpies flew until they reached the open cavern where Hades had created a haven for Daphne's grandmother. Once there, they spread their wings and soared.

"Agata!" Philos cried, when he saw his wife sitting peacefully at the hearth Hades had made.

Hades hadn't noticed the small, hunched shade riding one of the harpies until he heard him speak. Philos reached out for the grandmother, with everything he was and everything he would ever be. He would have fallen off the harpy, had she not maneuvered to keep him on her back.

"Agata!" he called again.

At the sound of her husband's voice, the woman was freed from her Underworld stupor. She turned. Her face filled with light and relief when she saw him.

"Philos!" she cried.

"We'll come back for her, Philos," the harpy told him. "We'll come back. But now we cannot waste a moment. We must get home."

Four harpies were flying, two carried Hades and Zeus. The other two carried the wounded harpy in their claws, sharing her weight between them. Hades didn't see any movement or sense strong life left in her. He felt responsible for her loss.

"Leave me!" Philos pleaded to the harpy on whose back he rode, who also carried half the weight of the wounded harpy.

"I cannot," the harpy refused.

"Leave me. Please!" he begged, nearly jumping off as the distance between them and Agata increased.

"Kerberos, lift Agata!" Hades ordered the hound.

Kerberos bounded over to Agata and lowered his heads to the ground. The howling of the wolves grew closer.

Zeus shouted, "Quickly!"

Agata grabbed hold of Kerberos and the hound tossed her floating figure upon his back. Philos turned around, not taking his eyes off his wife as she trailed behind on the Underworld's great guardian beast.

Hades and Zeus rode the harpies, exchanging glances but not speaking. Hades was filled with hope that the harpies were taking them to Persephone.

"She's dying," said the harpy carrying her wounded friend.

Hades knew she was right.

"We can't take you any further," said the harpy Hades was riding.

"Yes, you can," he urged. "We were on your trail. We've been looking for you, for you to lead us to Persephone. Please—take me to her."

"We have to take our wounded sister to Persephone. She can help her."

Hades almost couldn't believe he was so close to Persephone. He was too close to fail. Too close to her to lose her again.

"Take me too!" Hades pleaded, tightening his hold on the harpy.

"I can't," she said flatly.

And with that refusal, the harpies flipped upside down and dumped the gods from their backs, dropping them into a deep dark pit.

Another harpy swooped in and took Agata from Kerberos' back. The hound whined as he watched Hades and Zeus fall beneath him. They fell so far they were lost in the blackness, the light of the staff and thunderbolt disappearing into the dark.

CHAPTER 40

Hades and Zeus were in a free fall like the one that had brought them spinning and somersaulting into the Underworld. Only the distant howling of Kerberos connected them to the Underworld they'd been in before. Now they were going even deeper.

When they finally landed, it was noiselessly, and on their feet.

Hades crouched, his hands on the ground, his forehead pressed against his knee.

"I was so close," he whispered.

He pounded his fist into the floor. Then he flung his flaming staff across the narrow room. It wedged itself into the cavern wall, still flaming.

Hades bowed his head. Zeus sighed. He put his hand on Hades's shoulder, then stood and surveyed their surroundings. He saw a faint light from far above, where the harpies had dropped them into the hole. But in this new cave, only Hades's glowing staff and Zeus's thunderbolt lit the darkness. They were so deep now that Zeus wondered if they'd finally reached the bottom of the earth itself.

A shallow stream of water ran near their feet. Out of the corner of his eye, Zeus saw an opening in the cave wall. He grunted, perplexed—it hadn't been there a moment ago. Zeus patted Hades on the back and strode towards the opening, his thunderbolt poised.

As he approached the opening, he realized it was no more than a nook in the wall of the cavern, a dead end. It was barely large enough to hold the three stooped figures Zeus found there. As soon as Zeus saw the three women, he froze. He tried to back slowly away but one of them ordered, "Stop."

Her voice creaked. Zeus hadn't thought a voice could sound ancient, but hers did. It sounded musty and old and, when she spoke, fine grey dust flew out of her mouth. He had to obey her. He couldn't have moved even if he tried.

Zeus waited for her to speak again but she didn't, so he spoke.

"Are you?" he began, but found he couldn't finish. The three ancient, robed, veiled women wouldn't stop moving. They didn't stop their tasks. Ever.

Spin, measure, cut. Spin, measure, cut.

"Your brother is supposed to be here," the middle sister, Lachesis, said, not moving her gaze from the shimmering thread in her withered hands. "Help him. Don't fight him."

"I am helping him!"

"You cannot fight his fate," Atropos said, her voice a hoarse whisper.

"And what is his fate?" Zeus was angry now. "He is king of the gods!"

"He is king," the Fates said in unison. "And so are you."

Zeus was about to argue that Hades alone was king of the gods, when he heard a tremendous crack. He spun around.

The ground around Hades splintered, where Hades had smashed his fist into it a second time. Zeus watched Hades slowly stand. Hades summoned his flaming staff. It pulled itself free of the wall and soared to his hand, blazing brightly in his grasp. The fire from his staff spread to surround him, forming a protective shield around the king of the gods.

Zeus glanced back at the Fates, but they were gone. What had been their home was now a solid wall. Kerberos howled from far above. Hades smashed his staff into the cavern wall, where the Fates had just stood. Zeus jumped out of the way as Hades began to carve a new tunnel.

Hades ran into the new passageway he created, his shield of fire forging ahead. Every time he reached the end of the tunnel, he smashed his staff again, forcing the cave to yield to his will and expanding the tunnel, expelling himself out of the deep darkness and towards Persephone.

Zeus and Hades sped through the tunnel, splashing in the shallow stream that Hades was following. The stream grew incrementally deeper as they ran. Eventually, the tunnel Hades was making connected to one of the Underworld's enormous caverns. He and Zeus waded into the waist-high water that filled the cavern, but Hades's fire kept burning.

Hundreds of bats hung from the ceiling of the cavern. Zeus glanced nervously at the razor-sharp ears, glinting in the light of his lightning bolt.

"The water is rising," Zeus said, once he had to start swimming to keep his head above the rising water. "We're getting closer to those bats."

"I know," Hades said grimly. Then he heard an ominous roar. "Dive!" he warned Zeus. "Now!"

Zeus and Hades dove as Sisyphus sent a fresh onslaught of water sweeping into the tunnel with the force of a tidal wave.

Enraged that his wolves returned to him without the head of Hades, Sisyphus had opened the dam, vowing that he'd drown the gods—even if he had to deluge the whole Underworld to do so.

Hades and Zeus struggled against the press of water rushing into the cavern. Hundreds of bats drowned around them. Once dead, they floated in the water like seaweed. Those that were still alive were swept off the ceiling. Their ears and claws scraped and sliced the gods as the bats fought for their lives, not caring who they took down in their fight to survive.

Hades and Zeus swam towards the faint light of the surface, but the water kept coming. Wave after wave flooded into the cavern, pounding the gods down. Over and over, the gods surfaced, and over and over, they were dashed back down away from survival, from life. They had no power over the water, no power over anything. It felt as though their power over even their own bodies had slipped away in the water.

Hades saw through the murky and distorted water that strong, implacable Zeus was flagging. He grabbed his brother's hand and pulled him upwards, with all the force he could muster. But Hades's strength was flagging, too, against the seemingly endless water. He couldn't reach the surface.

Zeus's hand slipped out of Hades's grasp.

Hades shouted but, underwater, the noise he made was unrecognizable. And in vain. Zeus couldn't respond.

Hades watched, helpless, as disembodied arms suddenly appeared from the depths. They wrapped around Zeus's chest. Hades flailed and shouted as glowing, translucent limbs crawled over his brother, taking hold of his arms and legs.

Confused by what he was seeing, Hades tried to swim against the current, desperate to fight off these Underworld villains who were taking his brother from him. Hades roared uselessly.

Then Hades felt arms ensnaring his own limbs. He tried to fight them off. He tried to fend off the creatures who had a hold of him, but his strength was gone. His limbs felt as though they were made of kelp, swaying whichever way the current moved.

He closed his eyes in exhaustion, thinking if he could just rest a moment he could regain his strength and fight some more. He was telling himself it was not time to surrender—that he could never surrender—when he realized the creatures weren't trying to push him down. They weren't trying to drown him. They were lifting him to the surface.

They were saving him.

Hades let go and let them take him.

Once Hades emerged from the water, he took a deep breath, inhaling the formerly despised Underworld air. His eyes flung open as he felt the firm support of solid ground beneath him once again. He sat up and turned to look for Zeus. Relief washed over him when he saw his brother sprawled on the ground beside him.

"Zeus." Hades crawled over to his brother. He shook him. "Zeus!"

Zeus groaned and curled up on the black, rocky shore, like he was taking a nap. Zeus grinned mischievously, clearly having a satisfying dream.

Hades sighed with relief. He shook his head and managed a grim grin of his own. Then he turned away, leaving his brother to what seemed like a very good dream.

Hades sat at the edge of the water. It was silent except for the sound of water lapping against the rock. Hades dropped his head into his hands. He felt utterly defeated. Was Persephone slipping away from him forever?

Ever since her death, he'd desperately reached out for her the way he'd reached out for Zeus in the water—and yet Zeus had slipped out of his grasp. Hades held on with all his strength, but it hadn't mattered. He'd watched as Zeus was pulled away.

For the first time since she'd been sent to the Underworld, Hades was confronted with the possibility that he might never get Persephone back. He didn't know what to do with that feeling, a possibility he'd never let slip into his mind. He'd never accepted defeat before—he'd always outsmarted, outmuscled, out-thought it. Far-thinking Hades, he told himself—but when it mattered more than it ever had, more than it ever would, was he going to fail?

Hades felt a gentle tug on his arm. Startled, he turned to see a shade beside him, holding out his forked staff. Hades tensed. Then he saw the hopeful look in the shade's eyes.

Hades turned his attention to his staff. It had been extinguished. The shade nodded his round, bald head, encouraging Hades to take the staff. The moment Hades touched its dripping surface, the staff reignited in brilliant flames.

A thin female shade crept up and lay Zeus's thunderbolt by the sleeping god's feet. Then she backed away.

"Thank you," Hades said to them both, as a realization dawned on him.

He looked around the cavern and saw hundreds of small

openings, little holes like those woodpeckers carved out of trees to make nests. The shades had a vast city of homes carved into the layered strata of this cave, and they'd brought Hades and Zeus here to their refuge. Hades saw shades peeking out of the little cave homes, shades hovering in front of the openings. Most huddled together, some stood apart. All of them watched Hades, waiting for his response.

"Thank you," he said again, to all of the shades. "Thank you for saving us."

CHAPTER 41

"My darling!"

Persephone cried when the harpies reappeared, hurtling unevenly through the air towards her tower, one of them carried limply in between two sets of strong claws.

"Lay her here!"

She pointed to the stone floor of her tower. A bed of lush, green leaves instantly sprung up to cushion the harpy as she was set down.

Persephone waved her other hand. The wood door flew up off the ground and reattached itself to its hinges, shutting out Sisyphus's hulking, silent spider guards.

Philos and Agata embraced quietly, staying out of the way. Persephone bent over the wounded harpy, with the other four harpies kneeling silently beside her.

Persephone held Aiode's face in her softly glowing hands, and the harpy opened her large, golden eyes.

"My dear girl," Persephone whispered. "My strong, brave warrior."

"The akoniton worked," Aiode said proudly. "It killed the wolves...it was the bane of the wolves...wolfsbane..."

Persephone nodded, biting her lip, and caressed Aiode's face.

"I saw him," Aiode said, coughing, as Thalia cradled her head in her lap. "I saw him." Her feverish eyes were alight with impending death. "I saw Hades." She smiled at the recollection. "He fights like a hero," the harpy said, reaching for Persephone. "He will keep coming for you. I want him to come for you…"

"Shhh, my warrior," Persephone soothed. "My Amazon. Quiet yourself, love."

Persephone's eyes filled with tears as she felt the life draining out of Aiode. Her wounds were too deep, made by some godly forged weapon. Persephone couldn't undo them.

"I'm sorry we didn't bring him to you," Aiode murmured, attempting to raise her head. "You belong with one another…"

Philos and Agata came to kneel beside the dying Aiode. Persephone placed her head on the harpy's torn and wrecked chest. Persephone knew the harpy wouldn't become a shade. The harpies were creatures transformed, somewhere in between living and dead already.

"Transformed," Persephone said as the four harpies around Aiode wept.

Persephone sat up. Aiode's breathing was shallow. She had only a few breaths left, and then she would be gone.

"Farewell, beloved sister," Persephone said. "But not goodbye."

Persephone transformed Aiode as the harpy took her last breath. She turned her into a golden statue. Then she placed the statue at the top of her tower, where Aoide could keep watch on the island palace, her sisters, and Persephone, for the rest of their days.

CHAPTER 42

Zeus awoke, a wide grin still on his face. The grin melted off as he opened his eyes, remembered he was in the Underworld, and saw that they were surrounded by shades. The shades had closed in on him and Hades.

Zeus lept up, thunderbolt in hand.

"Back!" he roared and swept his thunderbolt in a wide circle to clear away a swath of shades.

But the shades didn't move.

"Brother." Hades put a hand on Zeus's outstretched arm. "They saved us." Hades pressed down Zeus's arm until it, and the thunderbolt, rested at his side. "The shades rescued us from the flood."

"Did they?" Zeus raised an eyebrow. "Well, they did that so they could keep you."

Zeus raised his arm again threateningly, his eyes fixed on the surrounding shades.

"Maybe we can help them in return," Hades said.

"Again?" Zeus asked, exasperated. He was poised to say more, when he saw that the cavern started to fill with a faint red light.

The light spread slowly, creeping silently and insidiously. It began at the floor, sliding in like water, and then rose, expanding until every crack and crevice in the cave glowed red.

The mysterious light carried with it the cold. The shades shivered as the light enveloped them, its cold piercing even the insubstantial shades.

"Run!" Zeus ordered the shades, quivering in the painful cold himself.

The light grew stronger. It deepened to the color of blood and the searing cold intensified.

"Go!" Zeus boomed, trying to rattle the shades out of their stupor. But the shades didn't move. They cowered. They shook and shivered as the light and its raw cold grew ever more intense.

"Leave!" Zeus shoved and pushed the shades, his eyes watering, the water freezing on his face and in his beard.

But his efforts were useless. The shades wouldn't flee.

Hades raised his flaming staff. He whipped it around and, as it moved, the shades followed it. Hades swung his staff here and there, rounding up the shades into a single, long line. Then he pointed the staff towards an opening into a tunnel that led out and away from the light. The shades went where Hades's staff pointed. They filed out of the intensely red, nearly blinding light and cold, towards safety.

Hades clung to his staff, eventually falling to his knees with the effort it took to fight off the red light. His skin burned in the cold. Zeus propped him up, his own face growing waxy and faintly blue. Both gods collapsed as the final shades were herded out of the light and biting cold.

. . .

The two gods lay there, frozen and barely breathing, unable to free themselves from the piercing pain of the enveloping crimson light. Motionless and numb, their eyes closed in exhaustion.

They didn't see the plants stretch and curl into the cavern. Vine after vine climbed the walls around the gods and spread along the floor of the cave, until the room was thick with Persephone's plants. Soon, the red light was extinguished.

Barefoot, Persephone approached. She sat beside the gods. She gently put Hades's head in her lap. She stroked his hair, kissed his cool, soft lips, and knew that he was dreaming. She breathed a soothing fog around him, comforting him, exposing his dark thoughts to root them out.

For Hades, the coldness of the red light had brought fear with it. The cold and fear dug in under his skin and spread searing, biting pain, infiltrating every part of his body. And in that pain, Hades remembered his father. He remembered the last time he saw him. It had been the last time anyone saw him.

Hades remembered how Kronos looked—like a rotting version of Zeus. Kronos once had a broad, handsome, and arrogant face like that of his eldest son, but now it looked as if it had begun to eat itself from the inside. Insects buzzed around his face. Maggots clung to open sores on his arms and chest. Yet his body remained strong and unwavering, the way he clung to his power.

"Who do you think you are?" Kronos had roared at Hades.

He and Hades stood across from one another, each poised to attack. Only one of them might hesitate when the time came to fight.

War had raged between Kronos and his children for an unknowable span of time. Islands and volcanoes were created. The world had been broken and re-formed and broken again. They would end the long war today. One of them would walk away victorious. The other would not walk away at all. It was time to end it. And begin anew.

Lightning crackled in the dark sky. Meteors spewed from behind the clouds, crashing into the earth and scarring its surface. The untamed wind swirled ferociously.

Kronos stood three heads higher than Hades, and the rush of his rancid breath made Hades's hair fly around his head.

"Who are you to defy me?" Kronos growled. "To rid my world of me? This is my world, not yours. Not your brother's or those other weaklings that cling to your ankles. Humans," he scoffed. "Yes, I know you're the mastermind. None of the others would have the sense or the daring to try to overpower me. They respect me."

"No one respects you."

"They fear me," Kronos spat, spittle flying from his frothing mouth. "And that's better."

"It doesn't have to be this way," Hades said. "I keep trying to tell you, Father. It doesn't have to be this way."

"But it does," Kronos grumbled. "Because you want my power and I refuse to give it up. So, this is where we're left. With misery and hate, each clawing our way to survive."

"You make it sound like this is about you and me."

"It is, isn't it? You want what I have," Kronos snarled. "You want to be me; the young lion wants to kill the old lion and take over the pride."

"I'm not thinking of you," Hades argued. "I'm thinking of this world. And everyone in it."

"And that's your weakness," Kronos sneered, tossing aside the half-eaten bone he was gnawing on. "You don't think of yourself enough. That's why you can't defeat me."

"You're wrong," Hades said, his hand shaking. "That's why I'll win."

Thoughts of his fellow gods and the humans, and the vision of the world he wanted to make possible for them all, ran through Hades's mind. They were magnified a thousandfold by his resentment and anger at his decaying father, who stood in the way, defiantly and actively blocking all their chances to move forward.

Hades howled. Pain and rage and guttural sorrow spurred Hades on, as he heaved his arm back and hurled the thunderbolt at his father.

The thunderbolt, freshly made by Hephaistos from the lightning Hades had captured, pierced Kronos's belly and soared out the other side. In a flash of light and a deafening roar of thunder, a bewildered look spread over Kronos's face. He stared down at the hole the thunderbolt had torn through his body.

Kronos looked across at Hades, and let out a startled snort. Then, shards of lightning—the thunderbolt split into a hundred pieces—splayed out from where he stood. And he was gone.

Hades caught the reformed thunderbolt as it circled around

and returned to him. He fell to his knees. He covered his face with his hands, overwhelmed with relief and sorrow.

It was over. He'd done it. He'd freed the gods. He'd freed the world. But he killed his father in order to do it, and that act would haunt him.

Before Zeus could stride out to congratulate his brother on their victory, Persephone was there. She ran to Hades before anyone else could reach him. She stood in front of a still-kneeling Hades with a benevolent look on her face. He looked up and saw her face, and felt safe and understood, like she knew the sacrifice he'd made. Like she knew what it had cost him to kill Kronos, and why he'd done it.

A foreign brightness began to peer out from the sky behind Persephone's head. Hades held up an armored hand to shield his eyes from the beautifully painful rays emanating from behind her face.

With Kronos gone, the clouds dissipated, just as Hades and Persephone believed they would. The sun crept out, strengthening as the darkness lifted.

Persephone beamed down at Hades, the sunlight glowing behind her head. It lit her delicate face with a brilliance mirrored in Hades's mind, when he thought of the honey-voiced goddess.

Persephone held out her hand. He paused before taking it in his own, which was still encased in an armored glove. She helped him rise to his feet and he found himself surrounded by jubilant gods. They sang and danced. They embraced him and slapped him on the back. They lifted him to his feet, each one happier and more joyful than the last, to finally be free of the darkness. They were prepared to make a new world. Their world.

Hades looked for Persephone's face in the crowd of celebrating gods, but was soon distracted by the raucous revelry and the unfettered jubilance at the end of the long war.

• • •

"Hades," Persephone whispered. Her breath warmed him, spreading through his body like a warm embrace. Relief flooded his senses.

"Hades, my love," she called. "Come back to me."

Hades felt her skin against his skin. He sighed. He felt as if he'd come home. Now, what was it that he'd been afraid of? When she was here holding him?

Hades opened his eyes.

And saw her.

Persephone looked down at him with a face full of love. Her dark hair enveloped him, sheltering his face. Her eyes were full of tears.

He reached up and pulled her towards him. He kissed her and the world felt right and good.

"Hades," Persephone whispered, tearing herself away from him so she could speak while she had the chance. She glanced around nervously. Then she ran her fingers again through his hair.

"Hades—. My generous and loving Hades. You're free of that act. You don't need to hold the weight of Kronos's death. We all bear the responsibility. We willingly share it with you. It had to be done for us to be free, for our world to be free. Only you were strong enough to do it."

Tears filled Hades's eyes—relief mingled with joy, with sorrow and release. Persephone clung to him. She pressed her face against his.

"Hades," she said. "We loved, you and I. We're fortunate that we found such a love. But now we need to let go."

She sat up. "Your place is up there—on the surface, in the world we created. And mine is here. Go, my beloved Hades. Go back to the sky and sun and the land we love. They need you. You're the best of all of us, remember?"

Persephone paused, her eyes bright, shining with tears.

"Go," she whispered. "But go with my love. Know that I have never and will never stop loving you."

Then Persephone massaged Hades's temples, and he drifted back off into a dream. She gently lay his head on the bed of leaves and kissed him. Her lips lingered on his, on their warmth.

Then she rose.

She turned to Zeus, who'd been watching from the moment he'd awoken.

"Take care of him," she said.

Zeus could only nod. He pulled Persephone into his arms and held her.

"I want to ask if you're all right, but you just saved us," he said, stifling a cry.

"It's not safe here," Persephone said, wishing she could melt into the solace of Zeus's embrace. She forced herself to pull away. "You have to take him home."

"I've tried."

Persephone looked at Hades and her heart thumped loudly. He stirred.

"I can't be here when he wakes," she confessed. "I won't be strong enough to push him away."

Persephone bit her lip to keep from bursting into tears. She wiped the grime and mud from Zeus's breastplate, and looked at the images engraved there of Hades and Zeus battling the giants.

"You cannot slay this beast," she murmured. "You can only live with it."

"Persephone," Zeus began, his brow furrowed. "Are you sure we can't bring you…"

"I'm sure," she answered softly. "Take him. Take him and go. Defeat Ares, who is battling Athena for dominance."

"What?" Zeus's eyes widened.

"Yes. Ares sent me here." She pointed to her chest, where Ares's spear had killed her, but she was too proud to show Zeus the wound.

Zeus cursed. "He was trying to lure Hades and me away from Olympus."

"Yes, but he has his hands full with Athena."

Zeus's face filled with pride. "I expect he does."

"I've sent a message up to Athena. Poseidon has joined Ares in his fight to be king of the gods." Zeus shook his head, not surprised by these betrayals. Persephone went on. "Ares has made and amassed weapons here in the Underworld. He's soon ready to take them up above. But I've sent help to Athena from here, too."

Now Zeus looked proudly, and a touch surprised, at the young goddess everyone thought was too sweet and lovely to be a warlike strategist. Persephone read his look and blushed, proud and surprised herself.

"And the land? Humans?" Zeus asked, a little startled that he cared.

Persephone shook her head. "My mother's grief…I've sent her a message, too, to tell her I'm…happy here. So she won't worry. So she'll let the earth grow again. Please tell her the same." Persephone took his face in her hands. "Lie for me, Zeus. Lie for me until what you say can be true."

Persephone heard the distant screech of one of her harpies. She looked over her shoulder. "That's my warning," she said. "I have to leave."

"How can I leave you here?" Zeus asked, suddenly angry.

Persephone smiled sadly. "Because I'm asking you to."

"I'll talk to Demeter. I'll do as you ask," he said. "Take care, Persephone." It was all Zeus could think to say.

"I will," she smiled sadly. "And you, take care of him."

"I will."

"You aren't far from where you came into the Underworld," Persephone told him.

Zeus was astounded. It seemed as if he and Hades had traveled across oceans beneath the earth.

"Kerberos!" Persephone commanded, and the hound came bounding into the cavern. He raised his six ears and sat up at attention. "Take them back to the entrance where you found them."

Zeus was surprised by the relief he felt at seeing the Underworld hound. Kerberos sat beside a still-sleeping Hades. Zeus scratched the dog's matted chest.

"Is there another way in and out of the Underworld?" he asked.

"There is," Persephone said, thinking of the waterfall. "Ares uses it. I have a plan for it. And for him when he returns."

"Be careful."

Suddenly, a swish of air and wings swept overhead. Kerberos lowered his heads and covered them with his paws.

"Some guard dog," Zeus scoffed.

Nike landed beside Persephone. Zeus recognized the fearsome and towering figure, who clearly served the goddess, from their earlier encounter.

"Yes," Persephone acknowledged her friend. "I know it's time."

"He's coming," Nike warned.

"I thought as much."

"Wait. Who?" Zeus asked, his hand on his rumbling thunder-bolt, his eyes ferocious. "Who's coming?"

"Ares's ally," she answered. "I have a plan for him, too. Go, bold Zeus. Save Hades. He will wake soon. Take him home. And save our beautiful world before it's too late."

With that, Persephone climbed atop Nike's back and they flew back into the tangled depths of the Underworld.

· · ·

Hades woke to see the harpy flying off into the distance. He saw a glimmer of light on the harpy. Persephone. She was looking back at him. He saw her luminous face for the briefest instant, her dark hair flying wildly behind her

And then she was gone. Lost again in the darkness.

"Persephone!" he yelled. "Persephone! Come back!"

He shook off the confusion of his sleep and of the healing fog in which he'd been immersed. Zeus stood calmly, feet firm, watching Persephone disappear.

"What's happening? Where is she going?" Hades leapt onto Kerberos. "Go! Kerberos, follow them!"

But the great Underworld hound merely whined and sank down onto his belly, his heads lowered submissively between his paws.

"Persephone told him to take you back to the entrance," Zeus told him plainly. "To make sure you go home."

"What? Why?"

"Because Ares is trying to take over Olympus, and we need to help Athena defeat him."

"What?" Hades was stunned by the revelation but quickly shook it off. "Athena can handle Ares."

"She may need our help."

"The other gods are there. Poseidon, Hephaistos, Hermes… Athena will rally them, and Ares's visions of victory will be short-lived."

"Poseidon joined Ares," Zeus said. He folded his arms and began to pace in front of Kerberos. The dog's six eyes followed him back and forth.

Hades remembered Poseidon's objection when Hades was crowned king of the gods. He remembered the look on Poseidon's face when Zeus had supported Hades as king.

In time, Hades nodded.

"You're right. You should go. Poseidon's loyalties have always been weak."

"Persephone told me to bring you with me."

"And I'm telling you to leave without me."

Zeus growled and threw his hands up in the air.

"And so, I must choose?" He paced again, this time taking long, angry strides. "I fear leaving you here alone, but now I fear for Athena. And our world. Imagine what Ares would do if he were king of all? And Demeter is still in mourning. She's letting the world die! Plus, Persephone said Ares has weapons here that he's going to take up above—what if they're like those wolves? With the metal teeth and claws? Nightmares like that released up above? Just imagine! Whoever Ares is working with here, he's a lot smarter than Ares, so that's a different problem entirely."

"Go," Hades said.

"I will," Zeus agreed. "And once I've dispatched Ares, I'll be back."

"Don't lose a moment. Go now. We still don't know how time passes here. It feels like it's been only days but, at the same time, it feels as though we've passed a lifetime down here…" Hades fidgeted with his breastplate and then looked up at Zeus, hopeful.

"How was she?" he asked.

"She's strong," Zeus assured him. "She has loyal followers here, so she has some protection." He grasped a handful of the shiny leaves that hung in thick bunches from the ceiling. "Not that she needs it…"

Hades was proud of Persephone. She was strong and capable and she'd saved them.

Zeus went on, unsettled by the wistful look that had come over Hades's face.

"And she has her own plan for Ares, since it was Ares who sent—"

Zeus caught himself before he told Hades that it was Ares who killed Persephone, and set this whole nightmare in motion.

"What?"

Zeus's evasion didn't escape Hades's notice.

"What about Ares?"

Zeus saw that Hades's face was reddening to the color of his flaming staff. He knew that Hades had likely already guessed, so he told him everything.

"Ares killed her, Hades. To drive you here. We did exactly what he wanted us to." Zeus cursed then bowed his head. "Persephone can never leave," he finished. "Never."

Zeus readied himself for a storm. He glanced up at Hades, but Hades didn't rage.

Instead, he was very still. He spoke quietly. Kerberos raised his head, ears pricked, listening as Hades spoke.

"I will take Persephone back," Hades vowed, undeterred. "They are forcing her to marry. She loves me still, as I knew she did."

Hades remembered what Persephone told him when he was asleep. It felt like a dream, but Hades knew, after seeing Persephone fly away—he knew the truth. It was real. She'd been there, holding him, telling him of her everlasting devotion.

"She loves me still," Hades repeated. "As I knew she would until the end of our days, until the end of all the days. I refuse to let this stand. She wants to save me, wants me to save myself. She thinks I cannot get her out of here, but we will not bend to the will of this place. And I will not bend to the will of Ares, who is by far my inferior."

Hades's voice grew louder and more powerful with each word he spoke. "I will not bow to anyone who thinks they have power over her, over us!" Then he quieted again. "Even death itself."

"Don't you see?" Hades asked, pleading to Zeus and to the Underworld and to Fate itself. "I am not myself without her. She is my lodestar—my guiding light. Without her, I'll be lost in the darkness."

Zeus threw down his thunderbolt and embraced his brother, his heart torn for him, anguished again to see his shining brother brought so low. After seeing Persephone for himself, watching her wield power in the Underworld, Zeus held out no hope that Hades could tear Persephone from the Underworld. She seemed too much a part of it now.

Not even you, Zeus thought as he held his brother tightly. *Not even you, for whom the world will lie at your feet, can undo what has been done.*

"She is strong," was all Zeus could bring himself to say.

"I know. She is strong. But I'm not."

Hades held Zeus by the shoulders and his eyes swam with worry and fear. Hades's fingers crushed Zeus's golden armor, making the metal crease and fold.

"That's my secret, Zeus," Hades whispered. "I'm not as strong as she is."

Zeus clasped Hades's arms and thought of what the Fates said— that Hades was meant to stay in this place. He remembered how Hades had herded the shades, how his brother felt passionately that humans deserved justice—even in death and darkness, and how he was driven to dole it out.

"Kerberos will take us back to the entrance together," Zeus said, determined to defy the mysterious, withered old women.

The Fates meant nothing to him. He and his brother had defied their own father, who had ruled the world with fists of rage. He and Hades were renegades who had crushed that dark, old world into pieces, making it brightly anew in their own design. The ancient Fates meant nothing to him. Or to Hades.

Hades and Zeus owned the world and the Underworld, too. They would defy everyone, and they would do it together.

Zeus made a vow to a disheartened Hades, refusing to give up hope, refusing to disappoint his brother.

"You will find Persephone. I will deal with Ares and be back for you both."

Hades nodded. After a longing glance toward the spot where he'd watched Persephone fly away, he and Zeus rode Kerberos back through the Underworld, to return to where they began.

CHAPTER 43

The clanking of Hephaistos forging godly weaponry was music to Hades's ears. He strode out of Hephaistos's workshop, clasping the thunderbolt the blacksmith made for him. It took tremendous focus and strength to control the thunderbolt. Hades had to concentrate his thoughts and will on the bolt, synergizing his energy with the energy of the lightning humming through the weapon.

Hades laid stones in decreasing size at the base of Hephaistos's steaming volcano. He walked away, then turned, aimed, and threw the thunderbolt, pulverizing the largest rock into dust. The thunderbolt returned to him. He squinted, aimed, and threw it again, repeating this action, until all the stones were gone.

Hades pursed his lips, satisfied.

He bent down, picked up a grain of sand and placed it on the ledge. He walked away, this time going all the way into the water. The waves lapped at his calves. He pulled the thunderbolt back until its tip was beside his eye. Then he tossed it at the tiny grain.

The thunderbolt sailed through the sky, a beam of light searing the air. It slid beneath the sand, lifting up the grain. Then it turned and sailed back towards Hades. Hades reached his arm out and caught the thunderbolt. He put his finger on the tip and lifted up the grain of sand. It looked untouched. It wasn't damaged, wasn't even singed. Hades nodded, pleased.

Hades was ready to practice with another group of rocks when he heard a scream. It was Persephone. He swung around in time to see Zeus yank Persephone out of the path of a massive wave that was about to hit her like a wall.

Zeus leapt to the safety of the cave entrance in the distance, Persephone in his arms. Persephone buried her face in the crook of Zeus's neck, her arms wound tightly around him. She looked so small. So delicate.

Hades's chest constricted as he dashed to the cave. Demeter beat him to Persephone's side, alternately weeping in relief that Persephone was safe and admonishing her daughter for being so careless as to stand so close to the unpredictable sea.

Hera couldn't decide if she should swoon at the romance of the rescue, or burn with envy that Zeus was carrying Persephone instead of her. She went with swooning.

"Oh, Zeus," Hera gushed as Zeus delivered Persephone into Demeter's frantic embrace. "That was well done! To think, what would have happened if you hadn't been there?"

Zeus leaned into Hera's enthusiastic admiration, comfortable as ever in the face of praise. Hera traced his muscled forearms hungrily, her hair as smooth and her face as clean as ever in the steamy, soot-filled workshop. As Hera fawned over Zeus, Hades saw his brother look over Hera's head at Persephone. Zeus's expression softened as he looked at the youngest goddess. Persephone mouthed her thanks to him over her mother's shoulder. Zeus reddened and nodded slightly before turning to submit to Hera's fawning.

Hades stumbled away from the scene, berating himself for nearly letting harm come to Persephone. He'd been so close to her on the beach. He knew she liked to stare up at the sky near the water, that she paid no attention to the waves. He should have known she was in danger—he should have felt it. He vowed right there that he would never let anyone or anything harm Persephone.

"Wishing that had been you instead of Zeus?" Ares smirked as he lazily rounded the corner, coming from wherever he had been slinking to avoid helping Hephaistos with the construction of weapons.

Hades tightened his grip on his humming thunderbolt as it vibrated and tried to attack Ares of its own accord. Hades withered Ares's with one fierce look and stalked off, the thunderbolt glowing and buzzing beside him.

• • •

"Zeus."

Hades stopped his brother just before Zeus began the climb back up to the world above.

"I know you loved her," Hades said softly. "Persephone."

"I still do," Zeus answered.

"No." Hades shook his head. "I know you really loved her."

"Well…" Zeus sputtered, lost for words. He flushed, feeling Hades's far-seeing eyes look into his very soul, if he had one. He had never told Hades of his feelings for Persephone, not once he saw how passionately Hades and Persephone loved one another.

"I could never love her the way you do," Zeus confessed. "No one could."

"Thank you, Zeus."

"I'll be back," Zeus promised.

"I'll be here."

"I love you, brother," Zeus said.

"I love you, too," Hades answered. "Now go remind Ares who's in charge."

Zeus grinned. "I will. And you—you will find Persephone. You'll be reunited." Zeus patted Kerberos and then turned to leap up into the funnel. He paused and said, "Just…"

"What?" Hades asked.

"Just be careful. Don't lose yourself in trying to find her."

"I can't find her if I am not myself," Hades answered sincerely. "If I was any less, I wouldn't deserve her."

Zeus looked at Hades and fought down the reservations that

cropped up again in his mind about leaving his brother alone in the Underworld.

Zeus wasn't used to inner struggles. Things were usually black or white for him. Simple, easy, straightforward. It was Hades who saw shades of gray. But Zeus knew this was the right thing to do. Ares had to be stopped. And Hades had to find Persephone. Zeus told himself to leave it at that. He could fight Hades. He could physically overwhelm his brother and forcefully return him to the surface, but he could never change Hades's mind. And so, he had to let him go.

Zeus clasped the thunderbolt that had once belonged to Hades's, the one Hades had given him before they began their journey into the Underworld. And with one last look at Hades, Zeus sprung up into the black funnel, a beam of light soaring up into the ascending darkness until it was beyond sight.

Hades and Kerberos turned away from the opening to the Underworld. Before they could take more than a few steps, an explosion ripped through the Underworld. Hades and his hound shook with the huge force of the blast and were thrown to the ground.

Hades quickly looked towards the funnel, afraid that Zeus was caught up in the explosion and would be sent barreling back down into the Underworld. But Zeus was nowhere to be seen. He would make it all the way back to the top.

Relieved, Hades prepared to climb atop Kerberos when a shockwave blasted into the cavern. The invisible force ripped Hades and Kerberos from one another and sent them flying to separate parts of the Underworld.

Hades helplessly rode the invisible wave until it dissipated and then dropped him. He landed hard, then slid along the rocky black ground.

He tried to stand but the cavern was so low-ceilinged that he couldn't. On his knees, he called to Kerberos.

He waited. He called again but neither saw nor heard any sign of the hound. Again and again, his calls were met with silence.

He was alone in the Underworld for the first time. All he had was his staff, his love for Persephone, and his commitment to find her. Without Kerberos, he had no one to follow the scent of the harpies. He had no idea which way to turn.

Everything was darkness.

CHAPTER 44

Persephone wore a wreath of fresh, bright flowers in her hair. She wore it the way Athena wore her battle helmet. Armed with this sign of Demeter's love, Persephone was ready to do battle.

Following Persephone's request, Melete had found Demeter in the world above. The ground was matted with dried, dead grass. The air was full of dust. It was cold and dark. No leaves grew on the trees, no flowers bloomed on the withered plants. The goddess of the harvest's long face was pale and drawn. Her eyes were red and sunken in her hollow cheeks.

Melete approached the goddess slowly. The kind harpy knelt by the goddess's side, bowed her head, and held out Persephone's gift.

Demeter turned slowly towards the harpy. Then she saw the dark plants making up the wreath Melete held in her outstretched wing, plants she had never seen before. She immediately recognized the glimmer of Persephone's light on them.

The goddess gasped and clasped the wreath to her chest. She lifted it to her face and inhaled deeply, drinking in the scent of the plants Persephone had coaxed to life in the Underworld.

Color rose softly in Demeter's face. She pressed the leaves against her skin, feeling Persephone's skin against hers once more.

"This is from Persephone! My beloved girl!" Demeter's face shone with relief. She put her hand beneath Melete's chin and lifted it. "You've come from the Underworld. My daughter sent you here to tell me she has power and she is safe?"

"Yes," Melete said. "She is well, though she misses you. Persephone is our Underworld now. She is our light and our strength. My sisters and I have vowed to serve her all our days."

Demeter bowed her head. Tears streaked down her shining face. "Thank you. Thank you! Tell her how much I miss her. I'm grateful to hear she is safe." Demeter smiled. "And I am not surprised to hear she is strong." Demeter nodded regally. "My devoted girl, your loyalty will not be forgotten."

Demeter turned away from the kind harpy. In doing so, she turned her back on the laurel tree for the first time since she'd made it grow, since the day she sent Hades along its roots to find and bring back Persephone.

The tree began to bloom. Leaves sprouted on its branches. The gaping hole left by Hades's furious search for an entrance to the Underworld filled with soil.

Demeter was asking Melete about how she came from the Underworld when Zeus burst up out of the new earth brandishing his gleaming thunderbolt. Clumps of dirt and dead grass flew in all directions as he soared into the sky, returning from the depths.

Zeus squinted, his eyes burning in the bright glow of the sun. His armor was polished to a gleaming gold once again as he winged through the vast open sky. He saw his helmeted daughter waiting below with a line of Persephone's harpies. He soared for a little longer, basking in the warmth of the sun. Then he saw Ares's and Poseidon's army at the base of Olympus.

Zeus did a nosedive, landing with a thud in front of Athena.

A smile came over clear-eyed Athena's fierce face as she stood, arms crossed, waiting for him to land. She reached out and touched Zeus's beard.

"I like this," she said. "It suits you."

Zeus grinned. He had missed his favorite daughter.

"Hades?" Athena asked.

Zeus shook his head.

Athena nodded, her grey eyes downcast.

"I'm going back for him—for them—after we deal with Ares."

Athena glanced up. She read her father's expression. She could tell he didn't believe his own words as much as he wanted to, as much as he wanted her to. Disheartened, she heard a familiar screech.

Her owl circled overhead. Athena held out her arm, and the wide-eyed owl landed on her bare skin. She saw Ares in her owl's shiny eyes, and refocused her thoughts. She had to leave Hades out of her mind, as he wouldn't be able to help them now.

Athena pointed out Nike and the other harpies to Zeus.

"Persephone sent these warriors to us from the Underworld. Listen to what they have to say about Ares's plans. Then I'll tell you my plan to defeat him."

Zeus put his arm around Athena.

"Tell me everything," he said hungrily, after acknowledging the familiar harpies. "Then you and I will defeat him together."

CHAPTER 45

A voice came out of the darkness.

"We meet again," it said, its speaker enunciating every syllable as if to show he had all the time in the world.

"Who's there?" Hades snapped. "Who are you?"

Hades spun around. Still on his knees, he couldn't see anything in the extreme darkness. His glowing eyes couldn't penetrate the damp dark of the cramped tunnel into which the shockwave had tossed him. His staff was out and he couldn't rekindle it.

Sisyphus shook his head and showed himself. He muttered, seeing how Hades looked at him blankly, "You ruined my life and you don't even remember..."

He hovered above Hades, half of his translucent shade body in the tunnel, half in the ceiling.

"You are disturbing my kingdom," Sisyphus accused the king of the gods.

"Your *kingdom*?" Hades raised an eyebrow. His staff began to glow as if covered with embers.

"Yes," King Sisyphus replied. "Since you sent me here, I've used my considerable skills to make it mine."

"The Underworld?" Hades shifted off his knees to sit with his feet out in front of him. He looked as though he was relaxing. "The Underworld is your kingdom?" Hades said dubiously. "I've been here for some time and I've not heard or seen any sign of you until now. Are you sure you control the whole of this place?"

"I control the parts that have value. Which brings me to why I brought you here."

"You brought me here?"

"Of course. You don't think that explosion just happened by chance, do you? Tut tut," Sisyphus admonished Hades, patronizing the god. "Not everything that occurs here is random. Or by chance. In fact, very little is actually caused by those forces. Keep a closer eye and you'll see."

"I don't plan on staying here long enough to learn any more about it than I already know. Now, you're telling me that you caused that explosion? That tremendous, destructive force?" Hades couldn't hide his dismay as he remembered the power of the resulting shockwave, and how it lifted him and Kerberos as though they were specks of dust.

"I did," Sisyphus boasted. "I've built a superb war machine for Ares."

"For Ares," Hades repeated, his anger rising at the mention of Ares. His staff burst into controlled blue flame.

Sisyphus gingerly moved away from Hades's forked staff.

"Ares and I are partners," Sisyphus cooed.

Hades took a careful look at the self-proclaimed King of the Underworld as Sisyphus lowered his transparent feet until they touched the ground. The ceiling of the tunnel was too low for Hades to stand, but Sisyphus could. He was not nearly as tall as the god, and the part of his body that didn't fit in the tunnel could simply manifest through the rock, a weightless transparent image.

"That was impressive," Hades said coolly. "I hope Ares values you and everything you can do for him."

"Oh, he does. In fact, that's why I'm here talking to you."

"Oh, really? You're not here because I'm the king of the gods and a pretty impressive figure myself?"

"Uh—no. Like I said, we've met before and it didn't work out that well for me."

"I can see that," Hades replied. "It looks like you were on the wrong end of my lightning bolt."

Sisyphus simmered with indignation. He clenched his fists in the face of Hades's lack of fear or remorse.

"Who do you think you are?" Sisyphus demanded through clenched teeth. "I know why you're here and you'll never get what you want."

The flames on Hades's staff grew red hot and wild when Sisyphus brought up Persephone, though he didn't yet dare to name her. Sisyphus backed away further, but kept talking.

"You think you can stomp and bully your way into the Underworld and that you can just take someone out with you?" Sisyphus asked. "You think the rules don't apply to you? You think you can do whatever you want because you are the great and magnificent Hades? And I thought you were the one who wanted everyone to follow rules."

Hades glowered from his place on the ground.

"Take me to Persephone," Hades said, his patience growing thin. "Or I will kill you again."

Sisyphus ignored Hades's command and kept talking.

"Well, I guess that's what power brings—privilege. That's certainly why I enjoyed it. I think, perhaps, you and I have more in common that I thought."

Hades glared at the despicable figure before him.

"You helped create humanity, but does that give you the right to control us?" Sisyphus asked. "I don't think it does. Create and then set free. Let go and let your creation do what it will."

"That's not what I believe," Hades growled.

"Obviously. Though I think sometimes you wish you didn't have a responsibility to keep watch on humans. It's a heavy burden. But it's who you are and you can't fight it any more than I can fight who I am."

"And who are you?" Hades asked, his hand flaming now along with his staff. He got up on his knees, a threatening figure even kneeling. But Sisyphus was too wrapped up in dreams of revenge to sense the threat that was right in front of him. Hades was not cowed.

"I'm the man who's ruined your immortal life," Sisyphus snarled. "The man who's taking his vengeance out on the one who mangled and deformed him!"

At this, Hades froze.

"I have your life now, you see!"

Sisyphus's voice was a high-pitched screech. His desire for vengeance, and now being able to dole it out to Hades in person, brought his glee to a fever pitch.

"I have a version of your life, anyway," Sisyphus boasted. "And I like it. I think I'll keep it. And her."

At the mention of her, Hades rose, flaming staff in hand. He spread his arms out as he bounded up, and smashed the unforgiving Underworld rock with his body. The tunnel burst open like a volcanic eruption. Sisyphus was hurled with tremendous force up along with the other debris, into a distant part of the Underworld. Hades neither saw nor cared where the shade had landed.

"Persephone!" Hades roared, and the vast Underworld quaked at the sound. "I'm coming."

CHAPTER 46

Hades was a god possessed. He stormed through the Underworld, full of noise and fury. Shades hid. Poison fogs dissipated into the walls. Rodents, Sisyphus's wolves, devouring insects, and every other creature fled from his approaching steps if they could. If they couldn't, he blasted them into pieces with his flaming staff.

There were no more obstacles for him. Hades, in his unmovable and inescapable determination to find Persephone, tore through everything in his path. He had no plan other than to keep moving forward. He toppled walls, shattered ceilings, and rerouted the Styx. The darkness of his mind matched the darkness of the Underworld. He submitted to its pervasive, unrelenting twilight, where the sun never rose. Where the perpetual, imminent arrival of nothing wore down his hopes, and his dreams died. Only anger remained, and Hades wielded it like his most terrifying weapon.

CHAPTER 47

The golden statue of Aiode watched from atop Persephone's tower with unblinking eyes, awaiting Sisyphus's return. As she stood watch, Persephone guided four harpies as they half-carried, half-rolled Sisyphus's explosive machine down the winding, uneven stairway. They moved through the waterfall, into the lava-lit cavern.

"Here." Persephone pointed to the ramp that Philos and Agata had designed and built, with the help of palace shades. "Roll it into the lava. We have to destroy it before Ares comes for it. He'll use it against Athena."

The harpies nodded in agreement, struggling to push the cumbersome instrument of death towards the ramp. It was on wheels, but the wheels barely moved under the immense weight of the machine. The ramp groaned and creaked under its new burden.

"Persephone," Aiode called, her voice urgent.

The goddess looked up.

"I hear Hades!"

The statue cricked her neck and focused sharply on Persephone. "He is close!"

Persephone froze, fearful that if she moved, Aiode's words would be taken away from her—blown away by the force of how desperately she wanted them to be true.

Persephone shut her eyes, remembering how he'd looked the

last time she saw him. His dark eyes were full of love, of relief to have her beside him once more. And then she'd left him behind as she flew away…

"He's calling for you," Aiode said. The statue blinked and tilted her head. Her face was full of pity. "It's a terrible and desperate sound."

"Aiode!" Thalia admonished as Persephone stared up at the golden statue, fixed like a statue herself, frozen with hope.

"You heard it, too," Aiode accused the other harpy. "But you weren't going to tell her."

Persephone wiped a damp strand of hair from her eyes. Her heart fluttered at the thought that Hades was close.

"We were going to wait until our task was complete." Nike swooped in from above via the waterfall to land before Persephone.

Persephone glared at Nike, angry to have been kept in the dark about Hades.

"We've won," Nike declared, triumphant. "We won, Persephone."

The harpy held Persephone's shoulders, then wrapped her wings around the goddess. "Ares is defeated."

Persephone's anger with Nike vanished as the harpy embraced her, her words of their victory sinking in.

Nike hummed with energy, the thrill of battle coursing through her body. As Persephone pulled away, she noted that Nike's quiver had only one arrow left.

"Athena?" Persephone held the harpy at arm's length, inspecting her face. "Athena was triumphant?" She glanced at Aiode and swallowed. "And Hades? Was he with you? Did he fight beside you?"

Nike shook her head. "Athena and Zeus led us and the other gods who stayed loyal to Zeus and Hades. But Hades wasn't there."

"Hades wasn't there? He didn't fight with you?" Persephone felt her face flush. She put her hand up to her reddening face. "He didn't return to the surface…"

Persephone looked up at Aiode. She felt her heart beat faster and louder, filled with hope that Hades had stayed. In spite of her best efforts, Hades had stayed. For her.

"He won't leave you." Melete confirmed Persephone's thoughts. "Aiode is right. He's still here. He tears the Underworld apart looking for you."

"I have to go to him!" Persephone ran to the steps. "Destroy the weapon!" she shouted behind her as she ran.

"Wait!" Aiode warned Persephone, but it was too late. A savage Sisyphus stepped through the waterfall just as Persephone was about to run through it.

Persephone stopped cold when she saw him. She backed away, but Sisyphus followed her, matching her step for step. Sisyphus had a terrible look in his eyes. He looked shaken but defiant. Fearful but angry.

Persephone's heart pounded at the harrowing look in his cruel eyes.

CHAPTER 48

Hades spun around. A sound penetrated the darkness. A faint noise broke through the rage and disappointment and unremitting pain. He dimmed his flaming staff, listening. It was like the beating of a drum. It called to him. It called him with each beat.

It was Persephone's heart. It was how he would find her. He would follow the sound.

Piercing the darkness like a guiding light, Hades turned and followed the sound of Persephone's beating heart.

. . .

Hades flew down the steps, Persephone's heartbeat growing louder and more urgent in his ears. He leaped through the waterfall, and then he saw her. He watched as Persephone took the last remaining arrow from Nike's quiver, and slammed it into Sisyphus's body. The tip of the arrow still had the wolfsbane on it, and she jammed it in between his bared ribs.

Sisyphus yowled and then froze. Everything, even his eyes, were paralyzed—held immobile by the poison from the akoniton-tipped arrow.

The harpies on the ramp had paused. Sisyphus's weapon lingered perilously close to the lava. They were poised to roll the weapon into the lava, but waited to see if Persephone needed them—when suddenly, Sisyphus's hulking spider guards swarmed in from all sides.

The guards dropped onto their bellies, crawling on their hands and feet. They skidded along the surface of the lava like terrifying water bugs, clattering and clamoring in their bulky armor towards their still-motionless master. The harpies screeched and the guards flicked their pincers, threatening to devour Persephone.

Watching from mere feet away, Hades swung his staff. He spun it around and around, over his head. The swarm of Sisyphus's guards were swept up in the air. Hades spun them around like a cyclone. They whirled around, accelerating so quickly they became a blur.

As they spun, the blur of darkness spread and expanded. It soon became a solid mass. Hades lowered his staff and the guards were gone. What used to be Sisyphus's guards now formed a mighty hill—a black, rocky mound grounded in the lava, almost as tall as Persephone's tower.

Persephone pointed to the hill, flinging Sisyphus to a spot halfway below the hill's apex. Sisyphus could only stand there, helpless. As he stood, still frozen by the poison on the arrow protruding from his ribs, he watched Nike lead her harpies away.

Moments later, they returned. The harpies flew towards the hill. They were all together now, fourteen harpies flying in formation. Each harpy clasped the end of a rope, which, when held together, made a net. In the net was a huge stone.

Persephone immediately recognized the stone. It was the door to the prison where Sisyphus had kept the harpies, the boulder that had once been the lock on the harpies' cage, until Persephone had set them free.

At Nike's command, the harpies released the ropes and the stone fell. It plummeted to the ground, smashing Sisyphus's explosive weapon. The weapon cracked and broke, its pieces flying into the lava and burning up in flames.

Hades watched the remnants of the weapon dissolve and burn into oblivion. Then he lifted the massive stone from where he stood, and hurled it at Sisyphus. Sisyphus managed to free himself from the wolfsbane just in time to duck.

The boulder landed on the hill above Sisyphus with a tremendous quake. Sisyphus dropped to his knees to keep from falling into the lava. When he looked up, he saw that the massive stone had begun to roll down the hill. It was heading directly for him. The self-proclaimed Underworld King scrambled to his feet. He reached out and pressed against the stone to keep it from crushing him.

He slid back on his heels, down the hill, with the weight of the stone. Then he grunted and dug his feet into the hill made from his former guards. Sisyphus heaved against the stone to keep it from pushing him off the tiny island and into the lava.

He heaved and grunted and pushed until the stone began to creep up the incline. There was nowhere else for the rock to go—only up. Sisyphus was afraid that if he released pressure on the stone it would roll back over him. So he pushed it all the way to the top of the hill.

Sisyphus paused at the peak, relieved. He looked down to where Hades stood, just on the other side of the waterfall.

A triumphant look crept onto his narrow-jawed face. He was a survivor, Sisyphus, and he'd survived again. He would rebuild again. He was already planning how to begin, when he heard a faint tap.

A vine had sprouted at the peak of the hill. The vine stretched. It reached over and tapped the stone. With that tap, the boulder began to move. It started to roll.

Sisyphus turned and sprinted down the hill, the stone chasing him like a nightmare. He ran until he reached the bottom, and the stone stopped. Sisyphus looked for a place to leap off the island, but there was none. There was only the sea of lava. He wasn't a god or a spider guard. He'd seen shades burn up in the lava—he'd pushed them into it himself. He knew the lava would burn him into nothing.

And so the hill was now his own private island, built by Hades, using Sisyphus's own creations.

Sisyphus glared at Persephone. Then at Hades. He watched them go to one another, and knew he'd failed.

In fury, he pushed the stone back up the hill, and strode down away from it. Then Sisyphus heard a scraping sound. He looked up and saw the boulder sliding down the hill towards him once more. It gathered momentum as it came, until it was careening straight for him. There wasn't room for both him and the stone upon the narrow, flat base of the island. It would hold only him or the boulder. And so he grunted as he struggled to keep the boulder from flinging him into the lava. And then he pushed the boulder up the hill again.

Sisyphus struggled and pushed, understanding this would be his fate for the rest of time. His punishment for the evil he'd done in this life and the last. Sisyphus heaved the stone up the hill. Against his will. He had no will any longer. He had only his punishment, immovable and everlasting.

The harpies screeched, circling around him triumphantly. Melete hovered beside Aiode, who was fixed, as the golden harpy would be forever, to her place on Persephone's tower.

CHAPTER 49

Hades and Persephone stood across from one another. They stared into each other's eyes. Hades caressed Persephone's glowing pink cheek. Persephone wiped away Hades's tears. When they finally embraced, the whole of the Underworld hushed, the power of the gods' reunion bringing peace to the lawless, untamed place.

CHAPTER 50

"It's as irritating down here as it was up above."

Ares swaggered over from the waterfall, where he'd just descended in defeat from above. His blood-red armor was dented and singed. It had a hole in the shoulder that looked like Zeus's lightning bolt had struck it but terror-inducing screams and wails still emanated from the armor with each step he took.

Observing Sisyphus's futile climb and ensuing hasty descent, Ares glowered. "It looks like I chose my allies poorly."

"You lost, Ares," Persephone said triumphantly, trembling in Hades's arms.

"If you want to call it that," Ares admitted. He pulled a bone out of his wild, dark beard and inspected it, as if trying to remember where it came from.

"I lost my woman as well," he said. "I lost Aphrodite to Hephaistos. Of all the gods—talk about embarrassing! I'm not sure he even has all his working parts."

Ares tossed the bone into the lava.

"Well, she'll be back. And my battle with Athena and Zeus isn't over just yet. Pretend I'm not here. Carry on with your insipid reunion. I have to get to the armory."

Hades heard Persephone's heart pound. She turned to him and kissed him passionately. Ares stomped away in disgust and envy, and a not a little bit of fear. Then Persephone pulled herself away from Hades, and put his hand to the place where Ares had killed her.

Hades felt the scar Ares had given her. For the first time, he felt the wound that had sent her to the Underworld. The hurt and anger at feeling Persephone's pain emanated from Hades like a storm, and made Ares pause. Hades's desire for justice and revenge for what Ares had done to Persephone coursed through him. But he knew Persephone was trying to tell him something. So he held onto her tightly and waited.

Persephone called to Ares. "No god had ever seen the Underworld until you. Tell me, Ares. How did you get here?"

Ares narrowed his eyes, suspicious. He sensed that Persephone was holding Hades back from killing him, so he decided to answer.

"My connection with the Underworld is strong," Ares said. "It needs me. I feed it. More than any other god, I give it sustenance. I asked for an entrance and it found me."

"I know where that entrance is," Persephone said. "I know it's the waterfall. Go to it now. Use it to leave here and never use it again."

"What?"

Hades tightened his grip on Persephone and she repeated, "I said leave here now, Ares, and never return."

"But I need my—"

"We destroyed your weapon," Nike said.

"And you can never rebuild it," Melete added.

"Go, Ares," Philos said in disgust.

Ares looked from Persephone to Hades to the old philosopher, who had his arm around some decrepit old woman, to the harpies and back.

Not letting go of Persephone, Hades stepped forward. Next to Hades, Ares looked like the insignificant lesser being that he was. Hades stood tall and strong and noble beside Ares's filthy, petty, need-filled self. Hades, using all his self-restraint—because he understood what Persephone wanted, what she needed—lifted Ares with the hand that wasn't holding Persephone. He held the god of war by the back of his thick neck.

"She said don't come back," Hades growled. And then he swung his arm back, and threw Ares with all his might.

The god of war went soaring up into the waterfall, and all the way up—until he was spewed out of the earth, and landed flat on his back before what was left of his terrified army.

At the sight of him, the pitiful remnants of his army dispersed.

Athena, the purple plume of her helmet fluttering in the breeze, Poseidon at her side, reached down and lifted Ares to his feet. Hera put her arm around Ares and the four gods walked away together. The conflict was over—for now. The gods, after all, were still family.

Zeus stayed behind. He stabbed his thunderbolt into the ground. Then he bent over the newly-built fountain in Nesos. He looked down into the water from which Ares had flown. He and Hermes exchanged a look. Then the two gods dove into the fountain, and down to the Underworld.

CHAPTER 51

The harpies spread out, standing at attention. Their arms entwined around one another's waists, Persephone and Hades looked approvingly upon the loyal, battled-tested warriors.

Philos and Agata stood just behind her, as Persephone named the harpies one by one.

As Persephone said their names, each harpy bowed her head and dropped to one knee. Persephone called Nike's name last. Nike, at the front of the line, bowed her head and knelt before her Queen.

"I am Memory," Persephone told the harpies, her voice loud and strong, carrying throughout the chamber. "I remember who you once were—my Amazon warriors, my stalwart and brave harpies. My daughters. And I know, too, who you will become."

Persephone turned to Hades, and looked lovingly into his eyes. Hades smiled down at her. Then he addressed the harpies.

"You will be our greatest gift to humanity," he said. "We ask that you leave the field of battle upon which you showed your prowess. Together," he beamed at Persephone. "We ask that you take upon your bold shoulders a new task."

Nike, her head still bowed, glanced up at Persephone. Persephone nodded at her.

"If we are to continue to make the world a place of light and beauty," Hades continued, "something must balance war. Something must provide humanity with a way to show their devotion to us, their devotion to one another. Something must allow them to tell their stories, capture their imaginations, fill the darkness of night and loneliness in a way that fighting cannot.

"That thing will be you."

The harpies' well-developed discipline kept them from reacting. They remained still, in spite of their eager anticipation. Aiode watched silently and proudly from her perch.

"You will connect men when Ares tries to break them apart," Persephone said. "Ares bombards humans with hate—you will teach them how to share their love, turning humanity from violence to its antitheses: creation." She paused.

"You will be the Muses," she declared. "Your task is to inspire humanity to create beauty and art. You will inspire them to seek and share knowledge. And by doing so, you will create war's greatest enemy. You will be the most effective warriors the world has ever seen."

The chamber was silent. All the shades hushed, awaiting what happened next. The only sound was the soft scraping of Sisyphus rolling his stone.

Their hands entwined, Persephone and Hades raised their arms. Golden light surrounded them like a cloud, then spread and filled the whole chamber. The harpies stood, holding their breath as the light filled them from the inside. Soon, the warm, bright light engulfed the harpies.

Hades squeezed Persephone's hand. She looked at him proudly.

After a few moments, the light receded. As it melted away, the harpies' shocked screams and cries filled the silent cavern.

They'd been transformed back into women.

The former harpies, the new Muses, stared, open-mouthed at one another. Their wings and talons had melted away. They stretched and bent and threw their arms around one another.

"Thank you, Persephone," Melete said, stepping out from the throng of joyous, crying Muses. She rubbed her foreign skin as she looked at Hades.

"Thank you both. But," she said, glancing down at her feet.

She wriggled her toes and wrung her strange new fingers.

Persephone and Hades waited as Melete gathered her thoughts. "But I'd like to stay here. In the Underworld. With Persephone. My lady," she said, holding Persephone's hands for the first time. "I vowed to serve you all of my days."

Hades's face grew serious.

"Persephone isn't staying in the Underworld," he said. Melete lowered Persephone's hands, a look of confusion and fear upon her new human face. "We are going back above," Hades told her kindly. "To the surface—to our home. We aren't staying in the Underworld."

The gods as well as the Muses and shades were reveling in their victory and newfound freedom. They had triumphed over evil and felt that anything was now possible. Persephone glanced at Nike, who was now a staggeringly tall woman with the same sharp eyes she'd possessed as a harpy. Persephone put her arms out, calling Nike to her. Nike hesitated, alarmed by Hades's words. She and Persephone knew the danger a journey back to the surface represented for Persephone.

Persephone took Nike's hands and squeezed them. Persephone smiled, and Nike couldn't resist smiling back at the radiantly happy goddess.

"You," Persephone said warmly. "Nike. You are to be the goddess of victory. You can travel up and back down to the Underworld as often as you wish. You will serve Athena well."

"What about the Underworld, Persephone?" Nike asked, furrowing her forehead. "What about the shades? If you leave, what of them?"

Persephone turned to Philos, who bit his lip and fiddled with the stylus behind his ear.

"I have instructed Philos in my plans to free all the slaves," Persephone answered. "He and Agata will serve the shades well."

"But why do you think now that you can leave? And how?" Nike asked.

Persephone's gaze went to the waterfall.

CHAPTER 52

ades turned to Persephone. His dark eyes focused on her glowing face.

After his long journey to find her, after her harrowing stay in the Underworld where he could see how much she had changed, Hades realized he had to make sure he was still what Persephone wanted. "Persephone? I should have asked." He was almost bashful. "Will you return to the surface with me?"

Persephone smiled. Hades heard her heart flutter and his hopes rose.

"Yes," she answered. "I will."

Hades was filled with joy and relief, but the harpies, now Muses, gasped.

"No!" Nike objected. "You cannot mean it! You've eaten the seeds. You're supposed to be here. Persephone, remember what happened to the shade? She became mist when she tried to climb the waterfall. She vanished—she became nothing!"

"I'm a goddess." Persephone squeezed Hades's hand, easily casting aside Nike's doubts. "It cannot be the same for me."

Nike shook her head, overcome with grief and anger. She knew her words would be wasted, that she would be unable to convince the stubborn goddess whom she adored to change her mind. She stepped back, defeated.

Hades's face beamed with joy and pride. Persephone embraced

Philos and Agata, and each of the harpies. She said her goodbyes, blowing a kiss to Aiode.

Nike stood apart, unwilling to say goodbye. She crossed her arms and turned away in protest. Persephone sighed and wrapped her arms around her.

"Thank you," she whispered. "You saved me, Nike. You helped me find the strength to save myself."

Nike was silent. Ever beside her since he'd found her again, Hades took Persephone's hand and led her to the waterfall. The gods turned and waved to the Muses, and to the shades who'd begun arriving and filling the palace cavern.

In unison, Hades and Persephone leapt, soaring up into the waterfall. Hades had one hand on his forked staff, leading the way. His other hand clasped Persephone's waist, pulling her along behind him. The two gods rose, until Persephone could no longer see the palace or gleaming Aiode.

They rose higher and higher, getting closer to the surface and the sunlight Persephone craved. Hades looked over his shoulder and saw Persephone beaming at him. Satisfied, he aimed his gaze back up.

Suddenly, he felt Persephone's body start to shrink. He tried to hold her tighter, but couldn't.

Soon she slipped from his grasp entirely. He dropped his staff and it fell into the distance beneath them. Hades reached his other hand back to try to take Persephone's vanishing hand, but it had become insubstantial, like mist.

Horrified, he turned back and saw Persephone disappearing, fading like a dream.

"No!" He dove on top of her, pressing her down. She was so thin, nearly insubstantial, like a fragment of cloth.

They tumbled down through the waterfall and splashed into the soft bed of lava.

"Persephone!" he cried.

Persephone was there, her body returned. Hades held her as they floated in the thick, viscous lava. He swam with her through the mud-like liquid until he could pull her up onto the rocky edge of the moat.

He lay next to her, not daring to look anywhere else but at her face. She lay motionless. She looked unharmed, solid again, but she was still, unmoving. Hades leaned over and pressed his skin against hers. Her cheek felt warm.

He waited. Afraid to breathe. Afraid to move. Afraid he had lost her. Again.

And then Hades heard it. The thumping of her heart. Tears filled his eyes and he clasped Persephone, pressing her to him, feeling her heart beat against his chest. And then he heard something else.

His heart thumped once. In response to hers.

At that sound, Persephone opened her eyes.

Persephone took a deep breath and smiled at Hades.

Hades closed his eyes, so relieved he couldn't speak. Persephone put her hand on Hades's heart and it beat again. Then again. Louder and more steadily. Then she put Hades's hand onto her heart.

"I came to life here. In the Underworld," Persephone said softly. "I see that now. My life can only be here. I cannot leave. I should not leave. I can make this a better place."

"And I came to life with you," Hades whispered, blinking away tears. He caressed Persephone's cheek and made a decision he would never regret, in all his endless days. "I will stay here with you. And we will bring light to this darkness together."

Tears of joy flowed down Persephone's face. She sat up and embraced Hades. Persephone and Hades held one another there, on the edge of the lava field, their hearts beating in unison.

Demeter stood across the lava, watching, until she could wait no longer. She burst across the gap that divided her from her daughter, and wrapped Persephone in her arms. Hades looked on, knowing what he gave up by promising to stay with Persephone, knowing that he would no longer reign over the entire world above.

. . .

The Muses lined up along the narrow walkway that led to the palace. Philos stood behind them, his wife's hand clasped in his. More shades floated in, filling up the palace cavern by the millions. The palace itself glowed white. Persephone's wall came tumbling down, melting into the lava. The gate to the palace vanished.

Zeus watched from a spot in front of the waterfall, having just made his way back to the Underworld. Hermes stood by his side. Kerberos howled as he joined them, joyous to see his master and mistress.

Hermes, who had made the journey with Zeus, ducked the drool that fell from the hound's huge mouths. Charon rowed up alongside the hound. The ferryman took his hat off and knelt in the bottom of his boat. A tear of joy slid down his withered cheek.

Eventually, Hades rose. He lifted Persephone to her feet. Hades and Persephone, their arms around one another's waists, looked first at each other and then out to their kingdom and its people.

Nike stepped forward and placed a golden crown on Persephone's head. Melete crowned Hades with a black crown forged from a piece of Zeus's lightning bolt, the one he threw into the earth when they first searched for Persephone. Hades's raw emerald radiated from its center.

Hermes, his head lowered and his face wet with tears, gave Hades the forked staff he had dropped when Persephone was fading.

Zeus stayed back, standing apart from the rest. He stood with his feet spread wide, his arms crossed. He listened to the cheers of the shades. He thought back to the Fates and what they had told him—that Hades was meant to stay, to rule in the Underworld. He was angry at the idea of losing his brother, who meant more to him than any person ever had or would.

But he couldn't ignore how happy Hades looked. How happy Persephone looked. How right he knew they were together. The

Underworld itself seemed to be celebrating their reunion and their promise to stay.

Zeus looked up at the dark ceiling of the Underworld cave. Resigned, he made a fist and slung his hand towards the ceiling. He opened his palm, and millions of sparkling stars floated out of his hand and hung in the sky above them.

"So you will know when it is day and when it is night," Zeus promised, striding towards the joyful couple. "You will see the heavens as they look from above. We will stay connected this way, gazing up at the same sky."

At that, Zeus embraced Persephone. Then he stood back, holding her arms, his face contorted as joy and pride mingled with sadness and loss. Persephone kissed him on one cheek, then the other. He placed a kiss on the top of her head and released her.

Zeus turned to Hades. "Little brother," he said.

Hades nodded, his eyes glistening. "Thank you, Zeus," he said, pulling his brother in close. "Thank you."

"I'm not sure what I will do without you trailing in my footsteps," Zeus said, clearing his throat and pulling away.

Hades laughed and Zeus pulled him in close again.

"I will miss you," Zeus said hoarsely. "You are the best of all of us. You made me better."

Hades couldn't speak. With tears in his eyes, the great bearded Zeus, the new king of all the gods, let his brother go.

The Muses bowed to Zeus. Then the numberless shades followed suit.

• • •

Hades and Persephone embraced the Muses, telling them goodbye one by one. Afterwards, they ushered them towards Hermes, who would return with them to the world above. But four of them, including Melete, refused to leave. Persephone nodded and turned them back into harpies. The four harpies took flight and soared over their heads, screeching in joy.

While Nike and Persephone embraced and said their goodbyes, Hades pulled Erato aside.

"Erato, you are the Muse of love poetry," he said, nodding at her lyre.

"Yes," she smiled, tilting her head and strumming a few notes on the stringed instrument. "That is the task that you've given me, and I am eager to begin."

"I ask one thing of you before you leave," he said quietly.

"Anything, Hades. What can I do for you and Persephone, who've given us so much?"

Hades spread his arms wide, indicating the Underworld. "I ask for this."

Erato looked puzzled. "I don't understand."

"I ask for our story. Persephone's and mine. I'd like it to be ours alone. Will you do that for us? Will you give us the gift of our story? I don't care what stories you and your sisters inspire men to create to fill the void of the truth. Just let us have our story to ourselves, for as long as we can."

Tears streaming down her face, Erato nodded. "Of course, I will do as you ask. But, it's such a beautiful story. The story of your love. It should be told someday."

"I know." Hades smiled. "It will be."

And then the King and Queen of the Underworld, Hades and Persephone, clasped hands and leaned their heads towards one another. Under the watchful eyes of Aiode, they turned and walked into their new home.

AUTHOR'S NOTE

I used to wonder why, in the classical myth of Persephone, did eating the seeds mean Persephone had to stay in the Underworld. In some versions of the myth, she ate six seeds, which meant she had to stay for half of the year, spending six months below (with Hades) and six months above (with her mother). This gives us a beautiful explanation for the seasons because Demeter mourns when Persephone is away (fall and winter) and rejoices when she returns (spring and summer). So, that's one possibility.

Other scholars interpret the myth, connecting it with the still-mysterious Eleusinian Mysteries. Connecting the Persephone story with this sacred festival, "tasting the seeds" might mean having an experience, like the festivalgoers did. Once someone participated in the mysteries, they would never be the same. What you experience stays with you and cannot be undone.

Our experiences change us and our new reality reflects a richer but divided self. We can never truly go back after we've had a new experience because we are not the same person we were before it happened. This is what my Persephone experienced—she grew too much in the Underworld to be able to go back to her old life up above. Lucky for her and our love story, Hades grew with her.

The beauty of Greek myth, and why these stories continue to be told and retold, is that the Greek gods were "gods in the making." For the ancient Greeks, making art and telling stories was a way to show devotion to the gods. There is not one definitive story of the gods because the ancient Greeks had no dogma, no theologians. Artists and poets were their theologians.

Inspiration for my version of Hades and Persephone came from Timothy Olyphant's portrayal of Marshal Seth Bullock in the TV series, *Deadwood;* Madeline Stowe's portrayal of Cora Munro in the movie *The Last of the Mohicans;* and Florence and the Machine's song, *Cosmic Love.*

Thank you for reading!

Laura

www.ingramcontent.com/pod-product-compliance
Lightning Source LLC
Chambersburg PA
CBHW031538150726
47990CB00001B/215